FLIGHT

C.A. Allen

Novels of Arborand by C.A. Allen:

A Dewdrop Away

Dewdrop Prequel Trilogy:
Flight
Fall
Overworld

Dedicated to my sister, Emma.

And always, to Mom.

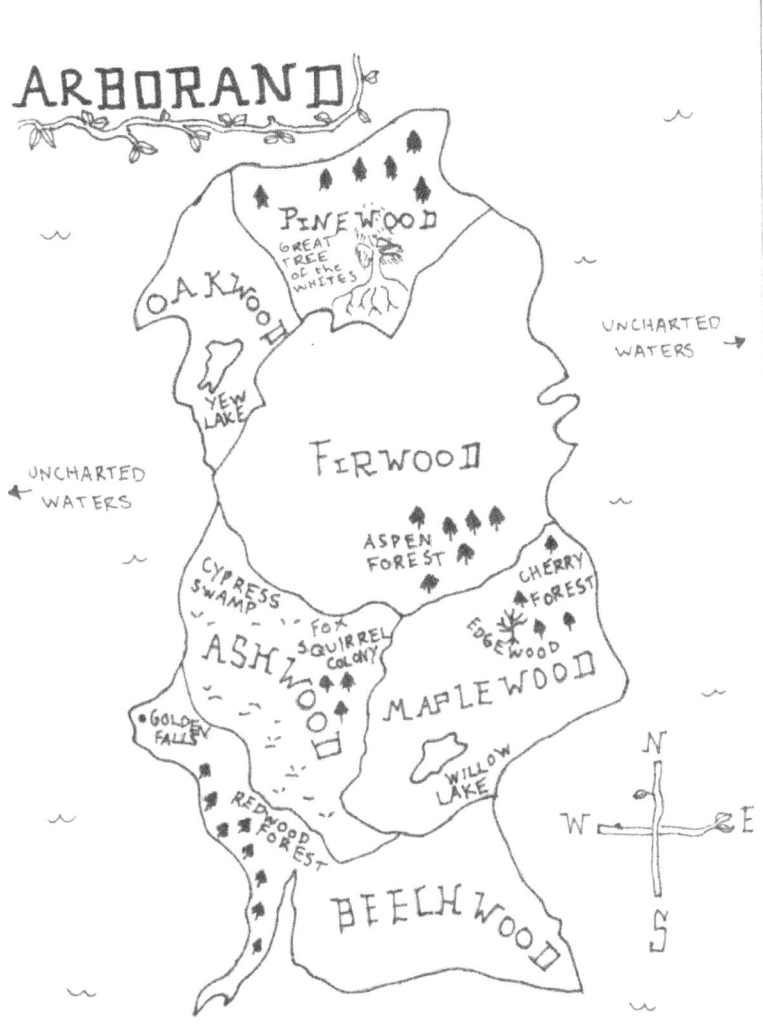

CHAPTER I

Eleven was suiting Tiallin Stormskiln very well. Glancing discreetly over his shoulder, he tried yet again for the eye of the young serving squirrel standing attentively against the wall some yards from him. She wasn't fooling anyone. He was sure he had seen her look this way at least once in the past quarter hour! Indeed, the sole reason he had not died of boredom yet today had to be her quiet congratulations on making 'another line in the book of his life.' Though he would not have worded it so laughably, Tiallin couldn't help but flush with pride at her words; reaching eleven seasons meant you were allowed to wait on the chamber of the King. Tiallin had never so much as caught a glimpse of King Sirius's throne room before today, and he had been eager for a look around, so much so that he had paid less attention than he normally would have to the squirrel maid's compliments.

Now, however, stuck waiting on the outside to be let in, he found himself trying in vain to put himself in her immediate line of vision once again. In the twenty or so minutes they had had to wait in the dimly lit corridor, he had not only lost the admittedly small bit of patience which had been allotted him at birth, but he had also not been able to fail to notice that his less fidgety companion was in possession of an pleasantly bushy tail. Tiallin did hope his own tail was shaping up—he knew his muscles were growing firm, from all the running about trees and personal challenges he set himself. Yes, eleven seasons might just equal luck for Tiallin Stormskiln.

In an attempt to loosen the cramp that had suddenly occurred in his left hind leg, Tiallin leaned to the side and back again, wondering what on Astrippa's forested land could be taking the King so *long*—didn't he want others to wait on him? And if he didn't, well, this was rather rude—but his thoughts were cut short by the image rendered to him from the corner of his eye. She *was* looking at him! Entirely discounting the possibility that it could be for a reason as simple as the odd dance he appeared to be inventing to ease the discomfort in his leg, Tiallin boldly turned to look back at the squirrel maid, who quickly looked away before evidently deciding she was caught in the act and turning back to meet his eyes.

"I'm—I am sorry," she said, "It's just—

"No. That's--"

They had both begun to talk at once, and Tiallin cut himself short, remembering manners.

She smiled at him. "I'm sorry for staring so, but you made me think..." She stopped and bit her lip while he waited on tenterhooks for her next words.

"What is your name?"

"I'm Tiallin." Tiallin puffed up his chest.

"Tiallin…?"

"Stormskiln."

The next two things happened so simultaneously that at first Tiallin could not make sense of anything. The heavy doors to the king's chambers swung open slowly, letting a good deal of light spill out into the corridor, blinding him just as the squirrel maid's voice continued to his right.

"…you have a brother?"

Tiallin experienced an odd sinking feeling in the region of his chest. As if to add insult to injury, the much-anticipated King's chamber was actually not much to look at.

She didn't even tell me her *name,* Tiallin thought grouchily, determined now to be angry with the pretty chamber maid.

She was older than himself, possibly by a good deal, something he wondered at not having observed earlier. To be fair, she *was* rather short. In the light her tail was also a lot fuller even than it had seemed out in the darkened hall. Tiallin knew he was silly, but he could not help but feel betrayed. Betrayed by this pretty squirrel with the bushy tail and the downy white fur, just as he was betrayed by the presence of the room about him, shockingly lacking in ornament. Tiallin had heard that King Sirius was a bit of an oddity, but really!

It was not that the king's chamber was ugly, or in any sort of poor taste. There were carvings, row upon row of them sitting atop one another around the walls, creating an atmosphere of brooding solemnity. The carvings looked as if they ranged in subject from great epic battles of the past and portrayals of the goddess Astrippa to mothers giving birth in typical drays and simple carvings of trees, or nature, or even bits of writing. One could spend all day staring at everything these walls had to say, Tiallin supposed, but his disappointment was ever present. Aside from the carvings, there was nothing that really stood out about the room. It was simply an extremely bright cavern with a honey-colored glow. Looking to the ceiling, he found with a start that there was none—or rather, that the middle of it had been taken out so as to let the natural light come flooding in. It was unique, certainly…but to one who had been spending countless hours the day before elaborating upon a mental picture of extravagant decadence…well, it was bound to fall short. Perhaps if Tiallin had been one for carvings and such, he would not have felt so utterly let down that day. Zerrith would be into this type of thing.

Come to think of it, Tiallin thought irritably as he followed the pretty squirrel maid to the center of the room into the direct warmth of the sunlight. *Today it would have been doubly nice to be Zerrith.*

His self-pitying thoughts were cut off abruptly by his almost colliding head on with the tail of the squirrel maid, who had stopped suddenly. By craning his head a bit, he was able to see over her to the offending distraction.

It was King Sirius.

Tiallin felt a double wallop to the stomach, a sensation in which he was sure he was alone, judging from the unfazed expressions of the two guards who had escorted them inside, and by the puzzled way in which the squirrel maid glanced at him as she gestured for him to stand beside instead of behind her. Huh. He didn't see how he could have missed the difference in their ages now. She was just patronizing enough to be his older sister.

Of course, unlike the others, Tiallin had never seen the king before. Sirius was not the most extravagant or stately, but unlike his chambers, the king did not excite any disappointment at all in the youthful squirrel who looked up at him in awe.

Sirius was an older squirrel, his white fur thinning so that the pink of his skin showed through when the light caught him at the right angles. His eyes were a curiously opaque pink in color instead of the darker red-black that was more common among their kind; they looked as if they held a constant smile somewhere in their misty depths. What Tiallin found odd about Sirius though, more than anything else was simply his lack of a throne upon which to sit. King Sirius was standing on a raised wood platform of sorts, a table with some fresh fruits laid out to one side of him and a pile of paw-woven cloth to the other. He was leaning against the wall regarding them from under eyelids half-closed, and in his paw he held a cane. Tiallin himself could not quite understand what made him find the king of Pinewood seem so impressive, but it seemed somehow despite every evidence of decrepitude, Sirius had a barely contained power to him, and a potential energy to match that of someone very, very young.

The King lifted his head slightly, and the guards left Tiallin and his acquaintance alone on the floor, trailing back to the doors. Tiallin only spared them a glance as they went, before turning back to King Sirius, who took that moment to address them at last.

"Ah, Lyrah, I see you have brought the fruit! Did you get any new varieties?"

Tiallin had no idea what the King was talking about, and it took him a moment to realize that Lyrah must be the name of the lovely squirrel beside him, who spoke in answer almost immediately after he had come to this revelation.

"Yes, I've got it. A few of those mulberries you're fond of and a couple blackberries—a little overripe, a fig. But I haven't been able to find anything new of late, I'm afraid. Would they do, your Highness?"

King Sirius looked disappointed for about a split second before breaking out in a little grin.

"Of course, of course…I do like those mulberries. Here, put them on this table right here…can you find it all right? Ah, of course, I forget that others are able…Well," he smiled again as Lyrah dutifully placcd the bundle of fruits on the table with the other fruit. "You are free to go now, if you wish. Actually, I must request some time with this fellow here," he nodded toward Tiallin meaningfully, who gave a start at being addressed, however indirectly.

Failing to understand the importance of fruit on any scale or context, he had let his mind drift. Interested though he was in the King and in what new service he was to perform, there was and had always been a part of him that longed to be outside, running along the branches of the pines as they interwove with one another, testing his body in every way possible...indeed, he thought he could feel a bit of breeze coming from the open roof. He tried to let it wash over him...

The sound of the door closing behind him alerted Tiallin to the fact that with the exception of the guards at the far doors, he was now completely alone with King Sirius, who appeared to be regarding him in that faintly amused fashion that he had as they had come in moments before.

"Tiallin Stormskiln," he said, slowly, carefully. "Do you know why you are here?"

Tiallin was a bit taken aback.

"Well," he hedged. "It's my eleventh season, and, uhm. My father...I remember him telling me that when this time came around I would find a job here. I've looked forward to it for some time, your Highness."

"Did he tell you why that is, Tiallin?"

"What? I mean, sorry your Highness. He said it was a family tradition, yeah. Or...something like that."

Tiallin felt impossibly lame. He could not believe how uncertain he could be, so in the dark—hadn't he ever thought of asking his father more on the subject?

"He told you that, did he?" King Sirius gave another of his small, quick grins, and leaned out from the wall, supporting himself with his cane. His back was not altogether straight, Tiallin noticed, wondering again why he didn't have a throne.

"You mean…it's not true?" he asked the King, puzzled.

"Your father certainly did not work as a server here. Your grandfather was a bartender. I knew him quite personally. His dew frosts were excellent, but I always rather thought he should have exploited raspberries a bit more. He would have gotten a good deal more visits from yours truly. Fruit, you know, is the key to anything lasting."

Tiallin frowned. "Then why…?"

The King shrugged. "Search me, as they say. Perhaps, as people often do when they are telling untruths, he did not want you to know the real reason you are now here. Which I must say is rather useless ruse because now I am going to tell you anyway. You are here, Tiallin, because I sent for you."

There was an uncomfortable pause in which Tiallin fidgeted, staring at a sunlit carving of one squirrel chasing another up a tree on the wall behind Sirius. His heart had begun to pound rapidly, and his next question was slow, more mechanical, as if he dreaded the answer.

"Specifically for me? All those years back, you asked for *me*? But…why?"

Sirius looked intent for a moment before answering. The vague smile remained in his eyes, but his mouth formed a straight line now, and his tone was serious when he answered,

"Because I want you to help me."

Tiallin was utterly bewildered. In what way could King Sirius require his assistance? To fetch him more fruit, perhaps? He seemed to have an odd affinity for the stuff. But was it not the case that if that had been all he had wanted, the King could have gotten just anyone?

King Sirius leaned forward over his cane, tracing the design carved into the handle with a thin white paw. He looked on the edge of speech when a loud, thundering knock sounded at the door.

"A moment!" the elderly squirrel called, and his voice was surprisingly cold. He leaned forward and said, very softly, "I think something is terribly wrong at this point in time."

"Wrong with what?" Tiallin asked cautiously. He looked about the spacious room with its honey colored wood walls and the series of carvings encircling them and wondered how anything could be wrong in a place like this.

"With us. The race of the white squirrel. With history. With fate," he said this last part darkly, eyes untrained, staring right past Tiallin at the wall beyond.

Tiallin stared at the King, waiting for more, but Sirius appeared to be done. He settled once more back against the wall and Tiallin cast a nervous glance at the door. To think he had woke up this morning thinking he'd be assigned some mundane chore like cleaning, or bringing meals to the king! But what he *was* supposed to be doing remained a mystery.

The sound of impatient voices issued from the other side of the door. He opened his mouth to ask something more, but it was then that Sirius began to speak, talking over his attempted words.

"I will call for you again tomorrow. Then I will make sure we are not disturbed." The smile came back to his face again. "You will not be otherwise occupied then?"

"No," Tiallin said quickly.

"Good, good. It is then that I will tell you what your task will be here. Have an eventful day, Tiallin Stormskiln."

Tiallin, figuring he was dismissed, moved toward the door from behind which the voices were bantering tirelessly, but Sirius held up a paw.

"Come this way, if you would," he said kindly but firmly, and pointed to a small door in the wall behind him, almost completely disguised so that it appeared to be a part of the wood. Tiallin dubiously obeyed, first pushing, then pulling, then at last sliding the door aside under Sirius's dead gaze. When he was out in the hall once more, he paused to listen despite himself, from the safety of the other side of the wall. He could hear Sirius's voice rise and then fall once more, and the sound of the grand door opening and shutting. Overly conscious of his own breath, and the fact that he didn't know where in the name of hailing acorns he was to go from this part of the Great Tree, Tiallin stood stock still, ear to the wall and listened as hard as he could through the sound of his own shame pounding heatedly in his ears, making him sweat. There were murmured voices, nothing he could make out, and then something that sounded like a cross between a scream and a laugh. The effect was frightening. Just as Tiallin's intrigue rose, a sound echoed from up the dark hall, a grunt as of someone pushing something very heavy. An old grey squirrel ambled into view, pushing a loom of fluttering threads. He stopped, and tilted his head at Tiallin suspiciously. Tiallin fled.

By some lucky chance, he happened to go in the right direction. Soon Tiallin found himself standing, shaking slightly, in the main atrium where he had been shown inside that morning. Finding it mercifully empty, Tiallin slipped out the front entrance and into the freedom of the brisk autumn air. For once the young squirrel hardly spared a thought for a romp in the pines, even when their scent was so close and pungent in his nose. He had far too much to think about.

CHAPTER II

Tiallin had some quick thinking to do when he reached home. His mother, Iskla, wanted to know how things had gone with King Sirius, and what Tiallin had been asked to do.

"This and that," he said, ducking his head. Iskla was one of those squirrels who could make a lie seem extra shoddy. She didn't inquire further, at least immediately, and Tiallin began to wonder why he could not have just told her the truth. For all the strangeness of the situation, it was true that he didn't quite know what the King had wanted with him. He was sure that she would not have told his father; lying was just easier.

"I'm making watercress salad tonight," Iskla told him, prodding some delicious looking green leaves. She raised an eyebrow. "What did you think of the king?"

"Erm," Tiallin began. "I liked him."

"Liked him, well." She paused, calculating. "There are some who would say he is losing his touch."

"Why?"

"Oh, well, you know. King Sirius has always had…odd ways about him, but they were far overshadowed by his keen wit, and his unusual insight. He could see right to the bottom of things, prevent disaster before it struck. But now they're saying…well, I'm not entirely sure I ought to be telling you this, Tiallin—"

"It would hardly matter with the odd jobs I've got," Tiallin interrupted dismissively. Lie number two. *Lovely*, he congratulated himself.

"Well then…some say the King's intuition has turned into something less like intuition and more like…seeing things that aren't there, that's all."

"Are you one of those squirrels?"

Iskla gave him a wan smile. "I...I don't want to be so quick to judge, Tiallin, understand that. But I do think...some of the recent news your father brings in..."

"Father hates the King."

"He does not," Iskla said, and there was real danger in her tone. "*I* personally believe it farfetched and a bit unfair to accuse him of 'seeing things' so fast, not to mention ironic, since he can't in the first place." Her mouth quirked upwards at the corner, but the humor was lost on Tiallin.

"What?"

"King Sirius is blind," Iskla said simply. "You didn't know?"

Looking back on it now, it made perfect sense. The wooden cane, the way Sirius had spoken to him while staring past him, the odd hue and blank, vague look to those misty eyes, competing to make Tiallin feel distinctly uncomfortable. Tiallin wondered, with a chill, how long it would have taken him to figure it out.

"Oh," he said at last. "But he seemed so—*sure* of himself."

"Well, you would be too if you'd never been anything else."

"What, you mean he was born that way?"

"I believe so. You seem unduly shocked, Tiallin."

He tried not to be offended by her amusement. Really, the idea that a squirrel could be born missing something as important as sight shed a new light on his own gifts. He was always comparing himself with people he considered to have held better cards from birth, such as Zerrith. But to be born without vision...Tiallin shut his own eyes and then opened them, shook his head. Maybe he should not be so quick to complain.

"Where is Zerrith?" Tiallin asked suddenly, reminded that he had not seen his brother all day.

Iskla looked up from chopping watercress leaves. "Last I knew he was in his room, working on something or other. That was around midday. I asked him if he'd like something to eat, but he sounded all preoccupied. He's getting too thin, you know," she confided, a faint worry line appearing on her forehead.

Iskla always talked about Zerrith this way, Tiallin thought, with an almost laughable reverence tinged with motherly worry. He wondered if Zerrith had remembered it was his birthday. Birthdays in general weren't as greatly celebrated among the white squirrels as they were with the other races, and if a birthday did not signify any one thing in particular aside from the turning of another season, it was often ignored or forgotten altogether. Tiallin himself often wished that his kind would be a bit more festive in these matters—it would be nice to get a gift or two today, but it looked like he might have to settle for watercress salad and a strange meeting with an even stranger King.

Starting up the winding, knobby, poorly sanded route that led to his own room, Tiallin thought about how different life might be if he had been born a grey squirrel. White squirrels were such solitary creatures that their small 'community' here in Pinewood was truly half-hearted in the sense of the word. Tiallin was curious about the others, the grays and the blacks whom he occasionally saw about the area, but as soon as they saw him, these others uneasily left the scene, or sometimes pointed, which made him feel uncomfortable. His mother told him to stop hanging around their haunts, but Tiallin could not seem to help himself. He was persistent in assuming everything everyone else did or had was somehow better or more interesting than on his side of the woods.

Tiallin stopped at the door to his room and let his eyes travel up the passageway to the end, where Zerrith's door stood firmly shut, immutable as always. After some time considering, he looked away. The simple wooden door seemed a larger barrier between he and his older brother today than it had any other.

Maybe it was a part of this strange eleven seasons mark, Tiallin mused as he entered his own space. But he knew birthdays didn't change a squirrel all at once, no matter how much he wished those around him would pretend they did. Maybe his painful feelings were simply part of growing. But instead of feeling elated as he did when he took on a bit of physical girth, Tiallin was oddly saddened.

Perhaps I am finally growing into my species. Don't celebrate, don't reach out to others, don't explain yourself unless you will benefit from it. It's high time to stop wishing I was anything but what I am. I am a white squirrel. Isolation. That is all. White fur, white space, white noise.

But *oh, oh, oh,* Tiallin thought as only hours later he lay on his bed in a pool of hopeless sorrow, watercress salad done and eaten, straining not to cry at the sudden melancholy that gripped him. There was something truly frightening in an isolation so cold it could not even be shared with the others who experienced it, even though they might be living under the same branches.

The morning could not come fast enough.

CHAPTER III

The next day found Tiallin back where he had started the day before, standing in the darkened corridor outside the King's chambers alongside of Lyrah, whom he was doing his best to ignore. Truth be told, he still felt a bit disgruntled over her dismissal of him the day before, even though he knew his childish attitude must only be proving her right to do so. Lyrah had another bundle of cloth gripped firmly in her paws, from under which a few large bulges could be seen. More fruit, he supposed.

"Lyrah," he blurted, breaking the stillness between them. She smiled over at him in answer. It would seem that she wasn't at all aware of his game of cold shoulder.

"What is it that you do for the King anyway, aside from, erm, bringing him fruit? What does he like so much about fruit anyhow?"

"You don't like fruit?" Lyrah teased, and he flushed.

"You know what I mean."

Lyrah shrugged, still grinning. "I honestly don't know. As to your first question, I think King Sirius will tell you eventually."

Tiallin was startled, not to mention more than a little annoyed. "What? Is it that big of a secret? And how can you possibly bring this guy fruit every single day and still not have any idea why he likes it so much?"

Lyrah's large, dark wine-colored eyes continued to laugh at him. Tiallin had the sudden urge to grab her by the shoulders, to shake her, to demand of her, "Look at me! I am more important to him than you are! He speaks to me in secret and he has you gather *fruit*!" But he didn't say anything of the sort, and gave himself over to silent brooding instead. He fervently hoped the King would summon them inside soon. No sooner had he had the thought when the large door creaked open and he found himself looking into the face of a supremely stuffy looking guard with an enormous amount of excess fur above his upper lip.

"His Majesty King Sirius will see Miss Lyrah now," he puffed, and Tiallin halted in his premature advance to the door, slumping down once more to wait. The guard fixed him with a beady eye. "All in good time, lad," he said. Lyrah did not look back at him as she was lead through the door, and then it shut once more on Tiallin.

It was a good time later that she came out again, no longer carrying her suspicious bundle. This time she smiled at him, but he refused to pay her any mind and followed the blustery guard into the chamber. The door made a great solid thud of a sound behind them, sealing him off from her as they retreated in opposite directions.

"Tiallin."

The King's voice floated across the chamber to him.

The guard escorting Tiallin maneuvered him rather pompously, paws on his shoulders, until he was facing King Sirius before he took his leave of them.

"And how are you today?" Sirius addressed him, as if they had merely gathered for some tea, biscuits and idle gossip.

"I—I'm fine, I guess," Tiallin said. "Could be better, I guess. Though it's an honor to be here of course," he added quickly. He snuck a glance at the King's eyes with their vague disconnectedness before reverting to staring at the table nearby, which was much less awkward and possessed as ever a goodly amount of fruit.

"We could all be better," Sirius mused. It seemed as if he said it more to himself than to anyone else, so Tiallin didn't reply. He looked about the room and noticed that even the guards were not about. He and the King were truly alone this time.

"I—I have some questions, your Majesty," Tiallin said hesitantly.

"About the fruit?"

The abrupt assumption took him by surprise. How could Sirius know what he had been wondering only minutes earlier about Lyrah's purpose? To ask it outright, though, would sound imposing, not to mention ghastly rude. Tiallin thought of how he could skirt around the issue.

"Well…" he began. "If you don't mind my asking, your Majesty, why *do* you collect fruit like this?"

Sirius raised his eyebrows.

"I use it, of course. The stuff is exquisite…it is all I eat, in my age. I am quite thankful for it. But--!" he said, as if to forestall any comment from Tiallin, "fruit has its other uses. Berries especially are very good for making dyes."

Tiallin was mystified. "Dyes? What do you need dyes for?"

"Ah, well," Sirius smiled, clutching his beautifully crafted wooden cane tightly as he began to descend the platform he seemed to use in lieu of a throne. Tiallin watched him apprehensively, but his worry was needless— the king was almost alarmingly graceful, full of purposeful poise. The cane appeared to make up for Sirius's old age, and not his lack of vision.

Sirius made it down the platform and came over to stand across from Tiallin. They were on equal par now, and though Tiallin was tall for his age, it felt uncomfortable to know that he and the King were within an inch of each other's heights. It seemed there was less distance between them now, which had probably been Sirius's intention.

"With most of my fruit," King Sirius confided, "I make dyes. With those dyes, I am having a tapestry made."

"Oh," said Tiallin. He was a bit disappointed with this answer, but felt he could understand the pile of cloths he had seen beside the king the day before.

"This tapestry," Sirius continued, "It is going to be very unique. A work of art. Just as fruit is the essence of life, this tapestry is the essence of *my* life. For though mortal life can be taken, the work of the paws will always live on." Tiallin could have sworn Sirius really looked at him then, but of course that was impossible.

"Now," Sirius continued, with a lightness that suggested he had only been discussing the weather and not issues of feeble mortality, "I had something I have wanted to ask of *you* as well. But first I must start by attempting to make you understand as best I can. It is hard, you see, when others will…but never mind." There was a long pause during which Tiallin feared Sirius might have changed his mind about confiding in him, but then the King spoke.

"I have been feeling…strange."

Tiallin waited. Sirius seemed to be having a very hard time with this.

"You can trust me," he blurted.

Sirius smiled at him.

"Ah, yes, I had a fair idea that I could. But the real question is, can you trust me?"

And suddenly Tiallin had an idea of what Sirius meant, understood his hesitation. His mother's words of the day previous came unbidden to his mind.

Some say the king's intuition has turned into something less like intuition…more like…

Seeing things that aren't there.

Tiallin looked uneasily at King Sirius, then quickly looked away again, ashamed. He remembered his first impression of the King; he had been so sure he had felt the power: the silent power the full force of which could only be manifest in someone who was in full control of his mental faculties. Besides, the King trusted him; he had said as much. To now denounce Sirius as mad based on rumor would be betrayal of that trust.

But could he trust the King, truly? He knew that Sirius was waiting for an answer, so with all the sureness of pure youth, Tiallin spoke before he could subject the matter to further doubt.

"I trust you," he said firmly.

Sirius turned full toward him and the absolute gratitude in the set of his mouth, the lines easing on his forehead, more than made up for Tiallin's straggling doubts.

"Can I trust you then to do something for me?"

Tiallin nodded, then remembering the King could not see his acquiescence, said "Yes you can, your Majesty."

"Good. For the time being, I would ask you to keep an eye on anyone you come in contact with. In here, out in the forest, at home. Wherever. I have been having many indecipherable feelings of late, but there is always the underlying sense of disaster. Impending disaster, coming ever closer. And it comes from somewhere within our very community. They are so *sudden*, these thoughts I have been having. It was only about a month ago that I first got the pricklings of anything amiss. But since then, I have been noticing trends, disturbing trends..." His milky eyes seemed to chase over the carvings along the top of the wall nearest to them. Tiallin felt himself shiver a little.

"I do not mean to frighten you," Sirius continued, "But there have been too many coincidences. Recently things have been taken from within the Great Tree itself. Stolen. So far they are things of no great apparent value, but that matters little. If there is someone in our midst who is able to do this with such ease, who knows what else of great consequence they may be able to steal away?"

A bell rang outside the door, which swung open a crack at Sirius's admission. An old squirrel maid stuck her head in.

"Will you be taking your tea, your Majesty?"

"In a moment, Cunlidde."

He began speaking again before she had even shut the door, his voice hushed as he leaned toward Tiallin.

"So. Do we have an agreement? I am not asking much, only for you to be watchful. And of course, not to speak of our conversations to anyone. No, not even your mother, lovely as she is."

Tiallin did not take much time to think.

"Yes," he said, "on one condition."

"That being?" Sirius's voice had changed; it was stiff and wary, almost angry and Tiallin spoke rather fast, fearful at this change.

"Oh! It's just—I would really like to know why you picked *me*?"

The frost dropped from King Sirius's tone at once.

"I'm sorry, my boy. I did not mean to be sharp. It is just that you must understand, I am entrusting you with a good deal. Often, sadly enough, suspicion is necessary…Well. As for your question, there comes a point, when you have instincts as chilling as I have had, that you must find someone to confide them in. If something were to happen and I had never made an attempt at investigating the evidence of wrongdoing I *do* have…well, you can see how that might work against us all, not to mention bring me terrible guilt. So it was that I had to choose someone I felt to be trustworthy; and that is a benefit of owning the *magic*, as it is called by some dimmer species, of intuition: I have excellent perception for rooting out who can be trusted and who cannot. My first choice was denied to me; a shame, since I knew him to be made of good stuff. And then I was led to you. Yesterday when I had you come in, I admit that it was only to test my previous intuition on you, to measure its stirrings with you at close range. The results were excellent. Indeed, I am almost glad that my first choice was denied...Tiallin Stormskiln, you are truly something unique. You have..."

But he trailed off. Tiallin, a bit annoyed by the sheer number of instances Sirius seemed to trail off as if keeping all the good bits to himself, was mollified all the same. He had never felt so singled out, so special, as strange as the circumstances were. Tiallin had never been a perfectionist—far from it--but the king's words instilled in him an absolute determination to do the very best he could at what was asked of him. He only had one question, a question that nipped at him just under the surface of his considerable pleasure.

"Your Majesty...if you don't mind my asking, who *was* your first choice?"

The King put a paw to his mouth in pause a moment only before answering.

"Your brother."

CHAPTER IV

Edelle Craswotch was hearing noises.

At first, she had thought it was her own imagination. She'd turned over somewhat restlessly, mind full of idle curses directed at her lumpy mattress of straw, and attempted to fall back to sleep. But now, for the fifth time that night, she was hearing the sounds, and she could pretend no longer. The barely audible scratchings were just as much a part of her imagination as the dim stroke of moonlight pooled eerily on the ground only inches from where she slept or the slow rotation of the night into day as she lay far too intimate with her own sweat, unable to sleep for the seventh night in a row…and counting.

It was not because of the noises; *they* had only started tonight. The insomnia had been sudden and seemingly irreversible. Edelle had reluctantly been to see the medic-of-sorts in the colony earlier that week, but the portly older fox squirrel had only shook his head and given her some crushed thyme and essence of parsnip root to mix with her soup each night. Not only did it taste horrible, but it had done nothing to help her disturbing trend of wakefulness.

A clicking, as of claws creeping on bark came to Edelle's ears, and she felt her body go cold. Someone was right outside her dray, she could feel it. And they were very close to her window.

Edelle was sensible; she hated the idea that there was anything which could reduce her to a whining mess like so many of the females her age. Nor was she helpless; there was a small blade, worked with beautiful, intricate carvings on the handle hidden just under her mattress, and her sturdy, solid build would be a definite advantage should she have to strike and buy time to run. But she could not help thinking of her little cousin Bench and her grandparents in the adjoining room, all of whom would be much easier prey should the thing outside go for them instead.

For this one night, her insomnia had turned out to be a good thing; otherwise, she might have slept through the sounds of the intruder. She wondered vaguely if the imposter outside knew that she was vigilant and aware of him—was he waiting for some sign or signal? It had been some time, and still he had made no move. She considered the possibility that this was someone she knew, playing some sort of ill-advised practical joke, but there was no substance to the idea; her instincts told her otherwise.

When a full ten long breaths had passed, each seeming to take longer than the last, Edelle moved quietly to the edge of the bed, and waited. The faint scratching sound had not started up again in a while, but she knew whatever was out there had not left. They had been out there so long--whatever it was they wanted, they must want it very badly. And Edelle was ready to meet them when they came to get it.

So she waited.

And waited. Until at last, there was the uncomfortable sound of something sticking in wood, then the faint grunt of someone trying to maneuver himself. Perhaps they weren't all too experienced, and could be dealt with easily. But as soon as she had the thought, a blur of darkness pelted into the room, shot across the moonlit swatch of ground, and overtook her completely. Any attempt at sound lodged deep in her throat.

"Augh…"

"Quiet and I won't hurt yew."

Edelle thrashed from side to side, very nearly successfully dislodging her captor, who sounded more than a bit breathless.

Trying another tack, Edelle went limp quick as a fish, then without warning struck her tail against his face. Sputtering against the blur of coarse fur, the mysterious other released her at last. Turning quickly, she caught him in mid dash toward the window from whence he had come and flung him against the wall unceremoniously.

"Like I said!" the young gray squirrel yelped, apparently unable to recognize a lost cause when he saw one. "Don't make a sound and I won't hurt yew!"

Edelle only held him patiently against the wall until he quit struggling.

"Please. Why on Astrippa's green earth would it do me any good to be quiet when you're making enough of a racket for the both of us? "

The squirrel glared at her, but didn't seem to have any retort handy. He looked off to his right as if distracted, then attempted a desperate feint to the left. Edelle, taken off guard for only a moment, recovered and tightened her unforgiving grip on him. She waited again patiently as her charge finally tired himself out. He slumped back against the wall, panting.

"Just—give me—what—I want," he choked out between breaths.

Edelle studied him doubtfully.

The squirrel was rather young, probably almost exactly her own age. He was almost certainly a gray, though his coat looked abnormally dark; she assumed this was just because of the poor lighting, but she was astonished all the same. Grays didn't normally partake in such ruffian behavior—they were reputed as the most noble of the races-- and something like breaking into the home of another and attempting an attack…well, there was nothing noble about that! Looking at the youth now, she could see nothing overtly threatening about him. He was skinny and scruffy around the edges—not combat material, it was no wonder that she had overtaken him so easily. But all the same, she imagined she could see a seedy, dangerously reckless glint in the eyes which glared back at her with alarming boldness. It was the mark of one who lives only in shades of want, and Edelle found herself thinking that this was not a squirrel she would trust with anything of more import than a hairball. What was she to do with him now? She could not let him go, not while he might threaten others in the small fox squirrel community. How had he gotten in anyway? They had set up guards around the area...

While Edelle pondered, the grey fidgeted in her grasp, persistent as the dawn light which had begun to crawl to the corners of her room. The prophets of Astrippa all condemned cheating and trespassing, and though she was loathe to the idea of it, she wondered if perhaps asking this ruffian what he wanted would be the best way to get rid of him. The tried and true strategy, talk it out, build a bridge and all that. It couldn't hurt. Without further ado, she addressed him, plain, direct, as was second nature to her.

"What *do* you want?"

The gray eyed the knife he had dropped on the floor like he could make it come to him if only he looked hard enough.

And then likely proceed to swipe it across my throat, Edelle thought, not without some discomfort.

Finally the gray looked from the knife to Edelle, and those hungry eyes were dark and intent, without a trace of fear.

"I want my knife back."

"Your knife?" Edelle said slowly. "You must think I'm crazy! I'm not thick, you know. You didn't come all this way from wherever you're from to wait outside my window for a good hour all to get something you had in your paw in the first place!"

"Not *that* one, the knife *yew* have. *My* knife. I want it back, and I want to know where yew got it!" His voice got slightly high on its last note, and she thought she caught a hint of anguish in it, which bemused her. He seemed unduly distressed; it was only a knife, after all. She was growing impatient, not to mention angry that he should think he could take that knife from her when it had been a special gift from—

She caught herself in mid-blush and snapped back to the business at hand.

"It isn't *your* knife. How many knives do you own anyway?"

"Plenty, and yeah, it is! Don't try to hide it from me, I saw yew with it today at...at that thing where yer pickin' fruit!"

"The harvest," she ground out. "You were watching me at the noontide harvest? Give me one reason why I shouldn't take the knife you're going on about and slit your throat!"

The gray's eyes widened into deep, swirling wells of anger mingled with fear. In a jolting movement that left Edelle little time to foresee, he pushed her from him, reaching for her wrist and twisting it, hard, then let go and moved away to stand at the far corner of the room, fur hanging in his face, breathing hard.

Edelle stared at the mad squirrel as he lifted his head and stared at her across her bedroom. There was real hatred in the eyes that might have been attractive had they been set in any other face. The gray's face was a distraught mess of emotion as he screamed.

"YEW DID IT! Yew, it was *yew*, yew killed him and now they all think—stupid, soft-arsed idjits—they all think it's me!"

"I can't imagine why," Edelle snapped, rubbing her wrist and backing towards the bed. If she could just get there she could take the cause of all this fuss from under the mattress where it lay at the ready and really give this crazy squirrel something to shout about. In the next room, she thought she could hear a stirring, and hoped she was mistaken; if her grandparents thought she were in trouble, they would be here in a matter of seconds, and there was nothing she could do to warn them.

Edelle took another step back and felt her back hit the bed, and reached under the mattress, pulling her paw back with a grimace. Her wrist was swelling alarmingly fast. Before she could go to use the other paw, she heard a definite muttering from the room next door, and her blood went cold.

No, no, please no. The gray was standing between her and the door, the door through which her unsuspecting family would come. Knife momentarily forgotten, Edelle frantically began to search her mind for a way, any way, to warn them, to stop them coming in.

The matter was taken entirely out of her hands by the rogue gray, who suddenly dashed forward and retrieved his knife from the floor with reflexes smooth as water. Edelle's whole body tensed as the grey leapt at her; she was sure he was coming in for another attack, but in the next instant he had passed her, leapt onto the bed and out the window into the night once more.

Edelle stood for a good two minutes, back to the window and body stock-still as her heart rate gradually slowed to normal. First she listened for any sound that might hint that the gray was lying in wait outside once more. Nothing. She turned slowly and poked her head out of the window and peered into the dark, searching…

Nothing, still. The night was a thick blanket of silence which received her tangled fear with reassurance, carrying it away from her into its crisp autumnal depths.

"Edelle? Edelle, is everything fine in there?"

It was her grandmother's voice; as usual, her grandmother had already begun to crack the door as she spoke, a habit that Edelle had found infuriating as a child.

Edelle counted to three mentally, preparing herself to sound perfectly cool.

"I'm fine. I've just been having trouble sleeping."

"We heard a lot of noise, missy!" Grandfather's voice chimed in from the background, chiding. "Bench woke up, and you know how hard it is to rouse that child! Like raising the dead…Weren't you tired from harvesting?"

The door was fully ajar now, and she could see them peering in at her, her grandfather now in front, large ear-tufts quivering and paws on hips in a fashion that would have made her smile any other day.

"I got a second wind, I guess," she said lamely, wondering just how much of the recent debacle they had heard. If they had awakened to the gray's screams…well, perhaps she should have taken the path of having had a nightmare. Edelle was no good at lying, and she knew it. Untruths always made her feel horrible. Even now, her stomach turned as she said "But now I think I'm beginning to feel sleepy. You needn't worry about being disturbed again."

There was a lengthy pause. Then her grandmother said, "Well all right. If you're certain." She scanned Edelle with a puzzled lift of her brow.

"No disturbance, my last year's nuts. Of course there'll be more noise, what with Bench up and all."

"Oh hush, Grenden. Let her be. Long day…"

The sounds of her grandparents' voices faded as they made their way back to their own room, and when she heard their door close, Edelle let out a long sigh. Perhaps she *should* try to get some sleep. Turning back to her bed, she could not help but take another glance out the open window. Nothing, not one hint of her mysterious visitor. She wondered if she had imagined it all, but it was not a real wondering at all; she knew with every fiber of her being that the strange gray squirrel with the coarse accent had been no part of anyone's imagination.

As she lay back on her straw bed, her paw—the uninjured one this time—slid under the mattress and felt about.

Edelle sat bolt upright once more, the meager strains of sleep that had finally begun to fall about her evaporating like so much stardust.

Her knife was gone. He had got what he wanted after all.

As dawn came stretching across Ashwood and into Firwood to the bounds of the Aspen Forest, its gentle light lit upon the gleam of something sharp and gleaming in the tops of one of the very highest trees.

Lute traced the swirling pattern of the hydrangea, the bumblebee and the hourglass, all exactly where he remembered them. Yes, this was it, there was no mistaking it. How *had* the hefty fox squirrel gotten her paws on it? His paw lingered on the handle for a moment before running ever so lightly once over the blade and back.

He shouldn't have yelled at her perhaps. Now the news might spread around, and everyone would know. There would be no doubt then that it was he who had slashed old Pember's neck, left him lying in the mud, in that joke of a half-swamp. The body only half in, half out, too, in a ridiculously near-amusing, macabre fashion-- mouth laid open, eyes strangely blank. They would say he did it. They had *already* been saying it…after all, was it not he who would have everything to gain? He would surely not miss the hard paw of Pember at his head or the sullen criticisms of small missteps. The others had never trusted him, oddity that he was…a result of the twisted intercourse of black and grey, raised among red thieves, and as good as one himself. Who else would have done it, indeed?

Left the throat bleeding, all…open, terribly open, like me when he first taught…

Lute shut his eyes against the stinging and clenched his paws tightly, forgetting the knife he held in his left. He gasped and watched the trail of red make its way down the blade to the wood of the handle, soaking in at first then running over the trail of the hydrangea's graceful stem, and down to the bumblebee, where it stopped, energy expended. Lute stared down at it for a while, his good paw moving to wipe the mess away before it ruined the craftsmanship—his craftsmanship—but paused and then simply held the handle against his cheek, letting salt mingle with salt.

CHAPTER V

Edelle's grandparents had quite forgotten about the incident the night before, or that was how it seemed to her. They didn't even broach the subject, which, knowing her grandparents, was likely a sign of forgetfulness rather than sympathetic tact. Her worsening insomnia was general knowledge about the dray, so she assumed they had just attributed anything they had heard to her inability to sleep. Though if they had heard *him* scream...

Edelle could not forget the way that shout had sounded, all at once angry and sad, predator and prey; pure emotion, thin skin broken to reveal bone. She was not sure whether it had scared her; Edelle was not accustomed to the feeling of fright, not since her younger years and the panic attacks that she tried not to think of, the anxiety that the doctors said would not go away; it was intrinsic, inborn, they said as they flicked their tails importantly, but they were wrong. All it took was faith for fear to vanish.

Edelle stared at the picture of Astrippa above her nightstand. In it, the squirrel goddess was pale, almost translucent in color, only her torso visible above the branches of some giant tree, paws reaching out and down to either side of her, on one of which stood an old squirrel staring upwards while on the other a young, transparent squirrel was reaching up, paw connecting with Astrippa's and melting into it at once. The picture had been a gift to her from her father before he'd left.

As she let her eyes wander over the familiar features of the picture, Edelle found herself saying a small prayer for the young gray from the night before, despite his seemingly violent tendencies. It had seemed that he might also be a bit afraid. She knew she should not be feeling sympathetic at all towards him; after all, he was crude and potentially dangerous…he had even confessed to owning a good stock of knives, though she wasn't so sure whether this had been just to scare her. Well, he would have one more knife to add to whatever he had already, since he had taken hers. Her heart tightened at the thought; the knife, too, had been a gift, presented to her only a few days ago in the early hours of the morning by a handsome fox squirrel who had blushingly stated that he had been told to give it to her with congratulations on twelve seasons. He had hurried away so quickly afterward that his tail might have been on fire, she thought in amusement. She hoped someday he would work up the courage to come out from anonymity—she had had her eye on him for some time, almost since he had moved in to the community a few weeks back. He was a quiet, sensible sort—the sort that Edelle would like to get acquainted with. And the knife itself had been wonderful, exquisite…she sighed at the thought of its loss. What would the handsome young squirrel think if he knew she'd lost his gift already? She dearly hoped he hadn't carved it himself, for the craftsmanship had been such as she had never seen in her life, with the curving graceful flowers and lifelike bumblebee. If he had carved such a thing…she felt herself blush again. Well, maybe she *did* wish it to be so.

As the day went on and Edelle stayed shut up in her room, dimly thinking of how she should make some attempt to join her family, to help with Bench, the whole incident of the stolen knife weighed on her mind. It all made no sense, and no matter how she tried to keep it from impeding on her thoughts, the situation played over and over in her head, a colorful jumble of images and sound, always pervaded by the hysterical shout she remembered most of all, ringing in her ears.

'IT WAS YEW! Yew, it was yew, yew killed him—

Killed who? Edelle had never harmed a soul, unless you counted the time she had made Bench eat sand when they were both younger. He had been sick for days. Though she tried not to let it, it bothered her that anyone would think her a killer. The gray had been on her trail for some time, apparently. He had seen her at the autumnal harvest, which made her exceedingly nervous. And whom was she supposed to have killed?

"*IT WAS YEW!*"

It was not *me!*

All alone in her bedroom, she stared around at the walls and the door and the window and the picture of Astrippa and everything else, the everything that began to close around her at once, until she closed her eyes. Breathe. Pray. Breathe. Pray.

After a time she opened her eyes again and sat in silence. So she needed answers. She would get them all in good time. She *intended* to get them, even if she needed to track down the scrawny gray to do it.

For now, though, it was high time that she got some fresh air.

She found Bench outside, alone, swinging his feet off the end of a particularly long branch. When he heard her coming, he looked up quickly and grinned.

"Why'd you spend so much time inside?"

Bench was only six seasons and started every conversational venture with a question.

Edelle shrugged. "I was tired."

"But you don't sleep!"

"I know. I was trying to. Why aren't you running around anymore?"

"*I* was tired."

"Ah."

"Dell?"

"Hmm."

"Have you ever seen a white squirrel? Like, actually seen one?"

Edelle caught the look on his face—eager and excited—and smiled.

"No, I haven't. I'm sure it would be fascinating, though. Why do you ask?"

"Oh. Then I guess you wouldn't know." Bench made no effort to keep his disappointment anything but obvious. "I was wondering if they had wings."

"Wings?! You mean like in the old children's fables? Oh, Bench…"

"What?" His tone was defensive.

"You know they're only stories, put out by elders with too much time on their paws. It's—"

"You don't *know* that!" he interrupted. "*You've* never seen a white squirrel, have you? They *could* fly! And they do protect all the others from danger up in Pinewood, right? I think it's true that they used to be messengers of Astrippa, and that they were banished and she made this place here for them instead, bounded by water and closed the heavens off to them, *and* made everything else here, all the plants and bugs and all the other squirrels different colors. But she didn't give the white squirrels color, and that's why they look so funny! It was a curse. And she told them that if they ever wanted to get back—"

"Bench. Please. It is an interesting tale, but that's what makes stories good! Truth doesn't have to have a hand in it. Besides, I think that if the white squirrels were really messengers of Astrippa, a story like that wouldn't be forgotten. They'd have it written in their histories, and we'd *definitely* know it for fact."

Bench looked sullen. "Well, then, how do you know Astrippa's real?"

Edelle turned to him, anger flaring up inside her.

"*Don't* say that!"

"Okay, okay...!" Bench eyed her nervously, and she knew she had scared him and should be ashamed, but somehow she couldn't eke out an apology. The blood was still pounding in her ears, and her tongue felt awfully dry. Bench shifted on the branch, then collected himself from the sitting position he had taken and left to go inside. Edelle stayed out for a long time after, just feeling the cold air nipping at her skin under her fur, making it prickle. A fall leaf came drifting past her, making weary circles in the air as it neared the ground.

I'm tired, too, she whispered in the safety of her own mind, unable to admit it out loud.

She did not see the figure watching in the trees opposite her.

CHAPTER VI

If Tiallin had been bothered by the discovery that it was actually his brother the king had wanted at first and not him, he had tried not to show it. In truth, he did not know what upset him more—the idea of Zerrith being chosen or the idea of his brother not accepting the invitation. Tiallin knew the reason already, or thought he did—their father had never been a fan of the king, and he would not have wanted his eldest son working under him.

His father confirmed this only a night later, stabbing viciously at a bit of parsley on his plate, eyes narrowed.

"Oh, I'll say you're in his bondage for good now, Tiallin my boy," he said shortly, "Sirius never gives out posts unless he intends you to hold them...for life. Not fond of short-term commitment, he's not. If you ask me—

"Datin," Iskla warned from her place at the table. Zerrith, until now seated in an odd, spaced out posture as if he had been dreaming of something much more interesting than the situation at hand, turned his head to look between Tiallin and his father, eyebrows lifted slightly.

Their father, noticing the new attention he was receiving, paused on the edge of his words and sunk back slowly into his seat. When he opened his mouth next, it was to shove the brutalized leaf of parsley down his gullet. He chewed, swallowed, paused to wipe his mouth, then said quietly, "All I mean is that I think there are better things for a young squirrel like you to do than to wait hand and foot on an old blind—well. He ought to have asked me beforehand. *You* could have consulted me."

"I know, father," Tiallin said, wondering whether he could leave the table yet. He was finished eating, and this conversation about his work for Sirius was making him uncomfortable.

"Now, when Zerrith was called to service, it was a different story," Datin went on, this time ignoring Iskla's pleading look. "Of course, Sirius made the mistake of telling me, and I told him no thank you very much, no sir. Now he's getting crafty, I suppose, sprung this upon you at the last minute when I wasn't around to stop it happening."

Tiallin, staring despairingly out of the window until now, stiffened.

That's not true, he thought. *I knew for a long time that I was going to work for King Sirius on my eleventh season.* He had never told his father, but that was only because Tiallin assumed he had known. But, he, Tiallin, had known! He had known since his mother—

Tiallin looked up into his mother's face across the table, and knew then. And though he did not understand, he felt a strong surge of affection for her quiet intellectual gleam. She had not told him. For whatever reason, Tiallin's mother had agreed to his assignment and not told his father…

"—Right, Zerrith?" His father appeared to have finally finished denouncing Tiallin's life choices.

"I'm not sure, father," Zerrith said, in the slowly thoughtful way he said everything. "I think that Tiallin could prove to be of use to us all by working for King Sirius. I didn't agree with my assignment more because it was not what I believe I am meant to do."

A respectful silence greeted these words, a silence in which Tiallin reflected bitterly on how if *he* had said such a thing, it would only have warranted a snort and a shrug from his father and a smile from his mother.

"Hmm," his father said. The discussion seemed to end there. Relieved, Tiallin immediately escaped outside for a breath of fresh air. Free at last from the eyes of others, he leaned up against their solid pine home and shut his eyes tight, counting to five. It seemed like ever since he had signed himself into Sirius's service, his life had consisted of tightly kept secrets and concerns, leaving little time for innocent pleasures.

A rustling sounded from a clump of brush some feet away, and Tiallin eyed it curiously. A moment went by and the brush crackled again, but still Tiallin could see no one. The fur on the nape of his neck rose uncomfortably; someone was watching him, he could feel it. Deeply unsettled, Tiallin stood thinking for a moment, then went to the other side of the tree out of sight of the clump of brush and picked up a good sized stick. Peering around the pine again, he took aim and lobbed the stick long and hard at the bush. Tiallin's aim was precise; he hit the bush from which the sounds had issued spot on, and was rewarded by a squeal and a frantic thrashing sound.

Leaping out from his hiding place, Tiallin was just in time to see the brush-like tail of a small gray disappear into the surrounding forest. A moment later, he spotted the same squirrel making his hurried way up a nearby tree.

Tiallin gave chase, determined not to let his quarry out of sight.

"Hey—Hey!" he called, winding his way around one tree and diving headlong into the resinous, prickly needles of the next. "I'm not going to hurt you! Hey, get back here, will you? I just want to—

But Tiallin was unable to speak anymore without feeling winded, and continued the chase in silence, keeping his eyes always on the bobbing, waving gray brush in front of him. He was getting closer, closing in now…

But then the gray all but vanished, and Tiallin was left standing rather foolishly in the high reaches of a towering pine, utterly confused and frustrated. He searched the area and grew ever more exasperated when he could not find a hole or possible means of escape anywhere. And still he was uncomfortably aware of the gnawing, uneasy sensation that there were eyes on his back everywhere he turned, as if the gray stranger had not really gone, but was merely watching now from a safer vantage point.

A weary fifteen minutes of fruitless searching, and Tiallin was forced to finally descend the tree and make his way back home. His mother and father were both still in the kitchen, which did nothing to improve his rotten mood—he had been hoping he could catch Iskla alone so he talk to her. He felt a deep need to know why it was she had given him over to the service of the King.

Alas, Tiallin thought grumpily as he ascended the narrow pathway to his room. *It looks like there will be no answers for me tonight.*

Secrets and concerns. Concerns and secrets. He was sick of it already.

When Tiallin reached his room, he was forced out of his brooding and into a kind of mystified shock by the note he found lying on his bed.

Tiallin—

Congratulations on your eleventh season! Present forthcoming.
~Z

p.s. don't listen to mother or father. Everyone has their own theories, but I think the King is only scared.

Tiallin folded the note in half and held it in his paw a moment before putting it in his chest of drawers for safekeeping. It was where all his other notes from Zerrith were kept, even as their number decreased dramatically over the years. It used to be that Zerrith would leave him notes while Tiallin was out racing in the trees, waiting for his younger brother to return and continue a game they had been playing. Usually the notes then would be about the next part of the game, some pretend element Zerrith had invented while Tiallin was away. Despite his genuine love of the outdoors, Tiallin could remember sometimes only taking a break from their games so that he would have a note on his bed to return to.

Even when they were not serving a purpose as part of some game, notes were Zerrith's chosen method of communication. He rarely spoke aloud unless he was addressed or else overflowing with passion over something or other. Over the years, Tiallin had come to notice that Zerrith never wrote meaningless notes. He wrote notes that might seem meaningless to others, but Tiallin knew better: each note was saying something his brother considered important, oftentimes too important for mere words.

Curling up in bed, Tiallin wondered what his present from Zerrith would be, at the same time hoping that Zerrith would tell him his secret. For Zerrith *did* have a secret. It had been Tiallin's ninth season when he realized this. It was not so much evident in the way Zerrith said things as in the way he didn't say things, which was just like Zerrith; Tiallin's brother was a squirrel of very few words and more passion than he knew what to do with.

He saw it always, this betraying evidence of something kept quiet, on Zerrith's face when they passed in the corridors and in his eyes when Zerrith thought no one else was looking. But something Zerrith didn't know was that Tiallin was *always* looking, ever since they were young, and Tiallin, a pudgy, over excitable and terribly plain youth had been thoroughly entranced by the quietly important reserve his handsome brother carried.

Even if he had managed to miss it somehow in all the half-movements and starts and demure smiles, Tiallin could not fail to notice that Zerrith had begun to lock himself in his room for extended periods of time which sometimes translated to days, only coming out to share a meal or to watch the sunset from the highest branch. Zerrith was big for sunsets.

Their parents had at first seemed oblivious to the slight changes in their elder son, and in this Tiallin took strange pride. No one, perhaps, was more skilled in gauging Zerrith's body language than was Tiallin. There had, after all, been a time when, as not much more than pups, they had been closer. A very short time it was, for Tiallin was separated not just by eight gaping seasons but by the same white space that seemed to separate Zerrith from everyone else. No, truth be told, most of what Tiallin had learned about his brother he had learned from careful observation.

Tiallin had known his brother had a secret, and even though keeping secrets was not exactly Tiallin's strong point, he had kept the fact of his knowing a secret as well. Perhaps Zerrith would now reward him by telling him what it was. It was clinging on to this excited notion that Tiallin finally drifted off into sleep.

"Do you know why I am king, boy?"

Tiallin started. He had been staring, mesmerized at one of the many dust motes floating in the brightly lit air in front of him when King Sirius's voice called him back into the moment. Thinking frantically on the question posed to him, Tiallin realized that he did not know, exactly. Kings were a custom of the white squirrels, but he had never pondered their exact purpose.

In Tiallin's hesitation, Sirius found the answer to his question.

"Ah, yes." The eerie, sightless eyes looked as if they were focused straight on the young squirrel, who shifted uncomfortably. This was Tiallin's third visit to the King, and though he knew Sirius to possess a generally benign, amused temperament, he was yet to get used to those eyes.

"I do not rule," Sirius began, stroking his carved cane up and down thoughtfully with an idle finger as he spoke, "So as to make rules or regulations for our colony. That, I think, would be useless and I have no personal interest in such things. No, I am here as a protector of sorts." He held up a paw. "Not in the way you are probably thinking. I…have a talent, which goes along with my intuition. I can not only sense most danger when it is impending, but I can sometimes *push* with my mind, and when I give that *push*, I can feel it draw back a bit. Shut your mouth, please."

Tiallin realized his mouth was agape, and closed it, flushing.

"I have been able to save more than a few terrible things from making their way to our doorstep over the years. This is the true tradition of the white kings. Now, this talent of mine is rather unusual, not in the least because it does not last. I did not possess it all my life, and I am not sure I will possess it much longer at all." His voice grew tired, worn. "Rarely have two successive kings of the whites," he said, extending a paw to indicate the walls full of carvings, "been father and son. No, this 'magic' of sorts would not appear to be hereditary. Usually someone, a prospective heir, will be born with the talent before the talent of the old King decides to up and leave him. This is a pattern that has been counted on through the years, and it has never yet failed. But Tiallin… no possible heir has been born for some time. And they should have by now. They should have. If they do not show themselves very, very soon, then I will die with no one to succeed me."

Though his voice was steady, Tiallin thought he could hear a subdued fear in the King's words and felt suddenly afraid himself.

"What would that mean for us?" he asked slowly.

"What would it mean? Why, it would mean that we would fail as a colony. Already, the signs of imminent failure are appearing. Less and less of us seem to be expressing innate…skill. And those who do," His voice grew harsh. "Those who do only want to use their gifts for selfish means."

Tiallin kept his silence. He was not sure he understood what the King was talking about.

"You see these walls, Tiallin?" Sirius went on. Tiallin turned his attention to the carvings on the honey colored walls of the cavernous room.

"Yes," he said.

"These walls are a history of the race of white squirrels in Arborand for as long as living memory goes. Each square, each carving represents a period of time that marks something new. There is the battle of the serpents, the crafting of the first illusions," he seemed to recite them from memory, and Tiallin looked back and forth between the carvings as he spoke, trying to find the ones he spoke of, but he soon gave up. They were far too numerous.

"—The reign of Tamen Nunquil and his disappearance…and then me. I could go on about these walls for some time, as you may be able to tell," he gave Tiallin a brief smile. "But."

King Sirius walked slowly over to the wall closest them. He placed a withered paw over the raised wood of one carving and began to walk along the wall in this manner, brushing each carving briefly as he passed it, until he came to the one where Tiallin noticed that Sirius himself was portrayed, standing in a proud fashion with the fingers of one paw placed on his temple and the other clutching what looked like an eye. Tiallin thought the King would stop at this carving, but his paw passed it over, lingering only for a moment on the miniature wooden face that was meant to resemble his own, and coming to rest instead on the wall directly next to it, a small wooden space no bigger than a picture frame such as the other carvings occupied— only unlike them, this space was unmistakably blank, the wall still smooth and unblemished.

Tiallin looked up into Sirius's face, trying to understand what the old squirrel wanted him to know, but his expression was unreadable. Finally, he felt the need to break the silence and said, "So what do you do when you run out of wall space?"

"Well, that is exactly the thing, Tiallin," the king said softly. "I do not think we will need to worry about that. I do not think we will ever need more wall space."

Tiallin wanted to ask exactly what the King meant, wanted to pretend he didn't already know. He felt impossibly sad at the despair he sensed in the older squirrel.

"You—but you—he struggled for words, and Sirius sat, his gaze that was not a gaze at all infinitely patient, staring always over Tiallin's head as if at something only he could see.

"You don't know that you won't find an heir!" Tiallin blurted at last. Sirius just smiled a bitter smile, fingers lightly tracing his cane.

"Oh yes, I know," he said. "Those who show the kind of talent that I have shown are very rare, and when they do show it, it is at a very young age. I myself was only five seasons when it first came to me. I could not too anything of great magnitude with my skill *then*, mind you, though occasionally I could sense when my mother was going to insist that I bathe and convince her to forget it before she even started off to find me. But that is not the point. Do you have any idea how rare your family is, Tiallin? Have you never noticed how few other young squirrels there are in this colony?"

Tiallin had indeed never given the matter much thought, but now that he did he saw what Sirius was driving at. It was true; thinking back to his childhood days, he could not seem to recall a single other squirrel of around the same age that he could have called a playmate. He was shocked never to have realized before now, but it had seemed normal to him at the time; his family was all. It was natural. He rarely even saw the other white squirrels of the Pinewood colony. They each kept to their own interests, locked away in their homes or alone with their thoughts in the treetops. Tiallin had often wondered whether most of his kind stayed inside because they didn't like being stared at. It seemed that every time he went outside these days, someone—he thought sorely back to the incident with the gray—had to disrupt his peace and stare. But why did the white squirrels stay together in the same place at all, if they felt so little connection to one another? Was it the King's skill, did they feel safer around his particular brand of magic? Or could it be that there *was* something that held them together, weak though it might be…like clinging onto the ghost of something that no longer existed?

Tiallin let a sigh escape him. How frustrating it was to understand so little of one's own species!

King Sirius had gone into a reverie of his own, and Tiallin brought him out of it by asking the question that, along with zillions of others it seemed, was weighing on his mind since he had entered these chambers.

"Your Majesty," he said cautiously, "If there *is* no heir…"

"Yes, go on."

"If there is no heir, well…maybe we can just *elect* a new King, erm, when the time comes, and. And the community can go on. I mean, not to say—

Tiallin, hot in the face, stopped himself. He should have foreseen how awful his idea, so poorly articulated, would sound to the King! Who knew how much time Sirius had left? And here Tiallin was, suggesting that his king might be more easily replaceable than he thought!

Sirius cut into his frenzied self-bashing thoughts to say, simply. "I could hope that you are right, Tiallin. But I know you are not. As I told you before, I have sensed a particular…disaster coming this way. Danger, and with my senses as they are, I cannot seem to stop it from coming."

He paused, and Tiallin understood then that the King had just admitted to something massive, something that would be a terrible weapon if placed in the wrong paws. And Sirius was entrusting this, the hint of his mortality, the crippling truth that he woke to every day, not as a powerful king but as a normal squirrel whose clock was ticking short, to *him*. Tiallin felt a strange sense of importance, of power. It frightened him and exhilarated him at once, and he had to close his eyes, glad for once that Sirius could not see what he was sure was written on his face.

"I need you to help me, Tiallin," the King continued softly, "I need you to help me find the source of my fears. It could well be that it is inside these walls. Remember when I told you that things were being stolen? Things like our rare hollow willow poles are disappearing from storage. They make excellent flutes, and tapestry hangings, but I am finding that there are less of them each week. I have not caught the culprit. It may have nothing at all to do with my fears on a larger scale, as they seem quite ridiculous and harmless snatchings. But they are still snatchings, *stealing*, and while there is much I tolerate, stealing is not on the list."

From his tone, Tiallin knew he meant it sincerely.

"This sort of thing, Tiallin, is why I told you to keep an eye out for me. Have you seen anything of late?"

Tiallin lowered his head. He hadn't, but neither had he been paying particularly fastidious attention to his new assignment. For a moment, he thought of the gray squirrel, but felt stupid for it immediately. The little sneak had to have been only seven seasons, if that.

Sirius seemed to have guessed the truth in his silence.

"Do not worry. I did not really expect you to, in such a short time. Very well, then, you may go."

Tiallin, silently resolving not to let the king down this time, stepped towards the door. No sooner had he opened it when he was accosted by Lyrah. She was not holding any fruit this time, which came as a surprise, and her face was rather strained. She did not look as if she had got much sleep of late, but it did not stop Tiallin from turning his back coldly, even as she shouted out.

"Tiallin!"

Tiallin continued through the empty passageway to the entrance of the Great Tree.

"Tiallin, please!"

She was following him. Rotting oak roots, she must really be upset. Inwardly cursing himself for lacking a soul of iron, Tiallin turned to face her at last, raising his eyebrows in what he hoped was a convincing air of surprise.

"Yes?"

Lyrah glanced about them both distractedly before saying, "Look, I know you don't like me very much. Oh, come on, don't look at me like that, I'm not thick. But I…I need to ask you a favor."

Tiallin's heart beat just a little bit harder within the shelter of his ribs, and he felt an absurd type of hope start to form.

I'm pathetic, he thought, just as Lyrah said, "Could you tell Zerrith—

Oh, in the name of acorns buried and lost!

"Tell him yourself," Tiallin said roughly, and shoved past her, out into a day that was colder than he remembered it.

Zerrith was watching the sunset.

Tiallin was not sure even now why he had decided to approach his brother tonight. Perhaps he just longed for a conversation that was reminiscent of familiar things, something ordinary in a life that had suddenly become anything but. Or maybe he was just hoping for some follow up on the note he had received the night before. Either way, Tiallin made his way easily out across the long knotty branch on which Zerrith was perched, until he came to stand beside his brother. The unseasonably cold afternoon air wrapped around them both, aware of one another's presence but not speaking. Tiallin was just reflecting on how Zerrith was probably the only squirrel he could stand in the same space with in complete silence and never feel the awkward need to fill it up with sound, when Zerrith broke that silence.

"The sky is very red this evening, don't you think?"

Tiallin looked obediently up at the horizon and saw the deep, wine-stained line running from clouds to treeline, like a void, or blood, or a solemn warning.

"Yeah," he said. "Yeah, I guess it is. The clouds are a sort of nice orange, too…What've you been thinking about?"

Zerrith turned to face him.

"Oh, a lot of things tonight. Tonight I feel very thoughtful." He looked down for a moment, and Tiallin noticed he was holding a maple leaf in his paws. There weren't many maple trees in the area.

"Where'd you get that?"

"This? Just earlier today, while you were with the King, I took a trip across the border to Firwood, mostly just thinking. There are a lot of gray squirrels there, you know. They seemed to find me very interesting. But they seem very shy as well."

"I know," Tiallin said.

"I did find this, though. I wish we had more leaves like this around here because I think they're very interesting." He traced the stem where it ran up the leaf and split into several vein-like branches. "You can see it's alive, I think that's part of what I like. You can *see* it instead of only smell it."

"Mm," Tiallin said. He supposed he could see what his brother meant. "Zerrith, why did you not want to work for the King?"

"I've told you, Tiallin. It wasn't my thing, that's all."

"It wasn't your *thing*?" Tiallin could hear the skepticism in his own voice, and Zerrith sure didn't miss it, for when he next spoke he was unusually short and condescending.

"Not everyone wants most to go high places, Tiallin."

The impact was as desired. It stung. Tiallin caught a gust of biting wind, prickling against his cheek, and suddenly he felt much less like staying out here on this stupid branch, staring at some equally stupid sunset.

"You've got a girl just *clamoring* after you, you know," he said acidly. "You might want to go talk to her, see what her problem is so she isn't constantly bothering *me* every time I step into the Great Tree."

Zerrith started, and his face seemed to go a shade paler, though it was hard to tell under his snowy fur.

"Do you mean Lyrah? What is she saying?"

"I don't know, I don't stick around long enough to hear it. But she obviously wants you to hear it, so will you please just shut her up? How do you know her in the first place?"

He knew his curiosity had ruined the effect of his previously sharp words, but as always, he could not help himself.

"Lyrah and I are—friends," Zerrith said simply. "We have been for some time. I will of course talk to her if she's bothering you so much."

"Fine," Tiallin snapped. He wasn't done being angry. As Zerrith moved past him to go inside, Tiallin called after him.

"Where are you going now? Back to your room? What's so much better about there than the King's chambers? You spend your life staring at things and thinking, huh, well I can certainly see how that's *much* better than what I'm doing!!"

"I'm not going to *stare*—"

Zerrith sounded indignant, and Tiallin felt a burst of triumph.

"I know you're not! You're going to do whatever you've been doing for the past couple of seasons! You've been working on something, and it's a secret, and I know it, and you know it, and no one else does, but I think you're taking a bit too much for granted. Maybe I'll just tell everyone you're up to something and then they'll find out all about it!"

It was the first time Tiallin had ever said this much of what had until now been implicitly understood out loud, and he wondered if he'd gone too far. Shouting at Zerrith made him feel sort of hollow inside, but he had been grievously hurt by his elder brother's words. He was also the tiniest bit peeved that the one thing he had achieved of high standing in his life was something that his brother had been offered first and had turned down for the most casual of reasons.

Zerrith stared at him across the branch, a paw resting on the trunk near the doorway, frozen in place. Tiallin half expected him to yell, or to lash back at him, or to say he never wanted to talk to Tiallin again, would never leave him another note. But instead, Zerrith just lowered his paw slowly, face lapsing back into thoughtfulness.

"You're right," he said.

"Yeah, well I'm glad you've finally—what?"

"You're right. You deserve to know. Soon."

Tiallin expected him to say more, but he just turned, and walked into the tree very slowly. He heard a door open and close, and then nothing.

Tiallin followed soon after. The clouds on the horizon were no longer pink but had succumbed to a deep red, like an inkblot or the end of a sentence, heralding the start of something new.

Soon.

CHAPTER VII

Lute did not know exactly why he had come back, what he had hoped to find by returning to the outskirts of the forest in which the young fox squirrel lived, the frightening one with the quick temper and the steady paw. He hadn't liked her one stinking bit, and what was more, he knew that she had *not* killed Pember. What he did not know was how on earth, then, she'd gotten her paws on the knife that had taken Pember's life.

Lute had spent a wretched night in the forest neighboring this one. Unable to find a hollow to curl up in, the young squirrel had been forced to make do with a sparse covering of leaves for comfort. It had all done little good in the end, for he could not sleep a wink, and had spent the whole night staring out into the darkness through the cracks in the leaves, wondering...

If Edelle Craswotch had thought Lute a bit different from most squirrels of his kind, she had been more than right. Lute, perhaps because he was raised by those who were not of his kind, did not really fit in with those of *any* kind. Despite his lanky build, he often felt all angles and awkward bulk when placed in the company of others. If Edelle had thought Lute reprehensible, she would have been right again. Lute was a thief.

He had been brought up in the trade, with the band of chickarees ("red thieves" as they were called in the south) that had raised him. When Pember took him in, this had all changed; the old squirrel had immediately insisted on complete respectability, belonging, as he did, to an erudite class of older grays. Lute had cursed it, hated it at first—he would steal things from Pember's friends just to spite them. But very soon he had realized one of the great truths of life: you did not cross Pember and expect to be happy afterward.

But someone *had* crossed Pember. Someone had crossed him and apparently won. And that was the reason that Lute was now standing here wearily, his paw against the trunk of the tree, feeling completely drained from lack of sleep the night before but persistent in staring at the tree he had visited only last night. She was sitting there, on a low-hanging branch, expression inscrutable from this far away. There had been another squirrel with her a while back, one who looked as though he could have been a younger sibling, but the smaller of the two had left, and she was alone again.

He knew she hadn't done it. He could not explain why; she had certainly seemed to mean it when she said she would kill *him*. Lute could simply not see the motivation a squirrel like her would have to go over the border to Firwood and off some older squirrel she didn't even know. Plus, she had all these whoopty-doo spiritual pictures in her bedroom, he had seen them. And now she was talking to kids—a family squirrel to boot! No, it didn't fit.

I ought to go home.

He quelled the thought quickly, as he had grown accustomed to doing ever since...ever since the incident. Each time Lute had to remind himself that 'home' was a very loose term for what he would come back to if he returned to the gray community.

There's nowhere else to go.

That's not true. I could find Saecka.

And now yer really going crazy. Bad idea, bad, bad idea.

Lute shook himself and turned to go, still without a fixed destination in mind. That was when a flash of movement out of the corner of his eye caught him and held him, frozen in place.

A young fox squirrel was watching him keenly from around the trunk of a tree a few yards away. Lute brought his breath back to a steady pace. The other hadn't noticed that he was aware of being watched yet. Lute intended that it stay that way.

Inching down from his perch, Lute cast glances back every now and again to see what his mysterious spy would do. Sure enough, the young fop was following him!

Cripes, that beats everything! Lute thought testily. *Now how do I shake him off?*

Unfortunately, he did not have a terribly long time to deliberate on this, for no sooner had he taken three more steps, than his follower had started to quicken his own pace, clearly meaning to rush-attack him.

Lute had just enough time to think how sadly inexperienced in this type of shenanigans the young squirrel was, when he felt something collide with his back.

"Ommpf!"

Lute turned to find the other squirrel picking himself up off the ground, flushed and winded. He noticed with a hint of amusement that a leaf had become stuck in the stranger's tail and that he appeared not to notice as he straightened up and looked Lute as squarely in the eye as he dared.

"Where did you get that knife?"

Lute raised an eyebrow.

"It's mine," he said coolly. "I suggest yew go get yer own if yer so keen on it."

The other squirrel shook his head, trembling from head to toe, whether with rage or fear, Lute couldn't quite tell. It was rather laughable, really.

"It's not yours, it's—

"Yew know, I've had rather too many people telling me that of late," Lute snapped, and without warning he made a quick movement of his paw, bringing the knife up and around in front of the others' face. The young fox squirrel, though a good bit larger than Lute, was by no means a fighter and was caught completely off guard. Crying out in shock, he jumped back, tail thrashing madly and (Lute noticed with that same streak of dark humor) dislodging the leaf that had hung there.

Lute did not waste any time. While his clumsy attacker attempted to gain his balance once more, Lute jumped on him and pressed the knife to his throat, speaking fast and with undertones of menace.

"Now, yer going to tell me exactly who yew are and how it is that yew recognize this knife. And yer going to tell me right *now*. Do yew understand?"

The fox squirrel squirmed underneath Lute's fierce black eyes, but he was held good and tight to the ground, and with every movement he made, the knife came closer to his throat.

"Don't think I won't," Lute warned. As if to make good on his statement, the tip of the knife grazed the squirrel's skin, leaving a spot of red against the deep brown fur. The squirrel froze, perspiring noticeably.

"Fine," he said. "It's—I saw it with Edelle, and I know you stole it from her!"

"Edelle?" Lute was surprised, and took the knife back a couple of inches. "Is that the female who lives...?"

But the other squirrel took advantage of Lute's moment of laxness to give a massive surge of his body, throwing his attacker off him into a nearby tree.

"Thief!" he shouted. "You stole it from her, you dirty, scrawny thief!!"

"Oh, please." Lute leaned forward and rubbed his head where it had hit the tree. "Yew wouldn't know a thief if he fell on yew. And what's it to *yew* if I *did* steal it?"

But the fox squirrel had taken this opportunity to attempt to run off again, and this time he succeeded. Lute cursed rather colorfully.

The young fox squirrel had not been telling the truth, that much was obvious. Lute personally would have suspected that he had been the culprit, except that it didn't do anything to explain how Edie-whatsit had ended up with *his* knife. Not to mention that Lute was having serious doubts as to the squirrel's actual capacity to commit cold-blooded murder. He considered, for possibly the duration of a second, tracking the squirrel in the hopes of forcing answers out of him, but Lute was too far wasted and the temptation to lie down was much stronger. After that he could plot his next move. But first he would need his pack, some provisions, and perhaps another clue, and though he didn't like the thought of it one bit, he knew there was only one place he could go to obtain all of the above.

"Edelle! Edelle, come here quick!"

Edelle's grandmother's voice was loud and panicked.

"Edelle!"

Edelle got up from her place on the branch and hurried inside, possible scenarios rushing through her head. Bench, hurt? Her grandfather? But when she got there, all that greeted her eyes was a seemingly mundane scene. Her grandmother stood at the round wooden table, holding a barrel such as was used to collect fruits and nuts from the autumn harvest in. She looked from her grandmother to the barrel, uncomprehending.

"Gran? What is it, is everything okay?"

Her grandmother, in a manner which was thoroughly uncharacteristic of her usual snappy self, sighed and shook her head, breath rattling out shakily, audibly. She tipped the barrel over so that a few berries rolled out onto the table. Picking one up, she held it between two fingers and squeezed. The juice that came flooding out was black, and the scent that reached Edelle's nose only seconds after, putrid.

Heart beating heavily in alarm, Edelle asked, "What…"

"They're all like that."

"All?" She felt faint.

"I checked every barrel. The nuts, too. Edelle, something very wrong is happening. This hasn't happened since my childhood, and then we called it…well, the rumor then was…"

Her grandfather came suddenly stomping in to the room and twitched his nose at the offending odor from the berry before weighing in.

"Yes, I recall it exactly," he said grimly. "The curse of the white squirrels."

It was not long before complaints began to be issued on the same matter elsewhere in the fox squirrel community. The panic was palpable as everyone began to realize that everyone else was experiencing the same fear as them—fear brought on by the black, rotted insides of fruit, of sweetness gone bad. The older squirrels, those like Edelle's Gran and Gramps, wasted no time on uncertainty; to them, it was the "curse of the white squirrel" Edelle heard the phrase repeated again and again, amid all the deliberation and chaos and organizing of meetings in the Meeting Tree.

But what was…

"…the curse of the white squirrel?"

"Well now, I'm glad you asked. Don't they ever teach you anything these days?"

Edelle shrugged, smoothed her tail out behind her, and waited. Her Grandfather got the hint. They were alone together for the first time in what felt like more nightfalls than it had been, and Edelle still felt sick to her stomach whenever she pondered their current situation or the fate of the colony for too long. Stuff like this, like potential starvation, happened to other squirrels. Those who weren't fit enough to gather. It wasn't supposed to befall a thriving colony like her own.

"The curse of the white squirrels was exactly that," her grandfather began vaguely, and Edelle leaned forward, all attention on him. Sensing it as a rare moment, perhaps, he continued with much more gusto. "When I was young, and this colony was young as well—just starting up in fact— our leader did something to make the white squirrels angry."

"What?"

"Shush, shush, I'm telling a story. Besides, that's not the point." He gave her a very disgruntled look that said he did not have the foggiest and continued as if there had been no interruptions. "Now, Cumin, for that was our leader's name, and he was a wonderful leader at that, was unusual in a way. He was one of the few of *our* kind ever to commingle with the white squirrels of Pinewood. You see, Cumin was born farther up north where apparently he fell in with a couple of the white squirrels, very unusual stuff since they're known for keeping to themselves. But they must have wanted him for something or other…Cumin did end up feeling used, I believe, but he never said much about it. Very honorable, he was. When he arrived here, our last leader Jarvul had just sadly passed away, and he filled the space quite admirably. Shortly after Cumin arrived however, the fruit started rotting and the nuts were inedible. It being the tail end of autumn, there was quite a panic. Cumin tried to console everyone, but it seemed as if something was troubling him. Cumin called a counsel one day to discuss the famine we found ourselves facing. He brought the whole colony before him at the Meeting Tree and told us exactly what was on his mind. It was not what anyone expected; he said he was afraid it was all *his* fault that this was happening to us, that he had had a quarrel with the white squirrels, a petty thing really, before he left his childhood home on the border of Firwood, and that they—the white squirrels, that is—must have put a curse on him with some dark magic...you know the types of skills they possess."

Edelle nodded, enraptured, and leaned even further in.

"At any rate, the white squirrels, whom we had thought of as protectors of a sort until that day—after all, they had saved us from several frights in distant years—would not be of much help in this case, it seemed. After all, we could not go to seek help from those who were causing our problems in the first place. But that was just what Cumin did. A handful of good, solid squirrels left with our leader in the wee hours of the morning a couple of weeks after the food had gone bad. They traveled all the way up to Pinewood to petition to the white squirrels, to plead with them to take the curse off. They did not come back for a couple of months. By then, it was winter, and several of the colony back home had fallen ill from hunger. Three had died. The worst thing was, there was nothing we could do—neighboring colonies had only collected enough for themselves to survive the winter, and it was doubtful some of them would have shared even if they *had* had plenty." He grimaced. "It was a terrible time. The time during which, by fate's odd sense of irony and a stroke of plain luck, I met your grandmother. We have never quite gotten along as well as we did that first day. Ah, well. We were all the worse for wear, and these were dark days in the colony, as goes without saying. Doomsday predictions were flying left and right, and many of us, myself included, thought that Cumin was not going to be coming back, that the white squirrels had turned coldly on the requests of our colony and in so doing fated us to a slow, withering death.

"But time goes by, and when the beginnings of spring were evident in the air, so was the first fruit and green budding acorns. We rushed out to them, biting into them feeling we had forgotten what they tasted like, without regards to the fact that they were likely rotted inside—we had no reason to expect anything different. But the fruit was wonderful and the acorns, though still bitter in their youth, edible. The curse was broken, it seemed. But still Cumin had not come back. Cumin never did come back."

"Then did you never have any idea *how* the curse was broken?" Edelle said desperately.

"Well, no, we didn't. Though one squirrel *did* make it back. He came straggling into our territory very early in the spring, and he didn't seem able to talk he was so traumatized. He did speak of how, upon getting to the ruling tree of the white squirrels, there was the general feeling that they were not welcome. It was all very nerve-wracking, and the journey had taken them forever and a day, because the exact location of the white squirrels—well, Cumin had been getting very frustrated with it apparently, because the forest seemed to be hiding it from them, making it hard to find. He started saying all this stuff about dark magic and the others with him were a bit frightened by it all. Some left on the spot, just went who knows where, to attempt to join other colonies nearby perhaps, take the easy way out. I thought that a damn cowardly thing to do, I'm telling you right now, Edelle, but anyhow... Cumin was only left with a good three squirrels in the end. When they came upon the place, the survivor told us that Cumin was immediately summoned to the King's chambers there, but that he and his other companions were asked to wait outside. Cumin never came out again. He had told them that if anything should happen to him, they were to save themselves, and so they left, distraught and lost, into the cold again, unquestioned and ignored by the white squirrels. Two of them, upon clearing Pinewood, decided not to go back to Ashwood, that there could not possibly be anything left for them there. They, like the others before, thought they were better off trying their luck elsewhere. The one fellow remaining was torn—he knew he ought to come back and tell us all what had happened, and his loyalty to his colony ultimately won out. He was a true hero of his time."

"What was his name?"

"Sachar. Not the brightest of squirrels, no particular talents, plain as could be. We had underestimated him, clearly. Only Cumin had seemed to see his value in choosing him to come along, and when only Sachar returned to us and we finally did see that value, well... it was too late. He died two days after delivering the news to us. He was unconscious most of the time, so we never even got to inform him that the curse had been lifted in his absence. He would never taste the ripe fruit of spring again."

Her grandfather looked blank for a moment. "I'm sorry. It's just that... I knew him. We were friends, and I was a bit resentful that he, for all his plainness, had been chosen to go along with Cumin, whom I looked up to so much. I'm afraid we did not part on good terms, and I never got the chance to make it up to him. He was incredibly forgiving though, I'm sure he would have understood."

Still he sat staring down at the table, held deep in some reverie he had opened up for himself in telling the personal bits of a well-known story. Edelle reached across to him and touched his paw.

"Astrippa knows," she whispered consolingly.

Her grandfather gave her a half-smile.

"Indeed She does. Ah, we're all foolish in our youth, aren't we? So mistaken in thinking it will be just one of many promised times for us."

They sat still for a long moment, Edelle almost afraid to speak. Her normally gruff grandfather was behaving in a way unfamiliar to her, and she was not sure whether to interrupt his thoughts would be intruding. Finally, her need for knowledge took control.

"Grandfather—what do you think happened to Cumin? Do you think that the white squirrels only granted his wish and lifted the curse in exchange for his life?"

"That is the conclusion, more or less, that we came to. It was the only thing that made sense. But now...now, I just don't know what to make of things. It seems so sudden." His voice was filled with a dull weariness but also with a throbbing anger held just under control. "What have we done this time?"

The outburst made Edelle jump.

"You're sure it's the same thing?"

It sounded stupid even in her head as she said it; of course it was, how else could the conditions the colony had now suddenly found itself facing be the exact same as those they had faced years back under the rule of Cumin?

"I'm positive it is the same thing. If it's not, I'll eat my tail. It may start to look very edible in a week or so, anyway."

For a moment Edelle was relieved that her grandfather seemed to be getting back to himself; the air lightened imperceptibly, but only for a moment before his face grew terribly grave again.

"Edelle," he said, "I was young the last time this odd curse struck. My body could weather the conditions of famine better. I don't think—that is to say, your grandmother and I—

Edelle understood all at once, like taking a gasp of air that she discovered to be noxious at the last second. She sat there, mute in her chair, and much as she tried not to think it, all that echoed through her head were two plaintive, weeping words.

Not fair.

She wanted to cry, but knew she couldn't. She hadn't since her father had left, all those years ago, in another lifetime now. Crying never changed anything.

"We'll be all right," her grandfather said, his words sighing.

Outside, a cry that was partly a scream sounded from far off, and Edelle, though she recognized a lie when she heard one, was grateful for the effort.

CHAPTER VIII

It was under cover of darkness that Lute came upon the gathering of tree houses, formed by slanting wood planks with light gleaming through the cracks, bunched together like several scared old beggars. This was home, or something like it. Lute approached it like a criminal.

What am I even doing here? Am I crazy?

In then out, just in then out. Shut up and do yer job, Lute. In and then out. Nothing more to it.

Coming around from behind the cluster of ramshackle huts, Lute zeroed in on one in particular and began to climb.

The wood siding was splintered and would have made noisy going for someone with lesser skills, but these were obstacles Lute was accustomed to, and easily overcame. As he crawled up the rear of the tree house, slow and slinking with his knife clasped between his teeth for lack of a better place to stow it, Lute could not keep his mind from flashing back to the night he had first come here; everything was much the same. The light through the cracks gleaming at him, the cool dark air all around him, shading his own silent, secretive movements. Saecka and Breshlin and a couple of others had been waiting for him in the branches of a neighboring tree—only to abandon him later at the scene of his capture. This time he was alone. And this time he was older, defter if unpracticed; he would not be caught.

Lute made it over the top of the roof and crouched down low, crawling on his belly, acutely aware of the houses directly across from him. These places were built to keep out intruders, and in the light of recent events… but even now as he questioned his sanity, even now as he thought of turning back, Lute had hooked his paws over the far edge of the roof, feeling below him to where he knew the rim of the window lay. After watching the ground intently for a telltale square of light that would tell him someone had taken up residence in his old quarters, Lute breathed out slowly, carefully around the knife he held in his mouth. He made the next move all in one fluid motion. Pulling himself fully to the edge of the roof, Lute held on tightly and flipped around, maneuvering his body into the small hole beneath him and darting to the side in one fluid movement. At last he stood breathing rapidly, standing to the right of the window, back against the wall.

Lute had quickly regained control over his rapidly pounding heart, and was waiting for his eyes to adjust to the untrustworthy dark when a light came on downstairs, spilling partially into the loft he was standing in.

Lute froze.

A horribly familiar voice came drifting up from underneath where he stood; he recognized it immediately as belonging to Gustoff, a fat prickly sort with a keen mind.

"Look, Walth, I'm not paying you with those lovely Dew Frosts you like for nothing," Gustoff said, leaving no doubt in the mind of any listener that he was terribly annoyed. "When I ask you to *look into* something for me, do you know what that means? No? Then you'd better learn, and learn quick, too. Pember was my friend, but he had a whole lot of connections, and I don't pride myself on knowing a whole lot about his personal history. I don't pry, but being who he was there are a load of possibilities on what could have happened for things to end up this way—

"I told you," The voice that broke in was plaintive. "The evidence all points to—

"I know what the evidence points to, and frankly I think it highly probable. But until you find some sort of *conclusive* sign, something substantial, the committee cannot decide on an action of any sort."

"But—"

"Yes?"

"Fine, fine. Give me tonight. I'll—try to have something."

A pregnant pause spread out in the room below, in which Lute became overly conscious of his own monstrous breathing in the darkness above.

"Leave the light on," the whining voice called, and Lute could have sworn he felt searching eyes stare upwards right towards the spot where he was.

A disgusted snort that could only have come from a nose as large as Gustoff's sounded, but a moment later he walked off, and Lute could feel that he was alone in the house with the other whom he could not put a face to. Cursing himself for choosing such a rotten night for his undertaking, Lute probed the darkness to either side of him, and found what he was looking for. A lump in the far corner of the small cramped room signaled the presence of his pack and blankets. Treading carefully, Lute made his way over to them and began to gather his things into his arms, discarding his knife on the floor to do so. A sigh sounded from below him, giving him only a moment's pause before he turned to the window where his next problem awaited him—how to slip out unseen carrying all of this? It was going to be a daunting task, but he did not doubt he could do it…there was only the slightly problematic possibility that Gustoff could be below, waiting for him.

"Lute, yew ninny," He could hear Saecka now, laughing in that cold, careless way that made you want to please her all the more. *"Yer thinking too much. Yer always thinking too much."*

Right, Lute thought grimly.

Swinging his pack over his shoulder, he peered out the window. The lights in the house directly across from Pember's old place were out now. As Lute situated himself on the windowsill, he stopped for a moment to stare back into the room where he had spent most of a rather miserable youth. He could not begin to explain why the emotions he felt at leaving it for the last time should be just as miserable.

A creaking of the floorboards and a heavy swinging accompanied by grunts informed Lute that whoever was downstairs was now making his way up the hanging ladder to the loft.

Immediately getting back to business, Lute backed out of the window, caught himself at the last moment on the side of the house, and edged his way around praying to all the possible gods and goddesses that Gustoff was *not* outside. Hitting the ground with a soft *thump*, he took off through the night.

A cry from behind him cut across his relief and he realized too late what he had left behind as the excited voice shouted.

"I know! I know! Gustoff! Someone! I know who did it! It was him, it was the boy, I can prove it!"

Lights in the surrounding houses were flickering on at all the commotion.

"Here now, what's all this?" someone called.

"It's his knife, and I think there's still blood on it…"

Lute, in keeping with the pattern that had become his life in the last few days, ran.

When Edelle woke up the very next morning the first thing she noticed was that she felt as if she had been frozen overnight. True enough, it was late autumn, but when had it gotten this cold? The second thing she noticed was that she had woken up, meaning that evidently she *had* slept the night before. How could it be that her insomnia had broken up, seemingly fled her on the very night that things started to look absolutely horrible?

Just the thought of her circumstances brought her to her knees by her bed, from which position she stared up at the picture of Astrippa, and said a short prayer for them all. The door to her room creaked open, and she jolted upright, instantaneously feeling shamed for the knee-jerk reaction as if this were her private moment, as if there were anything private about prayer.

Bench stood in the doorway, his countenance afraid and confused.

"Dell! Why is there nothing for breakfast?"

Edelle's heart sunk. Had no one told him yet?

"Bench," she tried to say calmly, giving him a tight smile. "There's not going to be much to eat for a while, I'm afraid."

"What do you mean?"

Their grandmother passed behind Bench in the hall and took him by the shoulder gently.

"Bench, you haven't woke your sister up, have you?"

"No, no, I was up," Edelle said quickly.

Her grandmother eyed her.

"But you slept."

"Yes…I did. I don't know what to make of it myself." Nothing was making much sense lately.

"Thoelen is holding counsel at the Meeting Tree today when the sun hits its zenith. The whole colony must come." She did not say any more on the topic, and instead turned to her grandson. "Come here, Bench."

Bench followed her mutely past the door to the adjoining room; it was as if he knew exactly the weight of what he was about to hear. Edelle saw a flash of an older squirrel in him, a squirrel that might be crafted roughly from too-raw materials, too early, and she was afraid for him.

Edelle exited her room and to the sounds of her grandmother's murmured voice behind the door at the end of the hallway, made her way up the grass-thatched tunnel out into the cold sunlight.

She was startled to see that not only had she slept, but she had overslept; she would have to head to the Meeting Tree in less than an hour's time. The sun glinted down at her, a cool impartial observer. Staring back at it hurt her eyes, and as she turned away she felt the orb dismiss her too; they would be feeling its warmth even less come winter.

Edelle's eyes, in avoiding the sun, came to light upon the dray nestled in the small ash across the clearing from her home. Her heart caught in her throat as she saw that someone was down there today, moving at the entrance.

It was him, of course, she knew it had to be—it was his house after all. The young male who had not yet told her his name was a mysterious face in her mind. He had lived here long enough that she felt she ought to know something about him, but he appeared reclusive. Apart from the time he had come directly to her door to deliver her the beautiful knife, the one she'd lost, he had not spoken to her. It was all very confusing. She had asked her grandparents about him, but they had seemed disapproving of her probing. "He's probably just starting out, and scared to be on his own, and in a new colony. It's not often that colonies receive new members, so maybe he feels like he needs to impress." Those seemed to be *their* sentiments, anyway. But Edelle wasn't quite as sure.

Maybe I just want him to be exciting.

Well, that sounded naïve and dumb. Besides, I know nothing about him. What if he turns out to have no faith in Astrippa, or something equally disappointing?

Go talk to him, then.

I can't do that!

Edelle, thoroughly pestered by this inner banter, tore her eyes from the form of the young male, who was jumping about and pawing at the branch on which he stood, as if to clear it of frost and up to the window in the top of his dray where her eye caught a movement, barely perceptible but there nonetheless.

Now *that* was interesting. She craned forward, putting her tail out behind her for balance, and attempted to get a better view, but whoever it was up there had edged away from the window into the shadows. Frowning slightly, Edelle looked back down to where the handsome young male had been, but he had evidently gone inside again, having gotten all the frost safely off of the branch. Guiltily, Edelle thought how she should have done the same thing this morning; if Bench slipped on the way out, what then? Edelle vowed to Astrippa that she would attempt to do better by her family in the future instead of thinking about childish things like the young male across the way.

Distracted by her own self-derision, she did not hear her grandfather come up behind her, subdued and grim until he broke the silence by telling her it was time to go. As she turned to follow him to the Meeting Tree at the end of the clearing, she still could not help but cast a last glance up at the window of the house across the way, where she had seen the movement earlier. Nothing but a dark, round hole stared back at her, but she could have sworn that a second before she had felt someone watching her, too.

The Meeting Tree was a buzz of scampering feet, carrying bodies all with one thing in common; they were coming apart at the seams. The elders squawked and squabbled about curses, the children clung to their mothers, gazing around with large eyes at the cavernous insides of the ancient tree, and still others tried to instill some order for the sake of filing into the meeting room presentably, an effort that was completely and utterly in vain. Edelle looked about the crowd, scanning it, then caught herself angrily and proceeded to march rather forcefully straight through the masses after her grandparents and Bench, heedless of the indignant cries of "hey!", "watch where you're going!" and "that's my tail you're stepping on!" Finally, she squeezed past one particularly plump squirrel wife ("watch where you're going, missy!") and into the open chamber beyond—which, considering the rate it was filling up, would soon be packed beyond its limit.

The Meeting Tree was a very historic site. Of course, she had been told that it was historic so many times when she was young that she had lost sense of what the word truly meant in its context. Her grandfather had made her visit this place when she reached seven seasons, and had explained to her its importance, this immutable ash with most of its branches raised upwards in a peculiar way, as if to hail some secret god. Her grandfather's words had fallen on deaf ears, much as she'd admired him as a child. They meant things to him, touched him in places that she had never been and would maybe never be...she had run her paws instead over the smooth, worn wood ridges along the walls, walking up and down the rows of them and imagining it full of squirrels while her grandfather talked.

Now as she stared out at the site again, she did not even need to imagine it full; but the place seemed to have developed meaning for her already. Now, looking up at the wicker chair from which the leader of the colony would speak, she tried to imagine it years ago, imagined instead the brave squirrel who had gone to his death trying to save the anonymous faces that stared back at him from these ridged seats. But though she tried to imagine Cumin, but there was no face to put to the name, and she felt oddly saddened that no amount of manufactured nostalgia could deliver it to her.

Edelle's wistful thinking was thankfully short-lived, for her grandfather gave her paw a sharp tug and she realized she was being lost in the continuously tightening clamor of bodies and voices. She followed her family to a space on the nearest ledge, and waited for the meeting to commence.

It took a good few rounds of the hourglass, but at last everyone settled into their place and all eyes turned with rapt attention to the front of the room, where a slim middle-aged squirrel was making his way briskly up to the wicker seat. The squirrels standing lining the way for lack of a seat moved aside respectfully to let him pass.

Everyone watched as Thoelen settled into his seat. Edelle could not help but notice how tightly their leader clutched the arms of his chair or the slight tremor in his voice as he began to speak.

"Good fellows of the Greater Fox Colony of Ashwood. You may have noticed by now that all is not entirely well here. In an unexpected turn of events, all that we have collected on Harvest Day, just four days past, has gone bad. The seriousness of the spoiling is so severe that we have found ourselves with no edible food aside of course from anything we may have held onto before harvest. I do not need to spell it out for you; this means we are in dire straits. This odd phenomenon seems only to strike the area that our colony inhabits…if others are facing the same problems, we have yet to hear from them. This has happened only once before in our history—those who are eldest among you and surviving will remember." He inclined his head as if in respect for those of whom he spoke. "I myself was lucky enough to have been born after that deadly time. Some say it was a curse, but regardless of the cause this time or that, if the implications for what will happen this time can be based on what happened the last, then we are in very serious trouble indeed. There may be no preventing it."

Edelle could see the fear contained behind his eyes, and felt bad for him more than she thought she had probably ever felt for anyone before. For she saw the terrible dilemma that was set before Thoelen, the dilemma which, judging from their still collected faces, most of the crowd hadn't caught on to yet. After all, their leader could tell his colony that this was happening, but what could he do to prevent it? What could he do to allay their fears in the face of something so stick-dry and circuitously terrible as hunger, starvation? In the eyes up front, the eyes to which everyone looked to keep their fear on low, behind the calm authoritarian demeanor, there was the secret whisper, the hidden trump card…the truth. And it said "I have nothing for you." And worse yet, Thoelen was about to reveal it. He had no choice.

A mutter had slowly broke out and was moving fast across the room, along the rows of seats as heads turned and whispered, children whimpering or raising their voices in whining questions.

"Some of you would say," Thoelen continued, and the noise immediately died down at the sound of his voice, "that this was brought on us by the white squirrels, like the time before. And if the time before was anything to go by—and I take the concept of learning from experience very seriously—well then, I would say that some of you have a point. The white squirrels have always been associated with magic of questionable alignment, shut off in the northern regions, unreachable by the common folk. We do not know how their minds work, or even if the blood that flows through their veins is of the same substance as that in ours, but we do know that fruit does not one day turn bad just as it should have turned ripe; it does not grow rotten on trees. These are elements of magic, and a dark one at that."

This time very few of those in the hall could keep from turning to one another and whispering, or drawing closer into one another's arms as they waited to hear what their leader would say next, what he would tell them to do to make everything all right.

Thoelen was quiet for a breath or two, and in that silence Edelle knew he was weighing his next words, choosing them carefully. She did not envy him his position one bit.

"I have somewhat of a suggestion for everyone. No, not a suggestion, an order." Heads raised at the stress he put on the word, and the stares around the hall intensified. "I would like for everyone to take their food, all that they might have from before, and bring it here, down to the cellar of the Meeting Tree. There, we will divide it up among us; we are a colony. We have prided ourselves on being closer than most colonies are, certainly more so than the white squirrels in their elitism must be. Now we must prove this pride not unfounded. We are in this together, and together we will share everything we have got. Not one family will have the disadvantage here. Are there any objections?"

The room grew deadly silent in the space that followed, and Thoelen smiled; Edelle thought the curve of his lips the bravest gesture she had seen in some time.

Their leader, who until now had been an abstract figure, almost just as abstract as the walls around her had once been, had become wonderfully real to her in a way that was both powerful and sad.

She felt she was with him, standing by his wicker seat looking down at them all when he said, "Good. I am not disappointed in you, then, my colony. I have a feeling that I never will be."

"Know this," Thoelen continued, "If there were anything I felt I could do for our colony, I would do it. But as things are—

A squirrel from somewhere behind Edelle shouted out suddenly.

"Why are the white squirrels doing this to us? I've heard the story about the last time, but Cumin is long dead, rest his soul! What motivation would they have for punishing us this time?"

Loud, angry cries of agreement could be heard all around. Thoelen shrugged his thin shoulders, and Edelle thought of white squirrels, gathered together in icy silence, having a silent laugh at the fate of those who could not help themselves with magic. Their red eyes burned a hole through her imaginings, sending her crashing back into the loud room she sat in, holding her head between her paws.

It did not come to her then, though perhaps it should have. It was only after the meeting had come to an end and she was helping to carry their meager food supplies that were not spoiled back to the cellar of the great tree that the thought came to her.

At first she ignored it, wrote it off as crazy and pushed it to the side; it only came walloping back down the path of her mind ever more persistently at each dismissal. And then, during the night when she woke gasping, drenched in sweat from a nightmare in which Bench was dying, skin stretched tight over his bones, Edelle finally embraced it as she lay shaking in bed.

The white squirrels. I need to go to the white squirrels.

It seemed a ridiculous thought, but the more she tried to ignore it, the more it seemed like the only thing she could do, the only thing left to her. Cumin had done it, back when her grandparents were young.

Yeah, well Cumin knew how to get there, for one, she told herself. She herself had no idea how to travel in one direction consistently, much less where she could find what she was looking for to begin with.

Well, they're somewhere in Pinewood.

Oh, very good, Dell. Trudge all the way up there in this near-winter weather and then what? What do you expect to tell them? Do you think they'd listen to you even if they did let you in instead of killing you on sight?

Edelle did her best to ignore the nagging, disparaging voice in her head. After all, what else could she do? She could not stand by and let her family die at the hands of some distant, corrupt sorcerers. It was unthinkable.

Maybe they'd take me in exchange. Maybe if I traded my life like Cumin did...

A chill went through her at the thought, and she felt a lump rise in her throat. *But you're not special to them like Cumin was. You're no one.*

Besides, there were a host of other problems with her plan. For one, she had no food to bring with her; she would be perhaps even less prepared than Cumin and his followers had been, and who knew how long the journey would take her? She might well die before she got there.

They *might die before I get there.*

No. Bench and her grandparents had *some* food; they had a portion of the pitiful supply the colony had lumped together. If anyone died first, it would be her.

Is this what it's like, living on the edge all the time? How horrible it is, when life is constantly considering the possibility of death, the where and the when.

Wrapping her tail around her body for warmth and feeling the slight emptiness already forming in her stomach from lack of a sufficient meal that night, Edelle stared at the picture of Astrippa hanging on her wall through the dark. The shapes of the squirrels to either side of Astrippa appeared to be moving with nothing but the moonlight to add clarity to their shifting forms; the translucent squirrel seemed almost to move upwards as if by magic until the whole of his body melted into Astrippa's unmoving form. To Edelle, the picture seemed to offer an answer to a question she had not yet asked even herself.

Yes.

Yes, the unmoving form of Astrippa said, her body coming up from the clouds as if it were the most natural thing in the world. *Yes.*

Edelle got up from bed unsteadily, her mind preoccupied by what her grandparents might think when they found she was gone. She found herself hoping that the colony would find a solution to everything in the time she was absent, that they would find some other, friendly group of squirrels with far more than they could eat. All of her rational senses were still raging against the decision she had made, but she would not allow herself to be deterred.

Edelle knew anger was not supposed to be a healthy motivator, but she could not help the rage she felt curled up under all of her worry. What right had the white squirrels to randomly do this yet again to them? She would have been outright spitting mad, had she not also been puzzled. She had sensed it in Thoelen too—there had been nothing to prompt this sudden curse thrown upon them— if it *was* a curse, she tried to remind herself, but a curse seemed all that made sense. She wondered briefly if she should wait, or at least tell someone of her departure, but it was too risky. She did not want anyone coming after her.

Crossing the room to her door, Edelle looked out and down the hall. When she saw that no one was there, she crept to where the door across from her stood open a crack, and, pushing it open a bit more, allowed herself to gaze in on her younger brother while he lay on his bed of reeds, his sides moving up and down slowly. She only allowed herself to look for one long minute

checking

then continued down the hall and out into the cold, forbidding night.

Edelle was halfway down the tree in the fork of which her family's dray was nestled when she heard a sound, as of a snapping of twigs from somewhere nearby. She froze and waited, whiskers twitching, but when no other sound followed, she hurried to the ground, setting off at rather a quicker pace than before. Trying not to think too much about what she was doing, lest she have second thoughts, Edelle was in the process of figuring out which way was absolute north, when the sound came to her again, filling her senses with warning. It was closer now, a rustling, twitching sound as of someone trying to keep still within an impossibly leafy thicket.

Wishing with more than a dose of annoyance that she still had her knife on hand, Edelle took what she hoped was the best course of action and pretended not to hear, putting on a blissfully unaware façade for any invisible watcher, all the while her mind turning in circles.

Who would...?

She got her answer within a matter of seconds.

"Wait!"

The sound came so suddenly to her ears that somehow she felt she should be shocked by it. But some sixth sense had whispered in her ear, and she knew who she would find before she turned. It did not keep her from being utterly bewildered.

The young fox squirrel, the stranger, the newcomer was standing discreetly to the side behind her as if awaiting permission to come closer. His face was fixed in an expression of suppressed pain that had every appearance of being wholly genuine. Edelle did a double-take and almost had to check to see if the voice had truly come from this new squirrel; he was standing so still now, seemingly afraid to move.

"Yes?"

The handsome young squirrel's mouth twitched, then he burst out, "Don't leave!"

"Excuse me," Edelle said, and she couldn't explain to herself why she felt so irritable. "But I don't even know who you are. Is this the way you get to know all your new neighbors, by coming to their doors with pretty gifts and then stalking them at inappropriate times? I see no reason why my going anywhere is any of your concern. Incidentally, were you even *at* the meeting yesterday?"

He turned a funny reddish color, to her satisfaction.

"Yes, I was. And—and well, I *hope* you're not going anywhere, because it's dangerous!"

"And what would you label the state of things *here*?" Edelle absolutely refused to let herself feel anything but aggravated, a task which was not proving hard thus far—

she had so hoped not to run into anyone on her way out, and here she already had. If this squirrel figured out where she was going and started babbling to everyone, it would ruin everything!

"Look," the squirrel said, keeping his voice down as if he had sensed the venomous nature of her thoughts, "I don't mean to pry, I know you should be able to go where you like, but…we're a colony, right?" The words slipped weakly from his lips. "We have to look out for each other. I—I know I've been less than polite, perhaps, since I've been here, but I have—there are conditions at home. I don't want to make excuses. I just—I—I really like you and I don't want never to see you again!" It burst finally from him, leaving him breathing a bit heavily, and he wet his lips as if in preparation for rebuke.

Edelle blinked. She stared at him hard, as though trying to see through him, trying to pick up the lie in his words. She came up dry.

"*You* look," she protested finally. "You don't know me."

"I've seen you…around, you know. Not like I was stalking, I promise I wasn't! I'm…I'm sorry, I'm not trying to get you to like me, I know you don't need to care and really I think it's better if you don't. But…I just can't let you go off and get yourself killed in search of them."

Edelle stiffened. Any softening up she might have felt in her chest for the strange, flustered young squirrel vanished on the spot.

"I don't need this," she said dangerously. "Look, whatever your name is, my family is in trouble. My whole colony is in trouble. I know the chances of getting any white squirrel to listen to my case are less than one percent, but I don't care. It sure beats doing nothing." He opened his mouth and she raised her voice, not allowing him an opportunity to get a word in. "You say you like me, whatever that means for you. Well, if you really like me, here's what you can do: you can just keep quiet about seeing me leave, keep your mouth shut about where I'm going. I don't know how you know about *that* in the first place…"

"Lucky guess," the stranger said softly.

"Yeah, okay. The bottom line is, I appreciate your concern, but I have to go—what are you looking at?"

The squirrel was staring around nervously behind him, and Edelle followed his eyes to the house where he had taken up occupancy. He kept looking around at it as if he expected it to sneak up on them as they were talking.

Why be afraid of your own house? Edelle thought, but her thoughts were many and going every which way and she did not dwell on it. It was time to be out of here.

"Additionally," she snapped, knowing it was rude and not caring, "I still don't know what your name is— couldn't think to give me that if you liked me, could you, huh."

She did not even wait to see if his eyes had come back to her. Turning from him, Edelle rushed off into the night, bounding silently as possible into the obscurity of the wall of trees beyond the path on which she stood.

The young male watched her go, his face pale in the moonlight.

"Felix," he whispered, staring miserably at the spot where she had stood. "My name is Felix."

CHAPTER IX

It had been ages since Tiallin had been summoned by King Sirius, and he was feeling a bit misused for reasons he could not quite put a paw on. Being alone in the house probably didn't help the new sense of bitterness that had set in his bones overnight, but Zerrith and his parents had all gone off somewhere and he was left with an overwhelming sense of boredom mingled with restlessness.

He had not forgotten his assignment from the King, but he was growing ever more jaded about it. Perhaps Sirius was not sending back for him because Tiallin had disappointed him by not having any information last time. The thought bothered him, mostly because he still didn't have any news of the type Sirius seemed to want. As far as Tiallin could see, there was nothing noteworthy or suspicious happening. He had even begun to wonder whether the King was not simply paranoid.

It was bitter and cold outside, so cold that when Tiallin awoke that morning, there had been frost encapsulating the needles of the trees all around him, making the whole forest eerie and frozen, like a beast gone to bed before its time, never to wake again. He had attempted to go back to sleep, but the cold had somehow stolen into his room as well, and he could not find a comfortable position. And so Tiallin had fallen to doing what he would continue to do all day: pacing the halls of his house, up and down the stairs built into the trunk of the tree, over and over, just thinking. After the time span of an hour, he felt that if he never had another thought in his life, he would be well shut of them.

Tiallin was in the process of his tenth round of the hallways, hoping desperately someone would come home from wherever they were—where were they??—and slap him out of this madness, when he noticed something that gave him pause.

Zerrith's door was open.

It was just a crack really, and perhaps it was only because Tiallin was insanely bored that his heart began to pound just a bit more rapidly in his chest. Zerrith never left his door open, not when he was in his room, and certainly never when he was out. Consequently, Tiallin had come to think of his brother's room as a secret of sorts, a place off-limits to everyone else in the house. His conceptions were not without foundation; he could remember being young and curious and venturing into his brother's room in the distant past. He would look through his brother's things, filled with wonder at anything that his childhood idol had considered interesting or worthwhile. When Zerrith caught him there, he would always get so upset—Tiallin still couldn't understand why, but a time had come when he no longer considered his elder brother's room worth the inevitable ensuing hysterics. It was only now, cold, lonely, and stewing with bitterness (and perhaps recalling what had been said between them nights before) that Tiallin realized he had not set foot in Zerrith's room for longer than he could remember.

Well now, here he was, and with nothing else to do. Tiallin made up his mind quickly; it wasn't as if he would be committing a crime. Taking the open door as invitation, he pushed it open a bit more and slipped inside.

He was instantly astounded at how much *stuff* there was. Zerrith's room was a medley of odds and ends; it seemed like his brother was an avid collector of just about anything and everything. From the grass stems and twigs of varying lengths that lined one wall to the collection of what must have been at least forty rocks, all different shapes, sizes and colors lined up against another, Zerrith's fascination with trivial things appeared to know no bounds. Shell-like cocoons that had been emptied of their occupants and now hung on hooks crafted from long, brown pine needles arranged in rows hung down from the ceiling. Some had what looked like writing on them, though Tiallin could not make it out from where he was standing. The room was so cluttered that it took him a while to spot the thing that made his heart leap into his mouth. It was at the opposite side of the room, hidden by a veil of knotted chains of wilted flowers—a large, bulky something covered by a nondescript sheet. He might have missed it entirely if he had not been looking carefully, but at the sight of the sheet, something overtook Tiallin. Some sort of fear mixed with wonder and even possibly the lightest kind of joy…it propelled him forward, toward the curtain of flowers...

Tiallin's body gave a jolt and he swayed on the spot, comically moving his arms in windmill circles to prevent him falling. His foot had come in contact with what appeared to be a large pile of junk. A pile of papers resting unsteadily on a painted vase came sliding down, scattering all over the floor about him. Tiallin snatched one of these up and paused to look at it, noticing with some surprise that Zerrith had drawn a picture of a leaf, similar to the one he had been so enamored with on the day they had fought. Underneath the drawing was written one word, underlined twice, the pen marks pressed hard into the paper excitedly.

Structure!!

Tiallin stared at the word uncomprehendingly. Next to the picture drawn of the leaf, there were a few other drawings, lighter sketches than the first, of things that looked like half-hearted attempts at other leaves, or the wings of insects, or both combined. After flipping over the paper and finding the back of it blank, Tiallin put it down, bemused, and his eyes caught on something else in the pile, something that made his pulse race. He put a paw on his chest and stepped back, and for the first time since entering Zerrith's room, he remembered how cold it was.

Four long willow poles stuck out from under a year's worth collection of what looked like dandelion fluff. Unmistakable in being what they were, the poles stared back at him, mercilessly solid.

"Things like our rare hollow willow poles are disappearing from storage... may have nothing at all to do with my fears on a larger scale... seem quite ridiculous and harmless... while there is much I tolerate, stealing is not on the list."

Stealing.

Stealing.

Tiallin's mind was reeling as the King's words echoed in his head, quiet and condemning, and still he could not look away from the willow poles sitting equally quietly in place, confirming Tiallin's dread, and all he could think was

You.

You...You?!

He saw Zerrith's face in his mind's eye, Zerrith looking down at the leaf in such wonder, silent intelligence burning as ever behind those eyes, denying the naivety others might attribute to him, others who did not know him. The room slowly seemed to close up about Tiallin. He saw Zerrith's face as he remembered it that night, denouncing Tiallin's pride in his work for the King, and now he wondered...

"I think something is terribly wrong...think they are among us..."

You. You. You.

"Tiallin!"

The voice was angry, and he turned to find that Zerrith's face wasn't just in his mind, it was staring right back at him from the doorway, now fully ajar. The cold air drifting through was more noticeable than ever.

Cold, cold, cold. It is very *cold today.*

"Tiallin, what are you doing in my room? You might want to learn to respect…I can't believe you would do this! After I told you I'd tell you—no, it's nothing, Mother," he answered a faint voice in the background. Tiallin has been messing with my stuff…"

Tiallin slid past Zerrith out the doorway not providing an answer to his brother or to his mother, who stood in the hallway, now remarking on how drafty their tree home had gotten, and had it been this drafty last winter?

Tiallin hardly paid them any mind, just walked and walked and walked until he was inside his own room, door closed now, down on the bed, face submerged in the blankets as he tried not to think and to concentrate at once, the pixilated blackness surrounding him now, making him dizzy.

"It just wasn't my thing."

"I think the King is just scared."

Scared of what? Scared of you?

Something is terribly wrong.

Tiallin felt the stinging in his eyes and could do nothing to prevent what followed.

CHAPTER X

Lute was dreaming, a fever dream of which he was half-aware, not entirely sure where his physical body lay during the cavorting of his mind. Maybe this *was* reality.

It seemed real enough. The wood underneath his fingers with its smooth curlicues and promises of a new design had a familiar touch to it and the self outside of his dream remembered he had been working on this one—this blade—just before it happened, the day he came to his master and realized his master was no longer capable of receiving him. He had used the blade with the bumblebee to carve this new knife; the bumblebee knife was his sharpest. There was always something ironic about using blades to make blades, Lute had often thought, a thought he shared with no one.

"Come here, boy." Pember's voice was rusty, seasoned.

Lute moved over into the light by the chair where the old gray sat, working on something of his own. The aged paws moved deftly over the surface of the wood, making small cuts, incisions, taking chunks of wood at just the right angles. Lute could have become mesmerized by this display, but Pember straightened up and put the box to the side when Lute moved over into his light.

"You're going over that too rough," Pember said. He took the knife-in-progress from Lute and pointed to a spot on a troublesome curlicue. It was persistently difficult, no matter how many times the younger squirrel, sweating in the heat of the shop with the dry smell of wood shavings always in his mouth and nose tried to go over it, to smooth it out.

"You have to go gentle, that's the trick." He took his own knife to it and managed to cut just the right portion of wood smoothly from the arch in the curling design, leaving it perfectly flowing. "Give it a try, will you?"

With Pember's eyes on him, Lute felt unnerved and sweating, less than perfect, but he attempted to concentrate anyway. As soon as his knife nicked the wood he knew he had failed. Pember saw it too, and his eyes narrowed. He grasped Lute by the wrist, hard, and the knife the young squirrel had been using to carve fell from his nerveless paw. He closed his eyes in anticipation of a blow that surprisingly did not come, and when he opened them again he saw that Pember was looking strangely pensive. Slowly unclenching his paw and releasing Lute's wrist, he began to speak very slowly, almost as if there was no one else in the dusty room with him.

"You're too much of a ruffian, boy. I can't train it out of you, I can't beat it out of you. Sometimes I wonder why I even bother. I could tell you right now that nothing that comes out of your paws is going to be suitable for anything grand, but perhaps it is the memory of my old days that keeps me at it. How things like this," He gave the small box he had been working on next to him a contemptuous glance, "ever keep me satisfied I have no idea. So perhaps we are both to be ashamed of ourselves. I am certainly not proud of the fact that I have any desire to go back to them. Sometimes I wonder why it is that the level of greatness could not be achieved anywhere else, but...ah..."

"...Them? Go back ter who?"

Pember looked up at Lute sharply, and he instantly wished he hadn't spoken. But a moment later the old gray's shoulders slumped and he picked up the box next to him once more.

"The white squirrels, boy. Did you never know? I used to work for them, back when Tamen ruled the locale up in Pinewood. Oh, don't look so surprised. Bring that knife to me and I'll try to fix what you've bungled up."

Lute brought the knife to him obediently and watched for a while as he worked at it.

"Why'd yew leave?"

Pember winced.

"Good gooseberries, boy, how many times do I have to tell you to get rid of that horrid accent? You sound like a blasted chickaree. And while you're at it, learn not to ask questions that aren't any of your concern. I left because I wanted a break. I did think they would call me back though. There were things left to do. At any rate," He handed the knife back to Lute, who took it but did not start to work again.

When it seemed like Pember would not continue, he said, "But what...?"

Pember's eyes sparked with a dangerous rage this time, and he raised himself stiffly from his chair and backhanded Lute across the cheek in an explosion of red heat. "What...did...I...*tell you*?"

As Lute held his throbbing cheek and the tears that had threatened to come, Pember sat back down, slowly, slowly, still holding the tiny box in his paws. He turned it about listlessly, and to Lute the box suddenly looked utterly forlorn, impossibly wrong in its smallness.

He awoke to the wind driving relentlessly through the trees, flinging specks of ice at his now unprotected body; his scant covering of leaves must have blown away overnight. He realized, with a start, that it was beginning to snow. If nothing else had succeeded in convincing Lute that this year was completely upside down, the light flurry of snow being blown aggressively about with each renewed gust of wind left him without a shadow of doubt.

Still feeling as though he should be back in the warm, dust filled air of Pember's shop, Lute sat in the cold on top of the sapling he had chosen to make his perch. He did not attempt to make another covering; instead he began rubbing his paws over his eyes repeatedly.

How long he had been asleep was anyone's guess. It was certain however that the time Lute had spent sleeping was time in which his pursuers might have managed to pick up his trail and consequently they might be very, very close by now. He did not doubt they could find it—he had been exceedingly clumsy in crashing through the trees. Was this the same night even, or the night after? His head felt light and confused. There was no telling how much time he had lost. And to think he had lain here, dreaming away…

The dream itself had been odd. It was more of a memory, really, the kind that got mixed up with dreams in a semi-conscious state. He had forgotten about that moment completely until now, the one day that Pember had ever mentioned his own past and the job he used to have working for the white squirrels. He had said they would want him back…well, they couldn't have him back now, Lute thought, they would never get him back because he was—

A thought occurred to him, quick and insidious like poison, and Lute gasped at the unexpectedness of it, the bald horror.

"No," he muttered, feeling the cold catch up to him at last and bringing his paws to his now damp chest for warmth. "No, no."

It made a sort of sense all up to the point of motivation, as to which he was stumped. Maybe the white squirrels didn't need motivation to kill…maybe their legendary magic had created in them monsters.

You're ridiculous, Lute-boy, he thought to himself. *Absolutely barking. Besides, you found the stupid fox squirrel female with the knife. How would that fit in with the crazy stuff running in your head? Give it up.*

"Fine," Lute said aloud to the cold, feeling foolish for talking to himself but too tired to care much. Still, the white squirrels had to be good for something, didn't they? Was it possible there was something they knew about Pember that he didn't? The more Lute thought on it, the more likely it seemed. Pember had never shared much of himself with anyone, least of all Lute, so it was not farfetched to assume that Pember's former employers might know more of him, more about his death. If they were not the cause of it, they might know, or be able to use their magic even, to find out. The prospect excited him, though he couldn't have said exactly why. He did not have long to think on it at any rate, as a sudden creaking noise caught him off guard. Someone was coming toward him, and quick, from the opposite direction through the trees. Before Lute could do so much as blink, they burst out in front of him, landing on the very limb he was sitting on and nearly bowling him over as they continued on their way.

"Hey, watch it!" he shouted, having recovered sufficiently from a near heart-attack. He had been sure for a fleeting second that it was someone come after *him*, that Gustoff's hired squirrels had found him and that he was finished. Apparently, it was only someone in one hell of a hurry to get somewhere.

The squirrel who had passed him was almost to the trunk of the sapling on which he stood when they heard his voice and turned around.

Lute immediately wished he had kept his fat mouth quiet. It was the same female fox squirrel from a few nights previous, the obnoxious one from whom he had finally wrested his knife.

She seemed to recognize him too. Her eyes widened, then narrowed, but before either of them could make another move, voices broke out below on the forest floor, in heated argument.

"I say we rest here!"

"Well that's all very nice, but you're not in charge, are you Walth?"

The first squirrel spoke again, a definite sulkiness to his voice. "I'm the one who found him out. I'm the reason we got this far."

"Oh, Walth, *please*. Spare me. We all know the only reason you ever did anything for Gustoff was so you could get your handsome pay of Dew Frosts every night at that disgusting Red Acorn bar, so don't even start with me like you're doing us all some big service…Now I heard something around this area—best I could with your yammering anyway—and I think…" Here the voice of the other dipped dramatically in volume, and Lute, heart pounding loudly in his own ears, had to listen hard to catch anything else.

"…should have a look before we think about sleeping, mm?"

Walth grumbled something inaudible. His companion ignored him.

"I think…I think it came from about *here*."

Lute knew it was his tree even before he heard the scratching of another's claws starting slowly up the trunk in an effort to keep quiet. He found himself hoping against hope that the fox squirrel female hadn't guessed it was him they were looking for, but one glance at her expression told him otherwise.

No...no... He shook his head emphatically but she only raised her eyebrows at him.

"Give me my knife," she mouthed, sliding closer.

"I don't have it, just don't give me away, don't!"

"And why shouldn't I?"

Lute spoke in a low, panicky mutter. "They're after me, they think I killed someone except I didn't, I don't have yer—*my* knife because I lost it, they're after me and if they find me—look, I'll explain later, just keep quiet!...Please?"

There followed a moment when they stared into each other's eyes, Lute pleading, the fox squirrel intent. Then the fox squirrel broke away, heading towards Lute's pursuers until he could no longer see her. Lute groaned, and tensed to make a mad and somewhat hopeless dash for it, but in that instant the voice of Edelle carried up to him. She was very close by.

"Oh, I'm sorry! Really I am."

Some unappreciative muttering followed this exclamation, then she began to speak, cutting it short impatiently.

"Oooh, looking for someone? Was he a seedy sort? Stringy, unpleasant to look at?" Lute winced and clenched his teeth together from his place in the tree. "I might be able to help you there, but I do hope you have a companion with you, he looked absolutely frightening to take on alone. Oh, well then. Still, you *are* brave. I had to hide really quick, he looked fit to kill. *Really?* Well if I had known *that* I would have panicked completely. Oh yes, of course. I think you're hot on the trail though. You might want to tell your companion it isn't the best time to rest. He was headed just that way. Yes, I'm almost positive. Fast, too. I think he knows you're after him now, so he might be a bit harder to follow...Okay, yes. I understand."

Slowly, the claws of his pursuer scratching on the wood got fainter and fainter once more, and Lute heard the sounds of the unnamed male striking up a conversation again with the cowardly Walth down below, their voices low, fading…

Then Edelle started back up to where he sat, moving almost without sound. Ignoring his astonished stare, she sat herself on a small stub of a branch nearby and assumed a dignified air as if only mildly interested in what had just gone on. Lute continued to stare in her direction until it became apparent that she would not be swayed to speak. Caving, he broke the silence.

"Thanks, er…" he blustered. "…Edelle? That right, is it?"

He caught a slight smile at the curve of her face, and she nodded but kept her silence.

"I didn't expect that, you know…I guess I didn't deserve it neither, what with breaking into yer house and screaming at you and such." He really wished she would talk, just to save him the trouble of blithering like an idiot, even if she only spoke to tell him he was a blithering idiot.

"You know," he said, keeping right on going, "I had my reasons. I don't do that to everyone. Just so we're clear on that."

"I figured."

The words cut so unexpectedly through his yammering that he nearly jumped. He looked to her for supplication, but she did not go on.

"Oh. All right then. I got to go probably, so—

"Where *are* you going?" Her smile was gone and she was looking suspicious and angry once more. "You keep right on like you're one of the good guys and everything, then you turn around and run away some more. What I'd like to know is if you're so innocent of doing what they say you did, why are you running at all?"

"Yew don't understand," Lute said. "It's not like that. *They* don't know I'm innocent, and there's no way they'll believe it wasn't me after they found—after I went back and—look. I'm not a murderer. I may be that fancypants word yew used back there, "seedy'…but I really haven't done anything wrong."

She appeared skeptical. "Why then, don't you just *tell* them that? They're your fellows, right?"

"Yeah, well, to put it loosely I suppose," Lute mumbled.

Edelle wrinkled her forehead. It didn't make sense to her, to grow up in a colony that would look for any excuse to hunt you down and kill you if you hadn't done anything to deserve their hatred in the first place…

Lute must have seen her critical expression, because he started up again hurriedly.

"I could ask yew the same, yew know. What're *yew* doing here?"

"I think it's clear," Edelle said, a tinge icily, "that you have no idea where you are. Am I correct?"

"Uhm."

"We're not very far at all from my colony, maybe a day's journey. How are you to know whether I'm not just out for a nice stroll, to enjoy the air?"

"The *air* is very *cold*," Lute said lamely. "All right, fine, if that's all yew want to say about that. Yew did save my entrails back there, even if yer regretting it and everything, doesn't change the fact that having entrails is nice. The truth about me is, I don't have a clue where *I'm* going."

Edelle blinked.

"You mean you've just been wandering around since the night you broke and entered on my house?"

"Well, not completely. Yew know. I went back to where I li—I mean, *used* to live and got some stuff…and I got them," he jerked a paw towards the swaying trees to the south, "on my tail. But I still don't…I don't understand how yew got my knife."

"Let's not be going into that again, or *I* may flip out on *you*."

"Fine! Okay! Everything's cool, it just floated into yer paws one night."

Edelle sighed. She had already faced one hold up since she'd left home, and her mind really had very little capacity for anything but what might be happening back there anyhow.

"'M'name's Lute, by the way," the skinny gray said into the silence.

"I'm Edelle. Pleased to meet you, I suppose. Now I'll be on my way."

As Edelle turned to leave, she heard the crunching of paper and looked back.

Lute had settled himself down on the branch and was squinting at a crumpled piece of parchment which seemed to have come from the pack beside him.

"Is that—a map?" she asked tentatively.

"Sure it is." Nothing could have prepared her for what he said next. "Don't suppose yew'd happen to know anything about white squirrels."

"*What?*"

Lute did not respond, still apparently intent upon reading the map.

"Lute—that's your name, right? You said something about the white squirrels?"

"Yeah. I mean, I've got nothing else to do. And I've had a—well, a weird feeling lately that there's something I need to know up there, like the answer to a question that really smart people ask yew and yer really frustrated because yew can't understand half the words in the question to begin with…" he stopped and shook his head. Edelle raised an eyebrow but made no comment. She was thinking she might need this squirrel, tasteless as he might be.

"Part of it is just me wanting to know who killed my father, and then—

"This 'Pember' was your father?"

"No. Cripes, no, did I say that?" He looked almost stricken.

"So you think going to the white squirrels is going to help with that how?"

"Well, cripes, I don't know. I only just came up with the idea tonight. That's the thing, though isn't it? I won't know until I figure in everything. I heard—well, I wanted to know if yew knew anything about them, like whether they can see the future or the past, or whatever kind of stuff they do up there. I always heard they were magic. And, yew know, there are some stories from the past where they've saved people and stuff. If that's true, maybe they can help me."

Edelle's mind was in a whirl. Where formerly she had been set on not telling a soul anything about her own plans, she could see that Lute could be an asset. And while part of her hated to think about any other living creature in such dry terms, it was only plain truth that she had not brought a map, or more importantly a single thing to eat. She bet that pack he carried with him was full of other useful things, as well. And if they were both going in the same direction…

The tables have turned on you, Dell. Shouldn't have been so insufferable now, should you have been?

"Lute?"

"Mm-hmm. Right. I think it's a bit north-west from here. Well, I should be going—what?"

"Would you mind if I came along?"

"Came along? Cripes, what for?"

She had been intending to tell the truth, but at the last minute surprised herself.

"I'm curious too."

Lute stared at her. She could tell he knew something was missing here.

"What, yew want to come with *me*? When yew have that nice colony back there?"

She shrugged, not meeting his eyes.

"Not everyone can stay around."

Lute thought he understood that all too well, though something in him never would have guessed it of *her*.

"Like you said, I saved your entrails. And you like having them," Edelle supplied.

"…Yeah. Yeah, that's true. Well, I don't see why not then. Just be aware, yew know, that I don't know what I'm doing so if I get yew lost or something and you can't get back…"

"It's okay." Edelle had thoroughly thought through all of *those* types of scenarios enough to dull herself to them. "Thanks."

She thought she saw Lute give her a funny look, but she wrote it off to her change of attitude.

Now that things were sorted out, Lute seemed to be very uncomfortable with remaining in the same spot any longer. Edelle, though she was fairly sure that his pursuers were not sharp enough to realize they were on the wrong trail for a while yet, saw his point.

A while later they had found a place to sleep—Lute made sure to deviate as far from his original trail as possible, and they settled at last at the base of a tree with sheltering roots to spare. He then fell asleep in record timing while Edelle stared up at the cold façade of the moon through the cracks in the trees, cracks that made it appear one big, shattered globe. With the sound of Lute's heavy breathing as a constant backdrop, she wondered at the mess such cracks could make out of anything, even something so distant. It filled her with a sadness that was preposterous—after all, the moon could never care for *her* in its white, milky isolation. But she turned her head all the same and buried her face in the leaves, losing herself in a familiarity so close and tried to ignore the cold. Lute's breathing went on; up, pause, hold, down, up, pause, hold—hold—hold—

And she finally managed to lose herself for the second night in a row.

CHAPTER XI

Tiallin was numb. He did not come out of his room for the next day after venturing into that of Zerrith, and no one questioned him about it either, which if possible made him feel even more alone and betrayed.

Betrayed. It was a perfect word for the way he felt: betrayed by the King, who he feared had forgotten him entirely, betrayed by Lyrah who never set her pretty eyes on him for any reason but to quest after his brother, betrayed by his mother for giving him over to the King without his consent, but most of all by Zerrith. Zerrith who had always seemed just a harmless dreamer, a squirrel whom everyone naturally seemed to admire for qualities that could not quite be named—was it surety of self, of the visions that he never shared with a soul?

The visions that might be more malevolent than anyone had imagined?

Tiallin shivered and stared at the floor where the note from Zerrith promising a birthday gift lay crumpled up. He had tried again and again to convince himself that he was just imagining things, but there was no doubt in his mind; those were the king's willow poles. Trivial, perhaps, but not enough so to cover up the fact: his brother had been stealing from the King. His brother, who had refused service to the King. That Zerrith might have his own agenda now, one that might be against the King, well, that just fit right in didn't it? And wasn't he, Tiallin in service to the King? Was he not bound to report anything amiss? He had sworn to it.

He had been locked up in his room because in a weak, faltering swell of panic he felt as if he could not face anyone, least of all Zerrith. He longed for the truth from his brother, for some rational explanation that might relieve him of his moral dilemma—more so, he just longed to forget what he had seen, to skip back the hours and the curiosity, come back to the boredom from which this mess had come. Only this time he would live with it. He could live with most anything but this knowledge, this painful burning in his chest, this staring at the crumpled paper by his bed as if it were a friend he had once trusted.

Why?

I love you. Why?

Zerrith's face laughed at him from behind a veil.

"You just like your high places," it said.

That's not true!!

What was *under that tarp?*

Tiallin could see it in his mind's eye, the cleverly covered object at the far end of Zerrith's room, lying in wait behind the curtain of wilted flowers. The feeling he had got when looking at it was beyond anything he could understand, but he did not dare risk going back to find out what the curtain hid.

Tiallin's stomach gave a complaining rumble and a pain shot through his midsection. Groaning, he rolled over onto his side and got up to fetch something to eat. He had been ignoring his steadily growing hunger for the last several waking hours, but it looked as if he could do it no longer. He would have to face the world beyond his door.

He could not say why he did it, but as he crossed to the door he glanced back at the note, still crumpled on the floor. Taking his paw from the doorknob, he turned back then with some hesitation, picked up the paper and smoothed it flat once more, lying it on his bed. Standing for a moment as if lost, Tiallin's stomach gave another vehement gurgle and he complied.

As soon as Tiallin pushed open the door, the sound of Zerrith's hushed voice greeted his ears, and he was taken so much by surprise that, hunger forgotten, he jumped a little before realizing his brother was standing further up the hallway and had not noticed him come out at all. Tiallin had almost turned to go in the other direction when he noticed his brother was not alone—he was talking not to himself, as Zerrith was sometimes prone to do, but to another standing outside with him, someone Tiallin recognized. She must have felt his eyes on her, for Lyrah looked to the side and met his gaze for a brief instant, held it.

"—will come back then?" Zerrith was saying.

Lyrah gave Tiallin a brief smile before turning back to Zerrith.

"Yes, I told you. I know how important it is to you. I just wish—Zerrith, consider it!"

"I'm not—okay, but—

"You say that every time," she sighed. "but—I want to see it through. You really ought to—

Tiallin moved off down the hallway, noticing he had paused to listen. It was all he needed to be suspected of nosing in Zerrith's business yet again.

Coming down the hollowed trunk of the tree, still drafty due to the weather, he stole a hunk of roasted chestnut from where it sat steaming unattended at the table and stuffed it into his mouth greedily. His stomach gurgled in pleasure. Tiallin was in the act of gouging out more of the nut's tasty insides when his mother came bursting through the entrance to their tree, breathing fast as though she had run a great distance in a very short time.

"Tiallin—oh thank Astrippa, Tiallin, I don't know what to do," Iskla exclaimed, trying to speak clearly and to catch her breath at once. A step sounded behind them and Tiallin saw that Lyrah had come downstairs. Her wide elderberry eyes took in the scene, the evident panic on

Iskla's features and she paused, apparently unsure whether to take her leave or not.

"What's wrong, mother?" Tiallin asked with some alarm. He did not think he could ever recall seeing his cool, reserved mother lose control, but she was certainly on the brink of it now.

"The King, it's the King," she said, forcing her voice to a calmer level. Behind her, Tiallin saw Lyrah's brow crinkle in apparent concern.

"He won't—well, he seems very ill and he won't speak to anyone, he keeps saying things we can't understand and he refuses to tell us how and when he got like this. He's just—he's been lying down and he can't get up. He seems terribly drained, and he refuses food or water. It is so sudden that no one knows what to do at all—just this morning he was seemingly in perfect condition. Everyone's been trying, oh, *everything* but nothing is having any effect, and you should see him, Tiallin, it's horrible, and the worst thing is he doesn't even seem to want help. I just...don't know what to do."

Tiallin sat in stunned silence in the wake of her news. It never even crossed his mind to ask why his mother had been up at the Great Tree to begin with. All he could think was how he felt awful now for feeling so childishly that the King had betrayed him.

Tiallin's eyes caught Lyrah's for a second over his mother's head and he saw she was looking at him, puzzled. He could not help feeling a bit the same way.

"Mother? It sounds terrible, really, but if none of the elder squirrels could do anything, why rush to tell me? What could *I* do about it?"

His mother shook her head.

"I don't know. But he mentioned you, Tiallin. He said your name."

Tiallin wasn't sure whether the faint gasping noise had come from his own throat or from someone else in the room, but suddenly he felt as if the nut he had just eaten so little of had swelled up to twice its original size in his stomach, twisting up into an uncomfortable knot.

"I'll—go then," he choked, and raced out the door, not bothering to see if Lyrah would follow. Evidently she did, for he heard her footsteps, nimble and light behind him and when he turned back she only shook her head and motioned him on.

"I was going there anyhow—don't mind me." Her expression was strained, and he knew the news of the King's illness was new to her as well. Vaguely, he wondered again what it was she did in his service, but now was not the time to ask such things. He felt he needed to get to the Great Tree as quickly as possible. He did not know what it was the King wanted him for, but if his condition were as serious as Iskla seemed to think, Tiallin would never forgive himself if he got there too late.

The Great Tree was standing where it had always stood, in its heart-stopping splendor; alone in its clearing in a forest where the trees were otherwise packed close together, it had always seemed to Tiallin almost as if the other trees had moved aside especially for it. Its thick, knotty branches rushed wildly out from its swollen trunk, the smell of pine thick in the air around contradicting what was evident from the jagged, broken top of the huge pine. The Great Tree was dying. It had been for years.

This fact had never caused a chill in Tiallin before, but now it appeared almost a warning, and he avoided thinking about it as he tore up the branch nearest to ground level, going up, up, up until he reached the entrance he had so nervously set foot through what seemed like eons ago, when he had first been assigned the task of waiting on the King.

Outside the King's chambers, he skidded to a halt and realized that at some point Lyrah had stopped following him and taken a different route, which made him nervous. Would he truly be alone with the King? The guard at the door did not recognize him at first and Tiallin had to do a lot of impatient explaining before the heavyset gray squirrel would let him pass into the chamber beyond.

It must be his first day on the job, thought Tiallin, trying now to keep his nerves at bay. He had not recognized the guard, though the King seemed to have a new one every time he came.

Tiallin halted his mind in its babbling and stared around the chambers, no longer lit by sunlight and seeming so much smaller for the lack of it. The room had to be lit with several firefly lamps, as the usually open ceiling had been sealed off with heavy rush netting to suit the weather, making it was hard to see. Squinting around nervously, Tiallin felt more like an intruder than someone who had been summoned properly. The room gave all appearances of being empty, and he peered into the corners, and at the mellow glow of the lamps' light on the carvings nearest them.

Then Tiallin heard a shifting coming from the platform on which the King had often stood, which had appeared to be clear moments before.

King Sirius was lying, apparently oblivious to Tiallin's presence, on a pile of pillows and blankets, his arms stretched weirdly over his head. Tiallin could not tell whether he was asleep or not until Sirius began to murmur under his breath brokenly, starting and then stopping, his words too soft for Tiallin to properly make out. Moving closer to where he guessed he would be in the King's range of vision but not mounting the platform, Tiallin cleared his throat.

When King Sirius turned, it seemed to take him forever. It took some control on Tiallin's part not to gasp out loud. Perhaps it was only due to the dimness around them both, but the King's face looked deathly pale; unnaturally pale. There were dark smudges lining the bottoms of his eyes and it made Tiallin's own eyes water to look at him. Whatever had happened? Utterly perplexed and lost for words, Tiallin continued to stare, unable to make his tongue work.

"Tiallin," King Sirius spoke in a rasping hush. Tiallin waited for more, but it seemed to take Sirius some time to summon up the strength for his next words. He spoke with his sightless eyes to the ceiling again, which Tiallin was thankful for.

"I have seen."

"Er…Are you all right, your Majesty? They've been saying—that you asked—

"I have seen, Tiallin, I have seen! I could not tell them, you know I do not talk to anyone of it. My gift. My loss of it, my losing it, no one knows, so I could not tell them what happened today or the truth about it, could I?"

"Uhm…pardon me, your Majesty but I don't understand. What *did* happen today?"

Sirius turned back in the direction of the sound of Tiallin's voice and said once more, "I saw."

"You…saw."

"Yes. The sight, Tiallin, remember? I thought I was losing it, that I *had* lost it, but I *saw*. And what I saw…it was horrible…horrible…"

His whole body gave a shudder and he lay still, drawing his paws to his chest.

"Tiallin, I think we are doomed. I felt it before, but now the feeling's stronger, now I have a sign. I think..."

But he broke off as if he had heard something, and Tiallin, listening, heard it too; a startled clanking from outside the room, muffled by the walls. The King kept silent long after the sound, apparently listening hard, but all was still and he hesitated before speaking again.

"You are familiar with the carvings of our history," he said.

Tiallin nodded, then quickly amended, "Yes."

"The squirrel who carved them is dead. He was murdered nine days ago."

Tiallin's breath quickened.

"The *same* squirrel did...did *all* of these?" He gestured around at the carvings on the immense circular walls, knowing that Sirius could not see him and not caring. His astonishment was simply too great—here he had thought that the carvings had been done one by one, over the many years they represented. He supposed, looking at them now, that they all had the same touch, the same magical air to them, and the same immutable presence.

"Yes," Sirius answered. "He was very talented. Tamen and he...had an understanding...however...It bothers me that someone would use his death to get at me like that, to play on my fears. In a way, it is quite brilliant. Brilliant yet twisted. It makes me think of—but no. I have only my suspicions, and there are some things that should be left in the past. That is one thing older people sometimes have a hard time doing, Tiallin...not losing the present to the tangle of the past."

Tiallin spoke slowly, as he doubted very much his understanding of what the King was trying to impart.

"What do you mean when you say someone's trying to get to you? Isn't it possible that this squirrel's murder could, well, just be…random? And I don't get what killing him would achieve if someone *were* trying to get to you. Sorry," he added, unable to help feeling thick.

Sirius only looked thoughtful.

"I think it likely," he said, "that they would know of my fear of…not having an heir. Of the line of white squirrels—*magical* white squirrels, that is…dying out. If that were the case, this killing would be a kind of cold symbolism, meant to frighten me, to confirm my fears. Without Pember Sigyl, there will never be a last square of a carving. No heir. No future. It is a message I believe someone meant to send, and they have succeeded. I saw."

"But if someone meant to scare you," Tiallin reasoned, "why would they just kill this…Sigyl guy, and leave him there? Wouldn't they want to find a solid way of making sure you found out?"

"Oh, they did," Sirius said. "I was not practicing the sight when that vision came to me. It was very brief, very cruel, and left me very weak—as you see now. I think someone had been trying to reach me, to show me this vision for quite some time, which I suppose in a way is lucky because it means they may not be as wholly powerful as they would like to think."

Tiallin was awed. "You mean someone *sent you* that vision? That's possible?"

"Not many can do it, but yes. That is why…I am very concerned. I used to be able to do similar things, when I…was stronger. But because my gift feels as if it has been drained from me over time, I am not very good at coping with receiving the gift of others, especially when it comes as an attack like this."

"Do you—is that why you're faring so poorly now? Are you going to be all right?" Tiallin asked, wondering too many things at once and also wondering whether Sirius would consider him annoying if he asked them all. The old squirrel was confiding in him, and all Tiallin had for him were more questions! In all fairness, he reminded himself that it was not entirely clear what the King wanted from him today—perhaps just someone to tell his fears to, someone to know the story of what was really happening so he would not have to bear it completely alone.

"I am sure I will be all right," Sirius said. "I am just very, very tired. They ask me what is wrong, but they don't really want to know. They don't want to know and they say I am wrong when I begin to tell them, that I am paranoid. I believe that is the latest rumor, at least." He gave a dry, brief smile to the thatched ceiling covering above. "Is it not, Tiallin?"

"Erm."

Hot and uncomfortable, Tiallin muttered, "Well, uh, yeah, some of them say that. But not all! I mean, I'm sure there are still many who would support you."

"But not enough," Sirius interrupted gently, "We are divided as it is. There is a chance, besides, that the enemy I sense is among us. Have you…?"

Tiallin felt something hot and heavy sink in his chest, and his whole face began to burn, but the question he was dreading never came. Sirius, perhaps finally exhausted beyond what his body could take, had fallen into a deep sleep. Tiallin stood a moment, at a loss, and then mounted the platform on which the King lay; his blankets had fallen aside from his frequent shivering, and the young squirrel moved them back into place. He stared down at the King for a good minute, forcing his eyes never to waver from the face that frightened him so. Then he turned and walked out the door, feeling the lamps' glow at his back, which became suddenly straighter as a strange sense of strength came pushing up slowly from his stomach, flowering out into his chest. Reaching the outside of the King's chambers, Tiallin spotted the guard who had let him in earlier up ahead, head bowed over a set of stones, rolling them about in his palm.

"His Majesty is asleep," Tiallin said, effectively snapping the indolent guard out of his little one-on-one game. "Make sure that no one disturbs him, but also maybe send someone in after a bit, just to see that he's okay."

To his surprise, the guard did not even question his authority, just shrugged and nodded, and as Tiallin left the Great Tree, the feeling in his chest surged and grew stronger, producing a giddiness that seemed entirely inappropriate in the context of everything that had occurred the past couple of days. It was strange, but not at all unpleasant.

When he reached home again, walking still in that leisurely, upright fashion in which he had left the King, Tiallin crossed over the threshold to find that this was not the end of the strangeness.

"Tiallin." Zerrith was standing beside the table as if he had been waiting for Tiallin there. His brother's face was a mix of emotions that did not know themselves, but Tiallin thought he saw excitement in there, and it drew him to Zerrith in a way that he had not had occasion to feel in some time.

"I told you I would show you," Zerrith said

Tiallin felt himself go numb. "Really?" he choked out.

"Yes."

"I thought that after…"

"So did I. But I'm not mad anymore. I think," he seemed to struggle for a second, "that someone else could see. That…would be okay. Our parents are gone."

Without further ado, Zerrith turned and made his way up the hallway. Tiallin followed him, feeling already part of something close and exciting, the way he had when Zerrith had played the games with the notes, the games he invented in which he gave Tiallin a really good part to play.

Zerrith opened the door to his room and crossed through, waiting for Tiallin to come across before closing it behind them. Tiallin knew where his brother would go before he started for it, and his heart went wild in his breast. Zerrith went for the curtain of wilted flowers, brushed it aside carefully and stood before the great, covered *something*, the shape that stood a bit taller off the ground than he did.

Zerrith only hesitated a moment; he placed a paw lightly atop the covering and pulled it free.

Standing at least a foot off the ground, planted on odd, claw-like struts made from stick, rose the skeletal structure of some large, mythical creature, exactly like something out of one of his brother's imaginary games of old. The thing seemed to be made from everything at once, and Tiallin was captivated by it, filled with the same indelible feeling he had experienced the day before when seeing this thing under its guise. It was made from wood, all carefully cut and pasted together very excruciatingly, and possibly even bone, clean and white the way bone that has long lain under the earth tends to get. Over these skeletal elements a covering of thatch had been made, integrating grass and pine needles and rushes all at once and woven into the bones to create a skin of some type. The makeshift creature was wondrous and frightening in its sheer size and the amount of thought that must have gone into making it—from the rounded body narrowing out into a graceful neck and head, to the sharp, pointed metal mouth. There were no eyes yet, but preparation had clearly been made for their inevitability by the careful sculpting of the head…they would be one to each side, he saw.

Tiallin was astonished. In all his life, he would never have guessed—would never have dreamed that this…*this* was the secret his brother had been keeping all these years. He could find nothing ominous about it. Tearing his eyes from the thing in front of him, he stared at his brother, knowing that words, so insubstantial to begin with, had deserted him.

"Now you know," Zerrith said softly.

It did not need to be spoken between them that Tiallin would not tell. Not now, not ever. Not even—his stomach gave a slight twinge—would he tell the King. There was something spoken, whispered really in the veins of this project that was alive and should not be exploited. It scared him a little, but oh Astrippa, who was he to lie, it was wonderful too.

"Thank you," Tiallin said quietly. It seemed the only appropriate thing to say.

"It's in progress," Zerrith said suddenly.

Tiallin nodded almost imperceptibly, unable to tear his eyes away. "What do you call it?"

A smile quivered on Zerrith's lips, so real and wonderful that it seemed to Tiallin he had been waiting ages for someone to ask him this very question.

"A Byrd," he said. "I call it at a Byrd."

CHAPTER XII

The snow came on the third day they were traveling. Edelle felt the world, which had seemed for a while as though it may have been possible to traverse, became one large, white expanse of eternity. It was coming down in flakes, slow and soft but continuous, until the ground became coated with an inch of the stuff, but still she and Lute did not dare to take to the trees. They knew that, aside from the danger of slipping on the newly fallen snow that collected there, they would be tracked easiest this way—or so Lute said.

In addition to being oddly knowledgeable about the most criminally indicating of things at times, Lute could be tiring as a travelling partner; they could barely agree on something as simple as where to camp for a night, although Edelle took a certain pride in knowing that she could usually make things go her way if she pushed hard enough. She also knew that it was probably not wise to trust a squirrel who knew ten ways to cover one's tracks and erase scent, and how to make crude weapons from rocks, sticks and thick grasses. But somehow she felt instinctually, inexplicably, that Lute would not be of harm...to *her* at least, and that was enough to be getting on with for now.

There were quite a few things she wanted to ask Lute, but felt she could not. If she asked him something, he might take it as a liberty to start asking questions of her, and she still was not sure she wanted him to know *anything* about her reasons for going to the white squirrels. After all, she told herself whenever she felt guilty for giving nothing in exchange for his honesty, Lute was probably keeping things from her as well. They were merely partners of coincidence and desperate times; she held no obligations to him—hadn't she saved him nights ago?

Edelle watched Lute's dark gray fur as he trekked, and wondered. She had never seen a squirrel like Lute. When she had run into him previously, they had both been cloaked in dark. She had assumed he was a gray then, but the first morning upon waking to see him she noticed that his fur was of a much darker hue than that of any gray she had seen. He looked indeed as if he were part black squirrel, which was certainly odd, as such mixings were generally frowned upon. But it was more than the color of his fur that threw her off—Lute did not possess the mannerisms that seemed common to most gray squirrels she had come across, and though she had not had occasion to meet many black squirrels, she knew them to be close cousins of the grays and she could not imagine that Lute's behavior was emulating theirs either.

While neither of them had brought up the topic of the knife and their first meeting upon her request, Edelle found herself wondering again and again about it. She kept thinking about how Lute had said the knife was his—she no longer doubted he was lying but she did not understand...

"Lute?"

Lute turned around, holding a paw to his face. He seemed to find the snow eternally obnoxious. Edelle found she did not mind it so much herself.

"Yew hungry?" Lute asked.

"No," she said, remembering guiltily that he had been sharing the food out of his pack with her every day. "It's not—

Lute shrugged. "I am." He plunked himself down in the impressionable new snow and went to sorting through his bag with a type of determination that might have been laughable had Edelle been better disposed at the moment.

"You're just going to stop right here then?"

Lute waved a paw.

"We're out of the mist," he said around a mouthful of candied walnuts. "We got 'em fooled."

"Oh, so simple caution doesn't apply anymore?"

He regarded her solemnly. "What's got yer nuts in a jumble?"

"That's crude."

When all she got for an answer was unnecessarily loud chewing, she sighed and went for it.

"Lute."

"What already? Yew going to just keep saying that?"

She bit off a testy reply, knowing he was trying to provoke her.

"No, I just wanted to know exactly *why*, that night when you came after your knife, why you wanted it so bad."

The face of the young newcomer to her colony kept coming to mind. How had he got his paws on it if it weren't his to give in the first place?

"I thought we weren't allowed to talk about that," Lute said rather smugly, and Edelle gritted her teeth.

"Now I suppose it's okay."

"All right, then, if *yew* think it's okay. It's *so* nice of yew to ask now."

She shot him a look; the effect was apparently quite chilling, for Lute nearly choked on his latest mouthful of food. He cleared his throat hastily.

"I needed to find the squirrel who took my knife, because basically whoever took that knife…well, they were the one who killed Pember."

Edelle tried to keep the fear from mounting in her chest.

"It can't be that simple," she said. "Anyway, whoever killed this Pember—couldn't they have done it with anything? Who says it has to be the knife?"

"Aah," Lute said, getting up and dusting the snow from his tail. "It's the only thing what makes sense, that's all. If someone snuck in to kill Pember, they would need to be secretive about it. So they wouldn't bring a weapon with them. In Pember's case, they wouldn't of needed to. He's got plenty of knives in the shop. So they just took one once they broke in, right, and—well, then they just went and done it, and it was damn bad luck that it happened to be my knife as well. 'Course, that could've been intentional. It could've been someone I knew…I could name fair a dozen of 'em that'd want to see me get the axe. But what I can't figure into *that* case, is why any of 'em would kill Pember to get me. Pember was well respected. He…" Lute stopped himself, faintly flushed. "He was well respected." Then, as if to save himself from some embarrassment or other, he blurted, "How did yew get the knife then? I know yew didn't do it."

Edelle opened her mouth, then closed it. She did not know why she should feel hesitant to talk about the young squirrel who had given the knife to her; after all, hadn't she been so annoyed by him before? Annoyed and…excited. She blocked the thought from her mind and said the first words that came to her.

"I found it."

Lute's raised an eyebrow.

" Yew *found* it?"

Edelle sat, terrified that he had seen right through the lie, but momentarily she realized that he was just confused, which did nothing for her guilt, and even made her feel inexplicably angry. *She* would have caught herself on that one; how gullible could you get?

Lute was looking thoroughly disappointed.

"Should've guessed. Whoever done it wouldn't have wanted to keep hold on the weapon what they used, would they? Probably would've left it lying around what for the next innocent person to find, so's *they'd* be framed, and then they'd be off the hook."

Edelle stared at him. It *did* make a good deal of sense, but it left her with a turmoil of sickness in the pit of her stomach. Why had she felt the need to cover up for the young squirrel? He was a shifty character, now she thought about it, and even though he'd said he'd gone to the meeting Thoelen had held, Edelle had a feeling he hadn't. Why did her mind seem to persist so insistently that he was not a killer? Was it only what she wanted to believe?

The thought left her very uncomfortable. After all, how much of what she believed was only true because she wanted it to be? Her mouth began to get dry, and she said roughly, "Come on, we'd better get going."

Lute blinked, coming up from a well of his own thought.

"Oh, er, yeah. I guess yer right."

They started off again, into the snow, which was now swirling with a bit of wind to pick it up, falling ever faster.

"Cripes, I hope there's not a blizzard," Lute grumped. Though her thick, rather wiry russet coat was rather better at keeping the cold out, Edelle had to agree. Even with Lute's pack and their hastily constructed weapons, they were ill-prepared for any unwelcome little surprise that the early settling of winter might bring. She lowered her head against the prickling flakes and nearly ran into Lute a split second later.

The gray-black squirrel had stopped for seemingly no reason, and was staring ahead, paws raised to shelter his eyes.

"Would yew look at that, we're in luck!"

Edelle peered through the snow, registering how fast it was now flying at them on the faint breeze, but she did not see anything.

"What? What is it?"

But Lute had plunged ahead, strapping his pack to his back and bounding on all fours now. Edelle, completely bemused, had no choice but to follow.

It was not long before she spotted what Lute was referring to. A compactly built one-room wood house was visible on one of the low-lying branches of a nearby tree. It looked rather newly built, so Edelle inferred that someone must still be living there.

Though her larger girth and thicker fur allowed Edelle excellent protection against the cold, there was a downside—plowing her way through the carpet of snow on the ground proved a lot harder for her, and when she caught up to her companion at last, she was panting slightly.

Lute was merely staring up at the house, a glint in his eye.

"What—Edelle began to say, but he turned to her, waving a paw.

"Shh, just be quiet for a sec, okay?"

Feeling highly offended, Edelle nevertheless fell silent and watched as Lute leapt lightly to the tree and began to scale it, finding all the right claw-holds with hardly a sound. When he reached the house, he moved carefully around behind it and peered into the one window. Then he turned and came back down to her, all in a matter of minutes.

"No one's there now."

"So?"

"It's a storehouse, Edelle," he said, as if this explained everything.

"So?"

"So let's go get some food. C'mon and help, someone needs to hold the pack."

Edelle's ears rang, and she sat still as in shock. Then she narrowed her eyes at him.

"I most certainly will not."

The look he gave back to her was not angry or exasperated, but simply confused.

"We're almost out. I'd say we don't even have enough for three more days. I mean, it wasn't like I expected to have someone else with me."

"Maybe so, but we'll figure something out. Just last night you told me we only had to cross Firwood. We'll just have to manage. That's someone else's food. We've got no right to take it, and I'm not going to help you steal."

Lute grinned.

"Oh, c'mon. They've got plenty, and we don't need much more. Yew don't pass up these opportunities."

"No." Edelle planted herself firmly to the spot. Lute, after staring incredulously at her for a second, shrugged and turned to go back up to the storehouse. He darted inside and she heard the sound of his pack unbuckling and a rustling as he stuffed it full. Edelle felt a boiling rage begin inside of her such as she was not accustomed to feeling. She wanted to pick something up and hurl it, or to run forever, and leave the shameful act she was allowing to take place, as if by doing so she could make it stop. They were just taking someone else's food, someone who might have a large family to feed through the winter—would this unknown family have gladly shared with them? She hoped not, as the thought only made her feel as if her insides were crumpling more and more. Would the nameless face from whom they were taking suffer for the loss? Would they go hungry?

Hungry. Like everyone she knew back at home. Was she right now taking from someone like Bench, another young squirrel who liked to run and play?

Lute stuck his head out from the storehouse and, shouldering his considerably bulkier pack, started carefully down the tree to the ground where Edelle waited, inwardly writhing.

"You make me sick," she spat. She wanted to strike the pack from him, to dump its contents out over the ground and to run off, try to fend for herself for the rest of the way—she supposed she nearly did so, too. At any rate, something in her eyes made Lute start, almost flinch back from her.

"I'm not eating any of it," she said. Her voice was colder than the day, than the flecks of ice that relentlessly drove down upon them. Lute did not argue. The silence between them was so incredibly thick as they continued past the site of the storehouse, that it was suffocating. Edelle longed to scream, to pierce it, to wound it as she felt wounded, but she kept control. She always kept control.

After all, they're not eating back at home—why should I?

The thought warmed her just as it frightened her. Very well, then. She would suffer with her kind, though the distance stretched between them. She would suffer, and she would hope that what lay in the distance ahead was better, that it would finally help bring some relief.

Astrippa, guide me. Help me not to fail…and hold them safe while I'm gone.

Please.

CHAPTER XIII

The next couple of days were the best days of Tiallin's life. Once he knew Zerrith's secret, everything else that had seemed to be of such import beforehand vanished. Time had spiraled backwards, and Tiallin could no longer understand how eleven seasons had ever been anything to aspire to—it was better to be younger, always younger, and under the constant spell of the creations of a mind that worked unseen.

Tiallin and Zerrith were no longer playing together, it was true; they were working together. The very next day after Zerrith had shown the Byrd to Tiallin, he had come to him early in the morning, knocking on the door of his younger brother's room and stepping back to wait.

"Would you like to help me?"

"What?" Tiallin had thought he misheard Zerrith at first.

"Help me. Make the Byrd. You don't have to. It would be mostly me doing the actual building, I think."

Tiallin had not needed to think about it. The ensuing days had developed a pattern which he enjoyed very much. He would get up, and before coming awake fully or breaking his fast he would be off to Zerrith's door, knocking and standing back impatiently, ready to be assigned any old task.

And most of the tasks were rather mundane. Zerrith seemed very hesitant about letting Tiallin touch the Byrd, preferring him to fetch materials from different nooks and crevices about the room instead. Indeed, it seemed as though Zerrith had been preparing for the building of this—thing—for longer even than Tiallin had first guessed, for everything was meticulously prepared, sorted according to its purpose. Tiallin didn't mind his job as errand-boy at all; they kept up some of the best conversation that he had had in a long time while they were at it. Once, as Zerrith was tightening the bonds that held two of the joints of the massive, make-believe creature together, Tiallin asked a question that had been on his mind since that morning.

"How do you keep it all together?"

The look Zerrith gave him was quizzical.

"What do you mean by that?"

"Well, I know you're tying it all up with the reeds, and I know they're strong and all, but I can't see how the whole thing holds together so well. It looks almost like—well—I don't know! Is there a secret to it?" He had been about to say 'like magic' but he felt stupid and childish saying so.

Zerrith shook his head.

"No. It's simple architecture. There doesn't have to be a secret to everything I do, you know."

Tiallin sensed the hint of defensiveness in his tone, and even though he did not understand it, he let the subject go, eyes traveling to where the skeletal body of the Byrd was gradually becoming obscured by the woven skin which was tenderly applied inch by inch as he watched. A smell of fresh grass, sharp and green in his nostrils filled the drafty winter air in the room. To Tiallin, it smelled of life. He could almost imagine the creature in front of him *was* alive, and later when Zerrith asked if he wanted to touch it, Tiallin felt so stupidly certain of this conviction that for a moment he truly feared closing the distance between himself and this part of his brother's imagination.

Tiallin never asked Zerrith exactly what he wanted to get out of building the Byrd, not once during the several times he stopped by to help or to simply watch his brother work at it. It never really occurred to him to ask, either—

that was the way it worked between them, and always had. Tiallin had come to assume that whatever Zerrith was doing held some abstract fascination for his brother that was just as well not explained, whether it was examining leaves and flowers or inventing monsters for them both to face.

"It only has two legs," Tiallin remarked on yet another day, bending a bit to peer under the Byrd. "Should it not have more?"

Zerrith's forehead crinkled, and Tiallin could tell he was once again annoyed.

"Why? It does not need more."

As much as his brother seemed to take quiet pleasure in having someone else survey his creations, he also seemed exasperated by Tiallin's inability to grasp what Tiallin could only label, rather resentfully and half making fun, as the genius of singularly weird ideas.

But weird as the "Byrd" might be, it also filled Tiallin with the strongest sense of lightness, of goodness, of something wonderful right around the bend. He still did not like touching it, for the act threw a bend on these feelings that he did not like or understand, but all his brother really required anyway was that he watch, so watch Tiallin did, and gladly.

As the days went on and the Byrd progressed, it gained round, beady black eyes from metal orbs and its body filled out so that he could no longer see the skeleton underneath, Tiallin found himself wishing fervently that the King would not call upon him again. It was not that serving King Sirius had lost its appeal so much as that going back to the Great Tree would make him have to face a reality that he had done his best not to think about. Of course, he could never entirely put the face of the King and his fears from his mind, but here, far away from the room that had once been so full of sunlight Tiallin felt it acceptable to believe that these fears might all be smoke and mirrors. Would it be too much to ask for anything to be coincidence?

Zerrith polished the eyes, staring into them as he did so, then ran a paw over the top of the head, stalling in his tireless craftsmanship, and Tiallin knew that it was time for him to leave for that day.

King Sirius called him the very next day, and it was on his way over to the Great Tree that Tiallin realized he was not alone. A twitch from one direction, an ungainly sneeze clumsily muffled from another, and he gathered he was being followed. Not letting on that he knew, Tiallin continued seemingly unperturbed to the Great Tree, through the entranceway where he stopped and stood in the shadows, eyes questing back out over the forest outside. For an instant, he thought he saw the leaves of a tree across from him shudder, but the movement stopped as soon as he fastened his gaze on it. Discomfited, he turned and went down the empty hallway to where the pompous, mustached squirrel he recognized from one of his first ventures here opened the door for him.

The first thing Tiallin noticed was that he was evidently not the King's only visitor. Lyrah was standing next to Sirius and by all appearances was in conversation with the King. At the sound of his entrance, however, she looked up and, voice seeming to die on her lips, turned to go. The King put a paw on her arm, but Lyrah pulled away in a manner that Tiallin found shockingly rude. She left through the small, hidden back door Tiallin had exited through at the end of his first time in this room. Tiallin turned to the King, eyebrows raised, but if Sirius felt as shocked at the behavior of the pretty squirrel maid as Tiallin felt, he did a very good job at hiding it.

"I am sorry for calling you here on what is very probably the finest day we will have this winter," Sirius began. "I really only had one question for you. Last time you were here, I was not quite…well, and I did not get the opportunity to ask you—

Tiallin's heart sunk. He knew what was coming next.

"If you had anything to tell me?"

Mind drawing a blank, Tiallin searched furiously for something to say. He thought of the willow poles, of the metal orbs, the latter of which he was sure Zerrith could not have got from anywhere but here—the crafting was far too impressive—but never once did he consider actually mentioning either of these things. Uncomfortably remembering his vow to the King, he brought up the only bit of other information worth telling.

"I think someone is following me."

No sooner had the words left his mouth, than he wished he could draw them back in. How incredibly silly and paranoid he must sound!

"Not that it's important," he amended.

Still staring past Tiallin at the wall beyond, Sirius said "On the contrary, Tiallin, it is very important. Did you see them?"

Tiallin was about to confess that he had not when he remembered the day when, coming outside his own house, he had caught the young gray squirrel watching him, the elusive one who had scampered as soon as Tiallin spotted him. But surely that one had been too young to be of any real threat? He mentioned it to the King all the same, and was surprised to see that Sirius appeared interested.

"Hmm…you did not get a good look at him, Tiallin? Can you remember any distinguishing features?"

"Er…no. I'm sorry."

"That's all right," said Sirius, looking disappointed all the same. Tiallin felt rather useless, and tried to keep his mind from wandering off to Zerrith and the stolen materials.

"This place borders on Firwood, that is the only problem," the King said. "There are a lot of grays living close by. Other squirrels, I believe…are fascinated by us. They tend to stare from across the border, but having one cross over *is* something unusual—for I think they are also afraid of us. And then, if this young gray were spying, what is it that he hoped to get out of it? Particularly if you were alone, as you said you were, Tiallin. He was not carrying any weapons?"

Tiallin shook his head.

"He was younger even than me. It was probably just curiosity." Tiallin was regretting having brought the subject up.

"It could be, it could be."

Somehow Tiallin doubted the King believed *that* for one minute.

Coming out of his momentary deep thought, Sirius said, "You may leave, now, Tiallin. Thank you."

His expression still troubled, he turned and started in the direction of his platform, the one on which he seemed to stand in place of a throne. Tiallin noticed that the fur of his tail was starting to become scruffy, as if tufts had been falling out of late from worry or stress. Tiallin was about to do as he was bidden and go when Sirius's voice came to him from across the room now, stopping him in his tracks.

"What does your mother think of this? Of my suspicions? Has she ever told you, truly?"

Tiallin was taken completely by surprise by the question. He looked back at Sirius, puzzled, but the old squirrel had his back to him still.

"She, er…"

He thought back to the conversation he could remember having with his mother, the last meaningful conversation they had had in some time. *She thinks you're mad,* would probably have been the most honest answer.

"She…doesn't know what to think. At least that's the impression I get," Tiallin said slowly.

Sirius's paw, clasped so tightly around the head of his cane, relaxed slightly as he said, "And here I thought she might have given you to me to say she believed."

Tiallin stood, suspended between leaving and breaking the ensuing silence. In the end, he chose the former, as he knew he would. Sirius did not call him back again.

Walking out into the blistering cold, Tiallin felt his heart lighten at the thought of coming back home and hoped Zerrith would be in his room, working on the Byrd and that he would be let in to help. It seemed such an innocent pleasure in the midst of a life that was fast declining into utter confusion.

About halfway home a loud, cracking noise from nearby sent Tiallin whirling around, heart beating fast. His mind had been on other matters, and he had all but forgotten the presence of his follower that morning.

As Tiallin resumed creeping along slowly, he could feel the eyes of the other presence on him, biding their time, waiting, and through his discomfort and muffled fear he wondered one thing.

Why? Why me? What do I have that would be of value to anyone?

Another cracking noise sounded, this time coming from almost right next to him. Tiallin jumped aside with a yell, but he was too slow. A thick gray paw shot out of the dense patch of shrub brush not two paces away and Tiallin felt himself dragged backward, bumping painfully on the frost-bitten ground, scratching frantically for a claw hold. It was no good—whoever had him had him by the tail, and they were no weakling.

With one last harried grab at the ground below him, Tiallin was encompassed by the dark and chill of the undergrowth, where he attempted to struggle free from his captor.

"Calm, calm," hissed a voice that made Tiallin anything but.

"I just want to know a few things."

The squirrel's face came into view, towering over Tiallin, who realized with a brief stab at his dignity that the other was standing on his tail. It was a gray squirrel. Not the younger one who had been spying on him days ago, but a larger, more powerfully built male wearing a necklace of raspberry thorns as if to prove his toughness to the world in case of any doubt. Tiallin hadn't had any. He did not doubt that this monstrosity could take him and break him against a tree, crush the life out of him with his bare paws.

The large squirrel was observing him with something other than menace in his face now, however. It was something like—curiosity.

"You whites aren't all that powerful, are you?" he said smugly, after a time. "I didn't believe the magic powers crap from the beginning, but you aren't even able to get away are you?" He laughed, the sound of it deep and roiling in his throat. Tiallin felt slightly sick.

"What do you want?" he choked out, trying to get his breathing back under control. Tiallin was not a weak squirrel. He had enough muscle mass to move the larger one if he took him by surprise, slide out from under him…but he would have to get his cool before making a move.

"Oh calm down, already," the larger squirrel laughed in amusement. He had the ugliest, throatiest laugh Tiallin had ever heard. "I'm not going to kill you. You're too young for that, and I'm not cold-blooded. I have a son. A son *you* threatened once, incidentally." His eyes narrowed, and Tiallin swallowed. "But I have some questions for you, and I *can* get pretty rough if I don't get my answers. I don't like to beat around the bush, though that may seem to you what I'm doing now," he gestured at their surroundings and laughed his ugly laugh.

Shut up shut up shut up, Tiallin thought, trying to see if he could inch his tail out from under the brute without making his efforts noticed. It was wedged tight between the ground and the gray's buttocks. He wondered if he were to die under this bush how long it would take for another to find him. He wouldn't want to smell…Tiallin gave a snort of strangled laughter, turning his head quickly into the ground to hide it.

"What are you doing for the King?" the gray asked, bearing down on him, and all humor was lost immediately as his mind drew a fearful blank on him. What was he to do? Would the gray know if he were lying? More to the point, did he have a choice?

"I do odds and ends for him. Wait on him. Get him some fruit, sometimes," he invented wildly, striving to keep his face free from fear. "Most of the time it's absolutely boring."

The weight on his tail drew back slightly, and when the big squirrel next spoke there was a hint of disappointment in his voice.

"You don't do anything—special for him? Anything—magical?"

Tiallin's eyes widened.

"You said you didn't believe in that!" he said, unable to help himself.

"I don't make a habit of it. But I know when you're lying, and you wouldn't be lying unless you had something worth telling me."

The weight started to descend again, only this time instead of just his tail it was his whole body under the attack.

"But that's all right," the gray went on. "I've heard you superior white squirrel types can crack under pressure. I've heard that if you get *pushed* hard enough, you can't hold your powers back." Now he was leaning into Tiallin, leaning hard, and Tiallin could not hold him back. The icy ground had sunk its cold through his fur and he felt as if his back were burning, burning, wet and burning.

"Put up any, say, *protections* around the King of late? Anything uniquely...*dangerous?*"

"N-no!" Tiallin choked out, trying hard to breath under the worsening pressure. And then, almost like the answer to an unsaid prayer, another sound broke into his consciousness; the sound, very close by, of another pair of feet on snow. The large gray darted away so fast that when Tiallin managed to lift his oxygen-deprived head from the ground, breathing hard, there were no signs of the other anywhere. Sitting trying to catch his breath, sucking the air in around him in gasping breaths and trying hard not to faint, Tiallin looked about him, at the dappled, weak patterns of the sunlight slanting through the dense brush around him. He listened, but whatever had disturbed the big squirrel did not seem to be in evidence any longer. Perhaps it had only been another passing white squirrel.

Still, Tiallin remained silent as he pulled himself over to the edge of the covering brush and stuck his head out, half expecting to be pounced upon once more. No one was there.

Get a grip on yourself, Tiallin. It's over, it's okay, no one's there. It's over.

Checking his breath at last into regulation, he dashed out over the dusting of snow on the ground, flinging it out behind him as he ran. He felt terribly out in the open, and even though he did not feel he was being watched anymore, Tiallin felt he could hardly trust his senses. Instead he hoped to death that his coat would blend him properly with the snow as he ran full-tilt toward his own home, not slowing until he had burst through the door and closed it firmly behind him. Trying not to entertain the notion of anyone tracking him *here* and what he would do if they did, Tiallin half-climbed, half-stumbled up the trunk to his room where he collapsed on his bed, laid on his back and shut his eyes.

Breathe. Breathe. Don't think about it. Breathe.

The panic still mounted in him all alone in his room, and he imagined that even now someone could be scaling his home, coming back to choke the life out of him and his family. What *had* the big gray squirrel wanted, and why had he had his own child spy on Tiallin earlier? What did they think he had?

But immediately after he had posed the question to himself, the answer came.

Magic. They think I have magic.

Didn't they know that very few of the white squirrels possessed such a thing? Tiallin had heard that once it had been common, but that had been years ago. The talent of the white squirrels was disappearing, and many were of the mind that it was a curse, the curse put on them by Astrippa for being too prideful, for failing to follow in her ways…or, for the more fantastical minded among them, failing to regain their wings and their color, and to soar once more to a place where they would not need to be so isolated. Where they would belong…

Of course, Tiallin and most others he knew didn't believe in this fairytale version of events. It dated way back, as such stories do, to older times when squirrel folk were more superstitious and would believe just about anything. But the story did hold a bit of allure. In it, Astrippa had warned the white squirrels that they must only use their given powers to help others, to care for the land she had created. If they did this successfully, then she would give them a place of their own once again. Tiallin rather thought that the white squirrels were making themselves out to be too important in the telling of this tale. *He* did not feel as if he were special in any way, and never really had. But whether or not the story held any truth, it was plain fact that the white squirrel colony of Pinewood appeared to be losing its magic. The King had confirmed this with his worries about not having an heir.

But it all came back to one point in Tiallin's mind, a thought that was gnawing at him with a frightening persistence: Why had the grey squirrel thought *he* had magic? He, Tiallin, of all squirrels? Had he perceived it as a threat and decided to kill Tiallin for it? He thought of the grey's face close to his, that horrible deep-throated laugh, and the words

I've heard if you PUSH hard enough, you can't keep your powers back.

It confused him. It was as if the gray had *wanted* him to harm him, to show some sort of magical defense. But to what purpose? He refused to pass it off to madness or a suicidal streak in the gray—he had seemed far too solid, too sure of what he wanted for that.

But what *did* he want?

Tired, sore and bemused by everything, Tiallin staggered upwards from his bed and out into the hallway, still half-expecting to see one of the shadows nearby leap into life and grab him.

Get a grip. Just…get a grip.

He needed someone to talk to, someone who he could confide his fears to, someone he could trust to keep silent as the grave. Someone introspective, someone who might come at things from a totally different angle, perhaps giving him insight he would never have stumbled upon if left to his own devices.

Someone like Zerrith.

Tiallin did not know why he hadn't thought of it until now. His brother had shared *his* biggest secret with him, after all. Didn't Tiallin owe him something?

Mind made up, Tiallin started for his brother's room at the end of the hall, already feeling better at the prospect of letting something out, something he had thought he would have to hold in, along with the jumble of other secrets he felt he was always carrying. Tiallin hated secrets.

Reaching Zerrith's door, he knocked and went back a step, waiting. A cautious hush answered the rapping, and he called out, "It's just me, Tiallin."

The hush persisted, and Tiallin began to think that perhaps Zerrith was not in at all when the door knob turned and his brother opened the door a crack, letting a sliver of light fall through onto Tiallin. He must have lit firefly lamps to work by—if work was what he was doing. Tiallin opened his mouth to ask, or to apologize for disturbing his brother, just as Zerrith pulled the door back the rest of the way and Tiallin saw that he was not alone.

"Hi, Tiallin," Lyrah said quietly, nervously.

Tiallin merely stood there in shock, staring at the far end of the room right next to Lyrah, where the Byrd stood in all its glory, the sheet under which Zerrith had been so careful to hide it crumpled below on the ground.

Tiallin looked from Lyrah to the Byrd, to his brother, the latter two of which were the only unperturbed bodies in the vicinity.

"*She*...knows?"

Zerrith made a sort of sighing sound.

"Tiallin, why don't you come on in."

CHAPTER XIV

"Tiallin, calm down. She's known for years."

That's supposed to make me feel better?

A small part of Tiallin argued reasonably that there was nothing to be upset about. But a much louder part screamed that it was unfair, that he had been slighted somehow. He had thought that only he and Zerrith had known of the Byrd, that they were alone on this secret.

"How many others know?" he said at last.

Zerrith shook his head. "No one. Lyrah—

"We've been friends for a long time," Lyrah broke in. She looked from Zerrith to Tiallin as if expecting one or the other to contradict her. "Ever since we were very young…I met you once before, Tiallin. You probably don't remember."

"You're right, I don't," Tiallin said flatly. The revelation was somewhat astounding; he had always thought of Lyrah as simply a squirrel maid—albeit a very pretty one—who seemed to have taken an annoying liking to his brother, someone who admired him from afar, perhaps.

"You were very young as well," Lyrah shrugged.

"How come I haven't seen you about in the past few years, then?" Tiallin challenged.

"Well…" Lyrah gave a sideways glance to Zerrith, who nodded. "Your father doesn't seem to like me very much. He grew suspicious of me for reasons undisclosed so Zerrith and I started hanging around outside instead. We both enjoy nature anyway. I should—I should probably go now. I'm sorry if I startled you, Tiallin."

She paved her way to the door and no one made any effort to stop her. Zerrith was leaning back slightly in an aura of calm and Tiallin still trying to cope with the fact of her presence. He should not, he supposed in retrospect, have been so shocked; hadn't he seen them together in this house just days ago, talking in the hall? He had been too distracted that day to ask her about it, to even stop to breathe as he had run upon hearing that the King was not well. Hadn't Lyrah been asking after Zerrith for some time?

"Tiallin."

Tiallin turned to his brother.

"...Yeah?"

"I did tell you we were friends, remember? The day on the branch when you were angry at me."

Cripes. *When* you *were angry at me. Way to make it sound like that argument was my fault,* Tiallin thought bitterly.

"Yeah, I guess you did say something about it," he conceded.

"Well then. That's settled. What did you come here to tell me anyway?"

His voice was oddly dispassionate, and Tiallin suddenly understood that his brother did not want him in the room. He was used to subtle dismissal from Zerrith, and as many times as he tried to tell himself it was only Zerrith's solitary nature that caused him to speak so, he still managed to feel a bit hurt each time.

"Never mind that," Tiallin said. "It's not that important." He turned to go, then turned back unable to bear it, needing to have an answer not to the question he had come with, but to something else entirely.

"Why did you tell her and not me?"

Zerrith did not speak.

"Why, Zerrith? We were close, too...once," He trailed off; it felt as though the lump in his throat had moved upward to sit uncomfortably on his tongue.

Zerrith shrugged.

"She got it out of me eventually. It grew hard to explain to her why I was inside so often instead of coming out to spend time together. One day she sort of cornered me." He laughed. "I got upset. I really hadn't wanted to tell *anyone*, you know," His eyes grew wistful, but he shrugged again as if to contradict this.

"She has given me lots to work with, I have to say. Lots of things I did not have access to before."

He walked over to the Byrd behind the curtain of wilted flowers and reached a paw up to touch one of its eyes. The glassy metal orb stared out at them, and Tiallin remembered suddenly his conviction that the orbs from which the eyes had been made had been stolen…stolen from the King himself. And who had access to the King's chambers on an everyday basis?

The realization came to him then that it was not Zerrith at all who had been stealing from King Sirius.

It was Lyrah.

The next couple of days were especially interesting for Tiallin. He tried as well as he could manage not to think of the incident with the large thug of a gray squirrel, pushing it to the back of his mind. He did not know when he had decided not to tell Zerrith—perhaps it was that by not speaking of it, he felt he could make it disappear, become less than fact.

Zerrith still let him come to work on the Byrd, and Tiallin grasped at the opportunity not only because it satisfied some deep inner part of him but because it was also a way to forget everything else but the impossibility of what was taking shape before him. His brother's fantasy creature was almost twice the size of him, causing Zerrith to strain at times to reach the top of the thing's head in order to fasten some dandelion fluff down, his slender body twisting, muscles tightened. The world held its breath in those moments.

Lyrah would come to watch, as Zerrith added a touch of this, or explained the appeal of that, and Tiallin saw it immediately, the truth her eyes held as she gazed on the magnificent scene each day. It was not the creation she was seeing at all, but the creator. Occasionally she would offer an opinion on an idea that Zerrith had pondered aloud, or laugh the slightly-too-loud, warm laugh that Tiallin had not forgotten from that day when, new to the King's court, she had laughed at *him*.

He saw it in the little things too, the way she would smile indulgently when Zerrith talked of his plans for the next step in his work or the way her eyes would sort of space out and grow almost sad when Zerrith looked away from her, the shadows drawing his face into angles as his mind floated to other things.

This new knowledge Tiallin harbored was uncommonly awkward, perhaps because he realized that Zerrith did not return Lyrah's feelings. It was hard to say whether he was aware of them to begin with. Zerrith's feelings were too busy being used up on this thing he had devoted years to, this thing that sat before them, for all its grandeur without a heart or breath to speak of. Tiallin watched the quiet interplay of words unsaid between his companions, and felt an intruder on the things he had never before been able to perceive. If this was what growing up was like, he did not want any of it. It made him feel small, fragile somehow, all bones and no fur to cover them.

Zerrith explained the hardened mouth, or the beak, of the Byrd to them one day, letting them both run their paws over its polished surface. Tiallin's paw rammed into

Lyrah's, clumsy and by accident, and he pulled back with a muttered curse. She didn't appear to notice.

"Why did you pick such..." Lyrah felt under the beak tentatively, where it curved into a wicked point, searching for a word. "...Such *carnivorous* features?"

"You think it's carnivorous?" Zerrith said it as though the idea were a novelty. "I always thought of it as a very misunderstood animal, gentle despite how fierce it can look. I think it would use the beak only for eating beetles and earthworms, things like that. It could also be a wonderful tool for crafting a home like the one in this tree. Or," his eyes lit up, "It could peck its beak against things like wood to make messages, as in a code."

"Hmm," Tiallin volunteered. "I never thought of that."

Lyrah merely looked quietly contemplative.

The Byrd, as odd an animal as it sounded to Tiallin, was filling out nicely. It appeared to be gaining more a downy substance all over its body that was not quite fur. Zerrith made the down from dandelion fluff, stored from two cumulative summers ago which indicated some lengthy planning on his part. But the biggest surprise was yet to come.

When Zerrith told them the most exciting of his plans for the Byrd, Tiallin was speechless. It was to have wings.

There would be two of them, Zerrith said, poring over a piece of paper littered with his own sketches and equations. They would be placed at either side of the round body of the Byrd, and they would be made from the willow poles, down and leaves.

"And I've got plenty of leaves," Zerrith had assured them, bending to reach under his bed in its corner of the room and pulling out a pawful to prove his point. He seemed to have been careful to get every single color of leaf under the sun, and Tiallin asked, "Isn't it going to be white? The Byrd, I mean? The dandelion fluff is white."

"Maybe the body," Zerrith said airily. "But that's just the body. The wings are going to be beautiful. They are going to have color."

The place between Lyrah's eyebrows creased at these words. She had been silent since asking about the beak, her normally open demeanor closed and thoughtful, even troubled. Not that Tiallin minded the break from her chatter. Not at all. But curiosity got to him as always, and as always, won out. He caught her halfway down the hallway as they both left Zerrith's room that day.

"What was on your mind today? You seemed quiet."

Lyrah focused on the ground, cleared her throat, seemed to think better of it and looked again at the floor.

"C'mon, tell me," Tiallin groaned.

She looked at him, then said simply, very quietly, "It's wrong. That's all. It's wrong, what he's doing. Can't you feel it? It's wrong, and I'm...I'm afraid."

Tiallin snorted.

"I meant for real, Lyrah. What is it?"

She turned and left him standing there, feeling mean but not sorry.

CHAPTER XV

It was amazing how much a body could weather with enough incentive. Edelle for one, would never doubt the distance she could go, the nights she could keep watch on the thick night with hunger roiling deep in her gut. She would never doubt it ever again.

She and Lute had made good progress. It certainly seemed that they had walked forever, and every time Lute pulled out his map (which was quite often due to the tension between them rather than an actual need to check their bearings), he would mutter something about not being very far now. Edelle, for her part, was still behaving coolly toward her companion, unwilling to forget his eagerness to take what was not his own. As they traveled, she had come up with at least five other quirks of his that really rubbed her the wrong way—the way he talked, for one. He held the air of one who was raised in aristocracy but did not belong there, his words all right and formal until he would slip up and spit out a string of slang or a nasty phrase that she might expect from a chickaree. He mumbled a lot, too, mumbled and shrugged. And he stole. In short, he was aggravating to the extreme, and if Edelle had seen any other option, she told herself she would have left him to strike out on her own.

Lute kept stealing glances at her when he thought she wasn't looking, eyebrows raised, always looking on the edge of saying something smart to really annoy her, but in the end he never did.

Probably he lacks the guts for that, Edelle thought scathingly. Her stomach had been woefully empty for far too long; she had followed through on her promise not to eat any of the stolen food, and now she was regretting it sorely, though not enough to admit so to Lute. She took satisfaction from seeing that he was vaguely uncomfortable with being the only one to sit down to meals.

And speaking of sitting down, it was about time that they took a breather, had something to drink—the patch of trees ahead looked tantalizing—a whole day of walking on flat ground had made her half-crazed. Lute quickened his pace a yard to the left of her, and she could tell he was thinking the same. The trees grew closer and closer and Edelle thought of lying in their branches, only for a bit; she could not afford to waste time, but it would be a blessed relief…

The arrow that whistled over her head seemed to come out of nowhere at all; stumbling backward, she heard herself give a little scream. She could hear voices now, more excited than angry.

"Eh, what've we got in our territory?"

"This is our territory, yer in fer it, yew are!"

We're being attacked, we're being attacked, Edelle's mind reeled off. She regained control of herself quickly and jumped to her feet, bristling in preparation for combat. Facing her were about eight chickarees, half of whom were armed and all of whom looked delighted at the appearance of the two larger squirrels. Edelle looked sideways at Lute. He seemed more annoyed than frightened, and his paws had tightened on the straps of his pack.

The chickarees were anything but silent. They were turning to one another and chatting up a storm, while the two eldest in their band, a male and a female, stared stonily at the pair of travelers, daring them to try and escape.

"What, are we going to kill 'em?"

"Let's do it then, I want to see!"

"Shuddup, you two don't know anything! That big 'un there is called a false squirrel, they'll eat yew real quick!"

"If yew don't stop blabbering ,*I'll* eat *yew.*"

A squealing match broke out between two of them, one poking the other with his bow and the other going all out with tooth and claw. A couple more of the little red squirrels gathered round and ending up joining the fray, which quickly escalated into a brawl.

"Stop, stop! Shuddup, *all* of yew!" the female leader shouted shrilly. When no one responded, she apparently decided that she could not resist the fighting and threw herself into the mass of squirming, kicking bodies.

The male leader stayed in place, though he looked as if it was costing him. He pointed his bow at Lute and said, "Where are yew headed?"

Edelle spoke up. "We're headed to the white squirrels, and if you so much as touch us we will tell them and they won't be too happy about it, I can tell you that much. And I'm not a *false* squirrel, I'm a *fox* squirrel," she added, glancing disparagingly over at the pile of fighting squirrels, though she doubted the offender was really listening.

It seemed like the best bet to make out like they were friends with the white squirrels, but when she looked over at Lute he was determinedly looking skywards as if willing himself not to roll his eyes. Edelle's annoyance with her companion mounted.

The male leader stared hard at her.

"Why are the white squirrelies going to care about *yew*?"

"Look, what do yew want already?" Lute said. "We've got a long way to go and we know this isn't yer territory."

The little chickaree glared up at him and tightened the string on his bow.

"Yeah?"

"Yeah. Should I just tell yew what's in the pack and we get on with it?"

In back of the male leader, the squabble was starting to break up. Edelle was shocked and disgusted to see some streaks of red across the snow. *They made each other bleed.*

Barbarians. She hoped Lute knew what he was doing. She wanted to get out of this alive.

The male chickaree eyed Lute for a moment. "Fine, gimme the thing." He held out a paw.

Instead of handing over his bag, Lute upturned it and let the contents fall to the ground, going over them lazily with a hindpaw, listing them off.

"Bedroll, food, map, food. Fascinating, right?"

The leader frowned. An impish young squirrel cried, "He's got nothing like the last one did!"

"Yew robbed someone earlier, then?"

"We didn't *rob*, we asked fer payment to pass our territory—"

"Yeah, and then we told him the wrong way to where he was going, stupid likkle thing he was, wasn't he, Brando?"

"Shuddup," Brando quelled the upstart squirrel, who snuck him a dirty look when he turned his back once more. "Yeah, we showed him, though. Couldn't have been more than two seasons."

Two seasons? Edelle was horrified.

"Oh, that's nice, you pick on people smaller than you," she snapped, unable to avoid opening her mouth. The chickaree called Brando gave her an amused look.

"Yeah, and there en't many of 'em, so yer going to have to excuse me, yew overstuffed lump." Someone behind him tittered.

Lute had turned back to his bag and was refilling it slowly.

"Well, we know where we're going so yew might as well let us on our way. And we know who those trees belong to, we're not stupid enough to go through that way."

This was news to Edelle, who felt sure they had been headed for the trees. She looked at Lute, but he was still avoiding her eyes, his attention fixed solely on the male leader.

"Dextis doesn't like outcasts lingering, does he?" Lute said maliciously, and Brando flinched back perceptibly, scowling. "Yer stealing from his selection, taking the possessions of those who come this way. Do yew honestly think he's not going to figure it out eventually? I could tell him now, I could give a call, a cry; I'm sure we'd both be heard if we both screamed this close to his wood. Even if yew silenced us it would be too late…he would see how yew robbed us, and then he'd have—

"Okay, I get it," snapped Brando, but all of his former bravado was gone as quickly as the winds of spring, replaced with a deep unease.

"If…we go…"

"Go?!" yelped another in the background. He turned around and nipped at the upstart squirrel, sending everyone into a fresh quarrel.

"Yew'd better go then." Lute raised his eyebrows. "We haven't got time to waste."

Brando jerked his head over his shoulder at his followers, and clutching his bow in his teeth, bounded away without looking to see if they were coming after. They did, rushed and messy, looking over their shoulders at the small wood behind them and at Lute. One of them dared to make a rude gesture, then sped so fast to the forefront of the retreating group that he might have been pursued by demons.

Lute made a point of watching them until they vanished on the horizon, then scooped his pack up from the ground and slung it over his shoulder once more.

Edelle burst forth into speech at once.

"Who's Dextis?"

"We should probably get moving, there's a good chance they'll be back." He saw the look she was giving him and sighed. "I'm getting there, d'yew mind? Dextis is the leader of the red squirrels in this particular neck of woods. He is very...large for a chickaree, so he sort of imposes his will on the others even though normally they've got no natural leaders. Basically. Are these the only times yer going to talk to me, when yew want to know something?"

"Probably. How do you come about knowing so much about the chickarees in the area?"

He did not miss her tone. Lute gave one look to the annoying persistent fox squirrel, took a breath for luck, and barreled on gamely.

"Right, so let's get this over with, I'm sick of questions. I grew up in this area. I was raised by chickarees. I was also a thief. The only reason I'm not right now is because I slipped up and got caught, and my captors would not let me go. Yew jolly with that?"

Edelle could only stand in the snow, gaping. It took her a while to notice that she had stopped in her tracks; Lute kept right on walking and she had to rush to catch back up to him.

"I can't believe you," she said after some time.

Lute shut his eyes. Could he not get a break from this?

"Really, I can't believe you. It's against Astrippa to steal, surely you must have *some* inkling of the seriousness..."

"A bit self-righteous, are we? Maybe I just don't care, try that one. Maybe I wish I still *were* a thief, even. Try that on for size."

He quickened his pace, pulling ahead of her.

Edelle's eyes were wide. "Take that back! You take that one back! You—you could burn for that one! You *will* burn for that one!"

"That's nice," he called back. "I'll deal with that bridge when I come to it!"

Edelle made no attempt to match his pace, and Lute forced a smile onto his face.

Cripes. Good riddance.

Trying to figure out why he wasn't a whole lot happier with all of that off his chest and Edelle out of his fur, he focused all of his powers of concentration on the land ahead of them.

He noticed it almost immediately, a small, jagged shape against the skyline, hobbling away from them, only to stop a second later and turn in another direction. Once he had gotten closer and watched the figure travel back and forth in this fashion several more times, he had figured out the truth; it was the little squirrel, the other whom Brando and his gang had robbed. Lute was wondering vaguely why a squirrel so young would have anything of value, when he noticed that the small shape in the distance had stopped under a lone tree, apparently confused. The tree's branches were crooked and bare against the sky, a stark contrast to the fiery brush that still clung to many of its brothers. Dead. The snow that had collected on the tree was solid, frozen, weighing heavily on one of its rotted old branches, a branch that was even now bending, bending slowly and inexorably toward the earth. Straight for the spot where the child stood.

There was a shout from behind Lute, and it was only when Edelle came rushing past him that he realized he had stopped, momentarily dumb as he watched nature's cruel joke approach its unsuspecting victim.

"Stop! Stop! Move out of the way!" Edelle called frantically, waving as she ran. The small squirrel regarded her with a mixture of fear and alarm, perhaps taking her for another thief come to have a go at him. He looked very young indeed, and Lute wondered what he was doing out without someone to attend him. Likely his home was nearby and he had gotten lost.

"The branch! Above you! It's going to fall!"

The little squirrel looked up and appeared to see the danger, but still he did not move, frozen to the spot in fear or fascination at the hardened snow and wood getting closer and closer to him...an ominous creaking reached Lute's ears where he stood frozen a ways away.

She was not going to make it. Lute could see it clearly. Cursing under his breath, he started after her, the cold air slicing into his fur and to his skin as he ran.

Cripes, what am I doing?!

Yew know what yer doing. Shut up and run like yew've just been caught on a job, Lute boy.

He took his own advice, and ran as he wished he could have run that night, the night when he had stumbled through a foreign window to the raucous calls of squirrels he didn't know, unable to get up in time, the fear thudding in his heart. He reached Edelle just as she reached in turn for the child. Pushing the child from her, she shouted at him, "Go!" Shaken out of his reverie by the contact of her paw, he needed no second telling. He was just in time; the branch fell at precisely the same moment, the loud cracking sound one with Edelle's short scream and for Lute, the impact as he moved to shield her, sticking out his paws at once to keep the weight from crushing him.

It was the snow, frozen and heavy, that hit first, perhaps saving them from the later impact of the branch, which by some other lucky instance did not hit them full on. Still, the force of it caused Lute to jolt forward, onto Edelle where she lay below him. Black threatened at the fringes of his vision.

Food's probably squished, cripes.

His head collided with something cold and he was out.

CHAPTER XVI

Felix lay on his stomach, stretched to his capacity across the thatched reed floor. It scratched at him, but he did not make the effort to switch position. He was feeling odd again, the kind of empty strangeness that he had felt sometimes before. It was not a bad type of feeling, this; he preferred it to how it felt when his Father was around, that blank, tilting, rapacious feeling, the one that felt like he had drunk too many Dew Frosts and their presence was giving him unnatural energy. It was the only way he could think to describe *that* feeling, and even though it did not do it justice, that hardly mattered. He only ever thought about it when he was not feeling it, which was not often anymore. And without it, he just waited for more, lay and waited for it to come back. It was a vicious cycle, really, a cycle that only watching her, watching Edelle, could break, but Edelle had left, left him disdainfully, and he was truly alone.

Alone except for Father. Always Father.

Although that was not quite right, Felix thought. There had to have been a time without Father, for now that he thought of it, he was sure he could recall—

But it was too much effort to think now. He had given up listening through the floor to the voices from the downstairs room, where Father had let in the squirrels, the gray ones with the nervous eyes.

"We're looking for a squirrel," the first one had said. "We got word he came this way. He's a killer, he's dangerous. And he was carrying this."

The knife the gray pulled out had made Felix's stomach lurch in a way he had not understood—until now. Father had sent him upstairs, and suddenly the knife seemed very important to him, it was the one Father had given him, the one with which he had—but what had he done with it? He had given it to Edelle in the end, he could remember that. She had seemed happy at the time, but later she had yelled at him for it. And then he had seen it again, later, with that dark squirrel, the skinny one with the smoky fur.

A killer...

But thinking on it tired him. There had been a time when thoughts hadn't been so tiring. Being outside helped, but now he knew he must wait. For the squirrels to go. For an explanation. For *something*. For Father. Father would help him to understand. He always did.

After an eternity of listening to silence grow below, Felix heard him come to the door, standing there for an instant before speaking.

"Get up, Felix. It is rude to lie about on the floor. Besides, I must tell you something, my dear son."

Felix felt the words slide over him like a film, and energy surged anew within him. He tapped into its stream eagerly, wanting knowledge now more than ever. He could not wait any longer.

"Felix, I have a bit of bad news."

"All right," Felix agreed hurriedly, staring hungrily into his Father's lined face. "Go ahead. I mean, this colony's been all about bad news since we got here, so it can't be anything that much worse than what we've got on our plates now, right?"

"You are very practical. But I am afraid that *you* may find it worse."

Something inside Felix plummeted, and he felt his face grow tight. Something was wrong, and his chest crowded with fear. "Father? What is it?"

"The squirrel you always watch," he said. "Edelle, you have said her name in your sleep—I do not think your obsession wise, but perhaps that is not my place—she is gone."

"I know. She left and I don't know what else I could have—

He stopped himself, feeling that this was personal somehow, a secret to keep even from Father.

"No, you misunderstand me, my boy. When I say she is gone, I mean that Edelle is dead. She has been killed. This..." he pulled the knife that the old gray squirrel had been holding from his lap, "was found beside her. They believe that she was killed by the one they were searching for..."

The words became a muffled hum, a song in the background as Felix gazed blankly at the knife, past the knife, past his Father even. But while all sound was on mute, he *felt* acutely, and what he felt was a rupturing somewhere deep inside.

"...Why?"

Father had not finished speaking, and Felix expected to be reprimanded for butting in. Instead, the older squirrel moved close to him, taking him by the shoulder in a grip that was firm, full of untold power.

"The white squirrels. They believe he was a messenger for the white squirrels."

Felix's knuckles clenched, the fur on his neck prickled.

The white squirrels. Of course. She was going to them. She was trying to save her family.

Edelle...

You don't know me at all, you don't owe me anything...but I feel I owe you everything. Everything, Edelle. And I'll never get to give it to you.

Before Felix could even register his own movements, he had jerked out from under his father's heavy paw.

"Come back here, Felix."

But he did not come back. He stalked to the end of the room because Father was blocking the doorway and stared out the window, across at the home where *she* had lived. He knew his father could not come quickly, could not cross this space in so little time; that was good.

Because you're a cripple, in your chair, and if I stare hard enough out this window I can disappear into all the things I've been missing and you'll never find me. Because you're a cripple, you can't follow.

But his thoughts were merely madness given shape as usual, and he turned back to Father in his chair, sitting straight backed, eyes unfathomable.

"I know I didn't believe about the curse of the white squirrels before," Felix said suddenly, meeting those patient eyes. "But now...now I believe. Something has to be done. Something *will* be done."

"It makes you angry then?"

"Angry?" Felix stared hard at Father, and felt for an instant as though he were seeing him for the first time. "I think I have always been angry."

He took the knife up from the arm of Father's chair, knowing he would never part with it again. Then, taking one last cursory look around, he left out the window. Running out to the end of the long branch outside, he turned back once and saw that Father had wheeled himself closer to the window. He was smiling.

"One last hug, Felix? You would not deny me that."

Felix stalled, then turned back and leaned in the window again at an awkward angle.

As they embraced, a cold fire ignited somewhere within, almost knocking the breath out of Felix and causing him to fall from the tree. The sounds of the wind and leaves were hushed and his head pounded.

For only an instant.

Felix stumbled back, looking at Father again, unsure, before his sense of purpose and direction returned to him.

"What was that?"

"What?"

The day could not have been more ordinary.

"Never mind. Right, I am going to call a meeting."

The Meeting Tree was crowded as it always became at such times, and confused as the squirrels of the fox squirrel colony pushed inside out of the cold, all staring at the young stranger up front. Felix felt as if he could read their minds, and he knew they were all thinking the same thing: what right did one such as him have to call a meeting? It was the presence of Thoelen alone, sitting some ways behind Felix, that kept them from getting out of hand or firing questions at him. If their leader was condoning it, there must be a good reason for it.

Felix stood up front, sharpening his knife with a rock he had found. Even before everyone had settled in, he began to speak, voice raw and breaking. He wondered why only moments before talking in front of the masses had not seemed so intimidating, and only then he understood that he would be saying what he had learned aloud for the first time, confirming it…making it real.

"I am Felix Gurtwater. You do not know me. That does not matter. I am not important. What is important is that…that…you may not have heard, but Edelle Craswotch is dead."

There was a hushed silence, exactly the effect he had expected. A cry came up from somewhere in his audience, a high keening sound, and there was a stir as two elderly squirrels, heads bowed, attempted to keep the young one between them from making a scene. They lacked enthusiasm in their efforts, and the child continued to cry, a wailing that persisted through Felix's next words.

"She was murdered by a messenger for the white squirrels. We were told by some grays earlier today. Most of those on the border of Pinewood are grays from Firwood, and seeing what the white squirrels have already done to us, I think there can be little doubt as to the truth of this. More so, my heart is…is…We cannot let this go. We cannot sit, and wither and die and let our young be kidnapped or killed by those who possess a hatred for us we do not understand. The time has come to take action. Do not take action for me, but take it for Edelle. She…she was gentle." His voice broke, but he caught himself, and his next words were strong, raw with a suppressed emotion that carried to all. He could see it in their faces.

"We must kill the white squirrels."

There was a silence of perhaps ten long seconds, stretching into infinity. Then the crowd began to cheer, starting up raggedly and growing strong as everyone joined in, clicking their teeth, flicking their tails, stomping feet or clapping paws. Only Thoelen in the back row behind Felix remained calm, a faint crease lining his forehead.

Felix looked around at the congregation, blinking, no longer minding the water in his eyes. He had called them here, he had made this. They might not approve of him, the mainly unobtrusive, quiet neighbor they had never got to know, they might never think of him as a proper member of their community, but they all shared a common pain, a common loss. He had made them realize it.

Well, he amended, *maybe it is not me at all. It is Edelle. It is Edelle they love after all.*

As do I.

"Come with me when I march to Pinewood, then! We've all heard history before, about the failed attempts to ask for help, to appeal to the cold white ones. But now there is a difference. There are more of us, and we are no longer only appealing! We will force ourselves upon them, and we will *show* them how much we object to their curses! Many of you who are older have lost those you loved in the last famine that swept this area. If we let this go on, everyone here could end up losing someone they care about to the white squirrels. So I ask you, come with me to Pinewood! If their powers are too great or they are too many and we are struck down even in such great numbers, we will at least have tried! The alternative may be death anyway, and a messy death fighting for what is honorable is better than a slow death living in fear and pain."

An even louder cheering and chattering greeted these next words, and Felix felt himself become one of them without their knowing. He felt at once more heartbroken and better than he had ever felt before, and wondered if he were the worse for it, if such a twisted thing were even possible. But the faces stared up at him, and he heard himself go on, voice stronger and more confident than when he had begun.

"Those who would go with me, go back to your homes and prepare. Bring anything you think might be useful, as well as anything we have left for food, however scant the rations are. We will share on the way, and pray to Astrippa we don't die before we get there, before we can at least leave a mark on the memories of those we seek. Go, now!"

They needed no further encouragement. The crowd poured out of the exits with such ferocity that being mowed down in their wake proved a valid concern. Felix scanned them, spotting the figures he was looking for, standing in a small huddled group against the wall, protecting the smallest one of them from being lost in the worst of the rush. They saw him before he was halfway to them, and the old male's eyes met his, seeking.

"Don't go," Felix blurted, when the sound of the receding crowd had died down. He made his way to stand in front of what was left of Edelle's family, feeling impossibly awkward. He knew they wanted to ask him questions, to demand details as he would have done in their place—but he realized that Edelle did not live with her parents, but her grandparents, and perhaps there was something in being older that made one cease to ask so much of life's mysterious turns, for the grandmother thankfully only addressed his remark and nothing else. The small child, watching them with wide, red eyes, was too shy to speak.

"You would not have us go to defend our granddaughter's death?" The old female asked.

"No, I wouldn't. But before you assume anything of me because of it, understand that it's because Edelle would not have liked to know you left. There really is a very high chance of us not coming back alive, and she wouldn't want that. I have no doubt of the fiber of your character, how much experience you have had of this life, and if it were just the two of you I would not feel I have the authority to tell you anything of the sort."

He gave a meaningful nod to their small grandson, still unable to completely meet their eyes.

"I believe she cared a lot for this one. Please, stay here. Once the others collect the rest of our food, I will give some to you. Wait for us as long as you can, and then…" he looked down at his knife. "…You know." Felix looked the grandfather in the eyes for the first time.

"We really do mean to come back. I promise you."

The grandmother nodded at long last, and taking the child by the shoulders, she steered him out the door.

"Good luck," the grandfather said gruffly, and Felix could see that it took all his effort to turn and follow his wife and grandson away.

He stared after them for a moment before a touch on his back informed him that he was not alone in the Meeting Tree even now. Turning around, he found Thoelen standing there, a sad smile on his face.

"I know what you think you are doing is honorable," he said slowly. "But sometimes people have the wrong conception of honor. I…I cannot tell you that I don't believe in the base of what you said. Sadly, that is all that makes sense to me. But I know that my people are now taken with you, that they will go where you lead. You've spoken to them in a way that gives them an answer. It makes them feel less lost, and I could not ask for more at this point. I would not ask you to stop what you are doing, but I would ask you to wait a while. To reconsider. It is not an order, it is just…advice. What you just said to that family seemed very genuine, and I have no doubts that you are…troubled by the death of Edelle. I am sorry I never got to know you while you lived here."

Felix stared back at the true leader of the colony and felt a great respect for him. There weren't many who would step aside for the happiness of their kind like this. But he knew at once that he would not do as Thoelen asked.

"No. I'm sorry, but I cannot reconsider. If I am mistaken in my judgment of honor, well…that remains to be seen. But I have lived a half-life here; you did not want to know me. Just today, I not only excited them, but I became just a little more alive myself in some way. I have to get away. I hope you decide to come with us, but if you don't...Edelle's family could always use support. I'm sorry."

He turned and left the Meeting Tree, left the squirrel not much older than himself in the middle of a hall where he had presided only a few times himself. He did not look back. In truth, he was afraid to.

CHAPTER XVII

Edelle came awake to muffled darkness, imposing on her from all angles, and for a moment she could not make sense of anything. Why was she lying down, her fur wet with snow? It felt as if she had only just come out of a deep, grossly enchanted sleep. She could not see the sky.

It was this last thought that jolted Edelle to her senses. Why could she not see the sky? Where was she anyway-- some cool tomb of ice? Had she died?

...And if I had, and this was all...?

Panic, crowding her throat like bile. She pushed it down. It would not win, she had promised herself that it would not ever again. If this were a dream, she wished fervently that she would wake.

Stretching a paw tentatively forward to test the air in front of her, Edelle felt something else, something gratefully different than the cold, hard caress of her entrapment's walls. Something warm against the chill.

"Lute?"

The sound of her own voice surprised her, but her relief blotted out all else. She was not dead after all, she remembered it now! The lost young squirrel, her efforts to save him from the cruel joke of the reds, the falling snow...had the young one managed to get away?

Yes, yes he had. Because—

"Lute?"

Still no response. Had the dratted gray gone to sleep on her? Fighting her fears, she reached over once more, this time peering down into his face. Hesitating a moment, she brought a paw up to his mouth and held it there, refusing to acknowledge the thought that crept into her mind unbidden. The breath that whispered past her fingers was faint, but there was no doubt of its existence. Lute was alive, but out cold.

Edelle leaned back against the hard packed snow behind her and tried to consider herself lucky. She knew she should…it was a considerable amount of snow that had fallen, and if it had fallen in any other way it might not have caught against the tree in this manner, preserving their lives in this pocket of air. But how to get out was the question. If she tried to dig her way out—and she was sure she could with some effort—she might end up causing some of the snow to cave in on Lute's prone form.

"Ehh…"

The groan startled her, and she stared over at the motionless lump beside her. It looked as if Lute was waking—he must have received a blow to the head, that was all. Surprised to find herself feeling guilty, she had to remind herself that it was his fault for interfering, not her own. He could have just as easily remained aloof and let her deal with saving the little squirrel. Yes, it was all the ruffian's fault…

"Wuzzhappenin?" The barely coherent grumbling took her off guard. She looked over to Lute once more and saw that he had his head up and was gazing confusedly about. Their eyes met, and there was an awkward moment of complete stillness.

"You…we got caught in a snowfall. You must've been hit full on."

Lute scratched his head. Then, much quicker than Edelle had, he caught on.

"Oh, that. Yeah. The young guy, is he…?"

"I think so."

Hadn't expected you'd care.

They fell back into silence. Lute took the time to straighten up and to gain a better position on the frozen ground. Last year's acorns, he ached! Staring up at the small bit of light filtering through the top of their snowy prison, he wondered where his pack had got to. If Brando came back this way, there'd be no doubt he'd take it…

"I guess we'd better—"

"Sorry."

The admission was so quick and without warning that he simply stared at Edelle.

"What?"

"Just…sorry. I've been—well, you *did* steal, I'm not condoning that…but you've helped too. I just feel like maybe I've been a bit—I don't want to say unfair…but I feel…you've told me things about yourself, and I've been maybe a bit too harsh but I'm under a lot of pressure and I didn't feel like I should tell you but maybe now I should, you're clearly not as bad as you seem—"

"Cripes, slow down! Sorry," he added at her look of recrimination for his language. "Just go a bit slower. I'll still be here and everything…not like I've got much choice."

"This is serious, Lute. All right, I've been unfair to you. You've offered to share with me, and you've got the map and you've told me more or less what you're after. I haven't told you anything." Lute opened his mouth, but she waved a paw impatiently. "I was only fabricating when I told you I was merely interested in the white squirrels. You'd have to be crazy to risk yourself going to them in weather like this. The truth is, I need to ask them a favor as well."

Lute sat watching her, expression unfathomable. Edelle took a deep breath and plowed onward.

"My family is in great danger. My whole colony is, actually. We've been struck by famine and no one knows what to do about it."

"So what're yew going to the white squirrels for, then? Do yew think they've got the solution?"

"I think they're the ones who caused the problem in the first place. Have you heard of the curse of the white squirrels?"

"No. What's that, a fable?"

"No," Edelle snapped. "It's—well, I suppose I can't expect you to know, you're a gray or— she gave him half a glance, "something like it anyway. But everyone in our colony knows, especially the elders. Basically, a famine exactly like this one has happened before."

Lute's eyes grew wide.

"Really? In this weather? How'd yew get by?"

"I wasn't alive to see it. But the leader at that time used to know the white squirrels. He believed it was his fault that the famine had been magically cast upon the colony, and he took a few others and went up to talk to the white squirrels, to try to get them to remove the curse. He never came back, but the curse was eventually lifted. No one knows exactly what happened, but they think he was killed by the king."

Lute was watching her steadily, his breath making little puffs of chalky white in the air in front of him.

"So yer..." he said slowly, thinking it out. "Yer going up there because yew think yew can fix it like..."

"Cumin. His name was Cumin. And yes, that's what I'm trying to do. I don't know the reason for it this time. Perhaps the white squirrels don't feel like they need a reason. In any case, I'm going to find out. There's a chance Cumin solved the problem by sacrificing himself...that's the common belief, anyhow. He's sort of a historical hero among us."

"But...but yer...?"

"If they'll take me," Edelle said shortly.

"For…for yer colony?" Lute finally managed to ask.

"Mostly for my family…for the colony too, but. You know."

"No," Lute said. "I don't." He could not explain why in that moment he felt more lost than he ever had. "But, er…I don't think yew have anything to feel sorry about."

Edelle gave him an incredulous look. "What, just because I'm being honorable in some small way, I should be absolved from blame in all things? I don't think so, so don't you do it to me. You have *no idea* how selfish I really am."

Lute knew there was probably something he should say but he found himself afraid to speak into the ensuing quiet. Instead, he shifted his gaze to the walls of snow around them.

"We should probably, er…"

"Yes, I think it's about time." Edelle gave him a small smile, which he found much welcome after the couple days of sullen glares of condemnation and stony silence. The undertone of disapproval had not quite left her voice, however, when she addressed him next.

"You're a thief. Is there any way you can think to exploit that hole up top so we can get free?"

Lute raised his eyes to the crevice in the snow above. The yellow sliver of light caught his eye at an exact angle and he looked away, rubbing it vigorously. Edelle waited.

"Well," Lute said, still wiping at his watering eye. "It's pretty easy. With yew here, that is."

"Meaning?"

"If yew don't mind, yew could hold me on yer shoulders and I could widen the hole, climb out and then help yew. That is, if yew think…"

"Of course I can manage picking you up," Edelle scoffed. "I'm only questioning the part where you pull me out. You're a scrawny thing."

Lute felt his face get hot.

"That—I could, I bet! And anyway, that's not what I meant. From above, I can dig the hole wide enough so yew can just climb out."

"Oh. All right then."

They set to, Edelle lifting Lute somewhat awkwardly albeit easily to her shoulders, from which place he proceeded to shower her with a sprinkling of ice shavings before his exclamation of "good, they didn't take it," confirmed that the job was as easy as he had said…and also that they still had food. Food which, despite all her efforts of earlier, Edelle could simply not refuse any longer. No sooner had she crested the side of the small pit than she hungrily dug into a wedge of bitter acorn, trying hard not to think of whosever food this *really* was. In a way, she supposed, it did not really matter. Relating her mission to Lute had refreshed its importance in her mind. Survival, merely for the sake of reaching her destination, suddenly seemed like the most important thing under the sun.

"We're not very far," Lute mused around a mouthful of acorn. His eyes were trained on the map he had pulled from his recovered pack, and they flicked up to meet Edelle as he spoke. If she saw tentative comradery there she ignored it.

"How much farther?"

"I'd say a few days at the most. If we go fast."

She caught the sidelong look he gave her.

"You go as fast as you can. I'll try to keep up. This is important."

Lute nodded, giving the map one more cursory glance before stuffing it back into his pack.

"Onward?"

"Yes, please."

The sun, now reaching its decline, kept its warmth just far enough from them to appear a baleful watcher on the horizon; if it held any answers about what lay ahead, it kept them well hidden. Perhaps, Edelle thought, they would have been worse off for the knowing.

CHAPTER XVIII

King Sirius's throne room was burning.

Waking in a sheen of sweat and with a fevered, bitter taste in his throat, the King saw him. The confusion melted quickly, and he realized with a plummeting acceptance that he had known it all along.

It was so *hot*, but the figure weaving through the flames hardly seemed to notice the heat—the licking embers pulled away from his skin as if he were even beyond their cold hunger. For a moment Sirius wondered whether the squirrel before him was actually alive, but that was foolish and something he should have learned not to question some time ago. There was no doubt. No doubt now.

My only regret…

How could it be too late?

But the other was laughing at him now, the laughter growing, spreading, feeding the flames. The heat, *the heat*, and when the figure spoke, Sirius felt a convulsive movement within his chest.

"Sirius, old friend, it is good to see you. But it will be so much better later. You won't have to wait very long at all. Then…then we shall be truly, how you say—reunited."

"Why…" Sirius gasped. It was so hard to breathe. The heat, the heat was burning his fur now, he could smell it. Why was no one coming? It was so *hot*…surely they would feel it rooms away…had he not placed a guard at the door?

"No one's coming, Sirius."

"Why are you doing this to me?"

"Oh, really, I'm disappointed you had to ask." And now there was a dangerous spark of madness in the other's eyes. "But, Sirius, I'm not doing anything to you. You should have realized but I suppose you never learn, do you? You've done this to yourself."

Sirius lay gasping, clutching at his sides with blistering paws.

I'm burning…burning alive.

"Perhaps you should ask why you have done what you did to me, shouldn't you? But you won't. You were never one to apologize, *were you?*"

Through the burning, the excruciating pain, Sirius felt a twinge of rage that was even hotter.

"I…never…did *anything* to…you."

"Is that so? But you're still using them, aren't you? Using them like you used me. Like you tried to use the female, like you're using *her son*…"

"Leave me."

"Oh, Sirius…"

Sirius sat up sharply and the fox squirrel staggered back, his expression blanching for a split second, unable to hide his surprise.

"Leave me, Cumin."

The other looked as if he might snarl or break loose from his skin a monster, but he turned his aged face away from that of Sirius and the flames seemed to subside.

"Very well. It is like you told me once. You are King, and you rule alone. It is tradition. Well. You are King. And you *are* alone. I have let you have that. But I will make sure you regret it. Soon."

"GO."

The face that faded from him, taking the flames with it, was grinning.

Exhausted, Sirius fell backwards into black.

It was the day they were adding wings to the Byrd that Tiallin felt the King fail.

The day that Zerrith told them that his creation would have wings, Tiallin had been filled with a strange excitement, and now as he helped Lyrah to lift one of the willow structures, copied from the design of the leaf that had so enamored his brother, he felt something cut through his happiness, silent but thick.

With a soft, startled noise, Tiallin watched the wing fall to the ground in a daze. It was only when Zerrith spoke that he realized he had dropped it.

"Tiallin, is something wrong?" His brother came around the edge of the Byrd, seemingly more concerned about the damage that might have befallen his project than anything else. But the room was coming back into focus for Tiallin once more, and he stood, confused, paws at his sides. Lyrah touched him on the shoulder.

"Tiallin?" she said tentatively. "Is everything all right? You frightened us."

Her eyes went to Zerrith for a moment as if asking him to agree, but he was bent low over the fallen wing and did not notice.

For a moment she frowned, and Tiallin spoke abruptly, not sure of what he was about to say.

"Has the King been all right today?"

Lyrah looked surprised, then shook her head.

"I don't know. I haven't been called to him today. I've been here all day with you." When he didn't say anything else, she continued. "If...if something was wrong, we would have been told. What makes you think...?"

"I don't know. I got a weird feeling just now. I think...when the King brought me into service he might have...bound me by more than words."

As Tiallin spoke, he registered only faintly that perhaps he should not be divulging this to the other two, but surely…surely *now* they all shared secrets in some way. He watched as Lyrah bent to pick up her part of the Byrd's wing once again, but Tiallin did not move.

"I think we should go see him."

"Now?"

"Yes. I feel—

"You think it's that urgent, then?" she whispered.

"I don't know. I— He flung up his paws, frustrated at his own inability to articulate what he *did* think.

"We should just make sure."

Lyrah stared at him.

"You said the King *bound* you—

"Never mind. I shouldn't have. It's not important anyway. We need to—

"No. We have to do the wings today."

It was the first time Zerrith had spoken since Tiallin's small fit and they both started.

"Zerrith…" Lyrah said.

Zerrith looked directly at her as he spoke. "You promised you would help with the wings today."

"Zerrith, the King might be in trouble," Lyrah said, and Tiallin could tell she was doing her best to return his gaze. "We can all do it later—

"I can do it myself," Zerrith said. His voice was unnaturally frosty. The Byrd, sitting motionless, suddenly became less of a wonder to Tiallin and more just a tall feathery fortress of childish imagination.

"Fine, then. You can do it without me," Tiallin said. Walking to the door in the heat of the moment, he felt as if something more should be added, as if he should seize the opportunity to have the last word for once. And he found with some surprise that he knew exactly what to say.

"You know, I never asked much from you Zerrith. No one *ever* asked much from you, maybe that's the problem."

He walked away then, rapidly for fear that Zerrith might come in with a word to top his or that he might be called back.

He feared that if he was, he would come.

Tiallin did not stop to see if Lyrah would follow, if she would decide to come with him to the King. He doubted it, the way she looked at Zerrith all the time...all the time they were building his odd dream. She didn't understand the Byrd either, he knew, she was only helping with it, keeping it a secret because Zerrith loved it. Because Zerrith loved it and she loved Zerrith. And Zerrith knew. He knew and he did nothing, too bothered with things that weren't *real* to bother with the lovely dark red eyes that gazed upon him so sadly...

It was only when a prick of sharp pain came to Tiallin that he realized he had balled his paw into a fist, claws digging into his palm. He passed outside of his tree and slowed his walk, staring at the fresh pinpoints of red against the white of his fur with vague disinterest.

The King, he thought immediately, and his pace strengthened and became purposeful once more. For still, the quiet force was pulling at him, ever so slightly but nonetheless effective, calling him in the direction of his ruler. Like a connection. A binding.

I should never have told them about my suspicions! About my vow to Sirius! Tiallin swore angrily at himself. Would he always be so painfully open, so afraid to keep secrets because of the loneliness it involved?

A loud crashing noise to his immediate left caused Tiallin to jump so high in the air that he was later thankful that no one had been around to witness it; it was only a bit of snow, sliding from its purchase on an upper branch and hitting others on its way down. For a moment Tiallin had thought...but he shook all thoughts of the big gray squirrel from his mind, until only one final idea clung to the inside of his skull, persistent and nagging.

You should have told the King!
What if it's the reason he's...?

Terrified now, Tiallin came to the Great Tree and barreled his way up its trunk and through the entrance, not bothering to apologize to the old gray servant standing there, carrying some threads of yarn with a listless look in his rheumy eyes...

Running nonstop to the door of the King's chambers, Tiallin began to pound on them, but the guard standing nearby grabbed his arm and pulled him to one side forcefully.

"What do you think you're doing, boy?"

"I need to see the King!"

"The King is resting."

Tiallin stared into the face of the gray holding him, who was leering oddly and the fear in his chest mounted.

"Let me go," he said, and even to his own ears his voice sounded new, different, controlled...even dangerous, as he had felt only one other time, and within the same place. Still, Tiallin did not expect the guard to listen, so when he was released it took him a moment to register his freedom. Resisting the urge for a backward glance at the gray, he burst through the doors of the King's chambers, prepared for a reprimand or rather wishing for one, for it would mean that all was well.

No one was within the darkened room. Tiallin felt his chest constrict even further...was it too late? What had happened? A slight sound, like the shifting of feet echoed across the room to him, catching his ear and Tiallin's attention was drawn to the small, nearly hidden door at the other end of the room which he had exited through at the conclusion of his first ever meeting with the King. It was open.

Tiallin stared at the small black square of darkness beyond the open door. He hesitated, though he harbored no doubt as to what he would do. Saying a silent prayer to Astrippa, Tiallin approached the door, ears pricked. Whoever had made the first noise seemed to have gone quiet, though, and when Tiallin stuck his head out into the hallway, fearing the worst, he saw nothing. Bitter disappointment began to set in and he was on the verge of pulling his head back out again when his eyes adjusted completely to the blackness and he realized that he was not alone after all.

It was not what he expected. Sirius stood with his back against the wall, his unfocused eyes betraying no hint of whether he was yet aware of Tiallin's presence. His mouth was half open, and as Tiallin watched, he began to mouth words softly to himself, as in song. Tiallin could not help feeling that maybe there was a grain of truth in what others were saying about the old squirrel. Lurking in his own halls and talking to himself, Tiallin thought, were not things that *he* would do as a King if he wished his subjects to believe him when it came to more important matters. But as usual, the King seemed to know of his presence, and as usual, Tiallin felt extremely shamed at his own thoughts as soon as Sirius addressed him.

"Tiallin," he said, and his voice held no urgency whatsoever, something that surprised and confused the young squirrel at once. "You have come. Good. For a moment, I had feared it would not work."

"Sorry," Tiallin said. "But what wouldn't work? Did you…summon me?"

Sirius did not give any sign of having heard his question, though Tiallin knew he had.

"Tiallin," Sirius said again, and still his voice was very calm, though Tiallin could see that his face was weary beyond imagining. "I know what is happening."

Tiallin felt strange. "What's Happening? What do you mean?"

"I may have triggered this," Sirius said, and his tone was dangerous. "But I will not take the blame."

Tiallin could only feel confused, and Sirius seemed to sense it at last and take some pity on him.

"Forgive me, Tiallin. There is a reason I asked for you, it will just take some explaining." He gestured to the door behind Tiallin. "If you would close that."

Tiallin stared at him then remembered that with Sirius, staring really did no good.

"Your Majesty…?"

"We have to be secretive, Tiallin. I would rather speak with you in here where there is no chance that he will…well, allow me to start from the beginning."

"Okay…" Tiallin was puzzled, but casting a glance down the narrow hallway in both directions, he complied, leaning against the wall opposite his King. The silence was palpable for one frozen moment, then Sirius drew in a long, tired breath and began. As the words left his mouth, it seemed that he was speaking as much to himself as he was to Tiallin.

"Once, when I was young, a squirrel named Tamen Nunquil ruled our Pinewood fortress. He was undoubtedly a great ruler, but…he was a bit unconventional. He believed that we should allow other types of squirrels to mingle with us at will, that we should not believe them any different than ourselves, and that this would be the key to our salvation, to gaining our access once more to another world that may or may not have belonged to us, to becoming one with Astrippa once more, so to speak. Or, as some of the more archaic tales would have us believe, to literally gain our wings once again."

Tiallin was surprised to note some type of half-formed bitterness in Sirius's voice. He wondered if it was disbelief, or something different. Tiallin himself had always had trouble believing that the white squirrels, however ill-fitted they seemed to be to this life, had some special place all their own. Usually only the elder squirrels stuck by these tales, giving them a fabled feel.

"Tamen believed," Sirius continued, "that his reign would be the one to liberate us. In keeping with the idea of guiding and protecting the other races, he allowed grays to come from across the border to live among us, giving them the best of food and living quarters along with it. He allowed some black squirrels from Oakwood to do the same. Tamen would call together the white squirrels in the area at times, and tell them the same thing—always that we were closer to going back to the place Astrippa had meant for us, back to home—to flight. And during the course of his ruling, even those who had been skeptical of the tales of old began to believe him, began to feel as if it were true. For a while, our community was a true community indeed. We were united by our belief in Tamen's cause."

Tiallin, who had never seen as many as three white squirrels in one place, had never even thought of this region of Pinewood as a community of any type at all.

"Where *are* all of the white squirrels now, then?"

"Oh," Sirius gave an odd sort of sigh. "There were never that many of us to begin with. But they've become reclusive, I suppose. I can hardly call my rule a kingship, countless though the times may be that I have pushed impending disaster off our backs with my skill without anyone being the wiser…" This time, there was a definite bitter tinge to his words, and Tiallin fell silent on the edge of his next question. When a few seconds had passed, he could not help himself and asked anyway.

"So what happened then?"

"Tamen, unlike I, knew who his heir would be. There was only one white squirrel in these parts who had the skills required, and that squirrel grew up knowing his place as heir. That squirrel was me."

Sirius paused, but only for an instant, as though he expected his words to have some profound effect upon Tiallin.

"I was told of my place as heir in secret, as was necessary. If the knowledge were to be made public, there was too much risk that someone would grow jealous and attempt to take me out before my time. So I waited, admiring my King and treasuring the secret that he had entrusted to me alone. When I was growing up, I had a close friend, someone that I would not have known at all were it not for Tamen's policy about the intermingling of the races. A young fox squirrel my age named Cumin, an orphan who the King had taken a particular fondness for and allowed to live within the walls of this very tree. Cumin and I were very close, so much so that we shared nearly everything with one another…

"Everyone liked Cumin. The white squirrels were okay with his taking up residence in the Great Tree, even though a lot of us believed the other races incapable of learning our ways. The other non-whites who lived here, the grays and the blacks, all especially seemed to like Cumin, not at all resenting his good placement with the King. Cumin was a natural leader, and I suppose that was a lot of it; he was a likeable squirrel with a good deal of charisma on his side. In the various games we played together, he often took the leading role and I fell behind contentedly enough. But we were both strong-willed, and that was where the trouble started. Well, that and Tamen going missing."

"What?" Tiallin, who had almost spaced out despite himself was now wide awake.

"Tamen went missing, and no one could find him. It was so unlike Tamen not to communicate things he believed to be of great importance to his followers that everyone was deeply disturbed by his absence. This placed me in an uncomfortable position: because I did not know whether Tamen's leave was only momentary or not, it was time to announce myself as heir. So I organized a meeting with a bit of trouble—I admit that I told Cumin beforehand so that he could help me to get everyone together. And then I made my announcement. Everyone wanted to know whether I knew of Tamen's whereabouts, naturally, but I had to tell them I did not. You could *feel* the dissatisfaction on the air that day.

'After the meeting, Cumin came to me and made a request. He wanted to rule with me if I should have to take over the throne from Tamen. I refused; it was not the tradition of the white squirrels. Tamen had explained things thoroughly to me, and as much as I loved Cumin, I could not go against what had been set in stone through past generations of Kings. Cumin would not give up; he told me that he had something he wanted to show me. I was confused, but I can remember following him into a room, a room in this very hallway, where he merely stood across from me for a long time. I couldn't understand what was happening and I was about to ask him when suddenly I was hit by a blast of images, images of the both of us, Cumin and I seated on thrones of wood, hundreds of faces turned up to us in admiration. The vision faded quickly, and I remember that after, Cumin's voice sounded as if he had exerted himself to a great extent. "I have it too," I can remember him saying. "I have it too.'"

Sirius gave an odd sort of shudder and fell silent. Tiallin felt a tremor go through his body at what he had been told.

"You mean he had magic? The skill?"

Sirius did not respond at first. Then, at long last he nodded.

"He did. I cannot explain how. I myself had always considered it only a trait of the white squirrels, and I had never suspected it of him myself, though after the fact I thought I could see more easily how he was able to win favor with so many others. He did not interpret the skill the same way that I did, did not save it for the sole use that I had been saving it for. Cumin had grown up with the skill and had experimented with it as he pleased. Still, I wondered…and still do wonder, how Tamen never figured it out. Or perhaps he had known. Much is still a mystery to me, Tiallin. The important thing was that Cumin thought by showing me his magic, he could convince me to let him rule with me. He said he had discovered interesting ways of using the magic that he could share with me, teach to me. He did get rather excited by it, but still I refused.

'That was when things started to go bad. Cumin had been so convinced that I would agree with him that he got very, very angry when I would not. We did not speak for the next few days. I noticed that the grays and the other non-white squirrels were acting particularly disdainful of me, and I knew Cumin must be telling them things about me, perhaps about how I rejected Tamen's ideas and considered myself superior to them. I grew angry…it was only natural," Sirius clenched his jaw tight and took a breath before continuing, "The privilege of ruling in

Tamen's absence was mine, so when the rumors about me became nastier and nastier, and I, in my young age, began to fear revolt, I was driven to do something which caused me great pain despite my anger. I had Cumin exiled. He was outnumbered, and had no choice but to leave. A lot of the grays and squirrels of other kinds who had expressed the strongest feelings against me left with Cumin, or simply chose to go back to roughing it across the border rather than live in proximity to someone whom they considered insulting to their pride. For the longest time, however, I had no idea where *Cumin* had gone; I half expected him to come back, wanting revenge or perhaps to make another proposition.

But although Cumin was gone, the impression he had made on some of the others in the colony had not worn off. As always, Cumin left his impression on a number of squirrels, and there were even whispers, the result of a rumor he had planted, no doubt, that I had killed Tamen Nunquil myself, due to my insatiable lust for the ruling position. As a result, we were not being saved by Astrippa as Tamen had suggested we would. Instead, we were damned by my actions. It was not only the other races that believed this; a lot of white squirrels seemed to give it credence as well. The whole disappearance of Tamen was such a mystery that it was hard to find much credible defense for myself. I spent a long time in the uncomfortable knowledge that perhaps the only reason attempts were not being made on my life every minute of the day was because I had magic and the others did not. My dreams of becoming a King whom everyone else admired and loved had already failed, withering prematurely without so much as a parting wave. Try not to be impatient with me now, Tiallin if I do not share in the pleasure of the old tales of salvation…if I do not appear particularly *warm* toward any of it. To be saved…with Tamen's disappearance and the fading of his promises to dust, I also lost my belief in such tales. To fly…well I would be bound to crash wouldn't I?"

Tiallin looked up at Sirius and seeing his tremulous smile, realized that it was the first time he had heard the king reference his own blindness. It was not a joyful revelation. Tiallin felt he should say something, no matter how idiotic.

"So, er…what does this have to do with now? Are you saying you think that…that Cumin is behind all of this—killing the one who carved on your walls—sending you images to scare you?"

Sirius almost smiled at him for an instant, but when he spoke it was somewhat condescendingly.

"I do not think. I know. What were the suspicions of yesterday have become the collective knowledge of today. It appears that while I am not as…potent as I once was, Cumin has managed to stay strong despite his age. Not that he does not need others to help him get to me…I believe he leans on them rather heavily, and this in itself could be his weakness. But I am getting ahead of myself, Tiallin. There are still things you do not know. Like the fact that Cumin has struck at me before in the past."

"He has?"

"Yes, in a time before you were born. When Cumin disappeared, he strayed rather far away from Pinewood, took up with some other squirrels, maybe even started a colony of his own—Astrippa knows he had enough influence to do so—it doesn't matter. What does matter is that he managed to poison the view of squirrels in locations remote from this place against me. They had all believed well of us white squirrels previously, largely due to Tamen's long and successful reign. But Cumin managed to taint their perspective, again through use of his magic."

"What did he do?"

"He brought some spell to the land to which he had come and caused the food there simply to…go bad, horribly rotten. He was then able to project the blame for the disaster onto me—it must have been quite simple for someone as persuasive as Cumin. I don't want to ponder the implications of the exact magic he would have had to use to make a thing of such propensity happen, or moreover the pure evil associated with doing such a thing to other, innocent creatures purely for the aim of getting at me."

Sirius looked angrier than Tiallin could ever remember seeing him, and Tiallin could understand why. It was absolutely chilling to think that anyone could bring himself to stoop so low as to cause death by starvation to innocents in order to get personal revenge. It was more than chilling, it was scary; if this Cumin was capable of what Sirius said he had committed, was there *any* limit to how far he would go? He didn't like to think about it.

"My powers then were keen enough that I was able to divert the disaster, to probe with my mind and find the problem, though it took me some time to undo what he had done. In that time, Cumin himself came up to me here. He had changed, and I could not help thinking that any trace of the squirrel I had known in the past was completely eradicated, gone for good. This was an evil soul, and I dealt with him as such. He brought a few others with him, who we unfortunately had to be just as rough with. Cumin and I then had another talk…he made the request once again that I let him rule alongside me. I don't know whether he thought I would actually be intimidated by his power and agree with him—he certainly tried to put me under his spell, and once I felt the intoxication almost take hold, but I was stronger than he thought. I thrust him from me with a particularly hard push and told him once again, for the final time, never to come back."

Sirius sighed, and in the darkness of the corridor he looked more tired than was believable, some of the anger flooding off of him and down his shoulders as he let them drop a bit.

"Even I do not know where he has gone this time. I was not foolish enough ever to bear doubt in my mind that he still lived somewhere, waiting for an opportunity to strike at me again. And now that I have begun to receive the messages, these images and foretellings of danger—

"But what do you think he would be trying this time?" Tiallin blurted. He was regretting ever entertaining the possibility that the king might be paranoid. The business with Cumin held a sort of terrifying pall over him, the sort that only truth could engender.

"I do not know what it is Cumin intends to do this time," Sirius said, tipping his head back against the wall, and Tiallin wondered if Sirius had chosen the semi-dark of this little-known back corridor to talk in so as to disguise the true severity of his fatigue.

"Cumin has come to me, recently, in a vision. It was very...real." Sirius seemed to gather himself before continuing and then he said "I do not think we have much longer to wait before we figure out what he is up to. And judging from his confidence in speaking to me, I do not believe he thinks I will be a challenge to overcome this time. I have tried to decipher what it is he is trying to do, but it is proving nigh impossible for me...which is why I summoned you in the first place, Tiallin. I realize it was unfair, perhaps. But there was no one else. There *is* no one else. My heir has not shown up, and I have come to doubt they exist. I searched among those in this colony and nearby very thoroughly, probed with my gift at the walls of their minds even—it is necessary for a king to do these things, Tiallin. But still, I found nothing. Except for once— The King paused, "I thought for the briefest moment that I saw something in—but no, that is not of importance now."

Tiallin did not ask whose name the king had been about to say; he thought he knew. Instead, he listened as Sirius went on.

"I thought once, Tiallin, that in selecting you I could get to the bottom of this, that I could figure out the plot against me. I confess to you now that I had suspicions of Cumin all along, and that I may have given you false hope of finding information. I suppose that in turning my attention to the idea that the trouble could be coming from somewhere else entirely than where I knew it to be coming from, I thought I could find peace. This was false, and I know it now. I ask, Tiallin, that you will not hate me for it. I have grown fond of you in my way, and I—you remind me more of your—well. Thank you for being loyal."

"What do you want me to do?" Tiallin asked. He did not know what had stirred him to say such a thing; after all, had he not just basically been told that there *was* probably nothing he could do? Should he not leave it at this and be glad for it? But somehow he couldn't. Some small part of him felt sure it owed something to the king, though he was not sure why, or what—but he just could not simply leave Sirius to face whatever a squirrel like Cumin had in store for him! Even if Sirius was leaving things out, even if he did not understand, he was in it now, for better or for worse. He had listened to the king's fears, and he felt he should do what he could...something of

Importance.
You just like your 'high places'.

Tiallin ignored Zerrith's voice within his head and watched Sirius, waiting for his response, thinking he would be denied.

He was surprised, therefore when Sirius said, "Help me only by knowing the truth. Know the truth and tell it to those who will hear, or to those who ask. There are many here, I think, that believe still, secretly, that it was my fault for Tamen's dying. We are disjointed and not worthy of being called a true colony. I believe that Cumin will come again soon, and that he will not come alone. If enough of us know the truth there is the chance that we will be able to make an effort against him, but I doubt that we can be united in such a way in such a very short time. I have become aware that all of our efforts at making the old legends come true have crumbled. This dispute is merely between Cumin and I now. I have tried to avoid it, have not seen its inevitability for what it was. No matter who else he brings with him or what strategies he tries, I must get to him…get to him and kill him before it is too late. It is all that is in my mind right now. I have confided in you, Tiallin, and I am not sorry for it. It has been of more use to me than you know."

Tiallin nodded in answer to his king.

"Of course I will," he said at last. Then something new occurred to him, and though he knew that Sirius had as good as dismissed him once again, the question refused to be ignored.

"King Sirius?"

"Yes," the King's voice was not inviting, exhausted beyond belief. He paused with his paw on the door to his chambers, waiting for Tiallin to speak.

"What *did* happen to Tamen? Does anyone know?"

"Tiallin, if anyone knew that, than perhaps Cumin's power would be a lot more limited. But no one does.

Tamen just disappeared one day, and his throne disappeared with him. Shortly before his disappearance, he dismissed the squirrel who had done all the carving for him, the one who I am led to believe Cumin has had killed. Pember Sigyl. He was a valuable asset to us and Cumin knew it."

Sirius turned again toward the door, but Tiallin was not done thinking.

"Wait! What if—do you think Cumin was the one who killed Tamen?"

It was a while before Sirius spoke this time.

"...It is a distinct possibility, but still only a possibility." Tiallin thought he understood his hesitation. If Sirius were to believe that Cumin had killed the former king for his own gain, it would mean that he would also have to admit that he had misjudged Cumin grievously in the earlier days of their friendship. He remembered how aggressive Sirius had become when he had defended his ability for determining who could be trusted or not; it was amazing really how much more Tiallin thought he understood now in light of what he had been told. Well, the king could think what he liked, but Tiallin personally believed that if Sirius's former magical friend had been at the root of everything else, why not the disappearance of Tamen to boot?

Sirius had turned away from him yet again, and Tiallin had the distinct impression that the king was trying to be rid of him now that he had eked a promise from his lips. Tiallin knew Sirius was tired, and that he was perhaps being selfish, but he could not seem to contain himself.

"Your Majesty!"

"...Yes?"

"Do you miss him at all? Cumin?"

He did not know what fool impulse could have swayed him to ask such a question, or why standing waiting in the dead silence that followed he felt only discomfort and no regret. He thought the King might snap at him, or yell, thrust Tiallin from his presence at last, spitting out the sharp words that Tiallin could sense on the edge of the old squirrel's tongue.

Sirius turned so that his face was completely out of Tiallin's line of vision. When he answered, his voice was soft yet controlled.

"When he showed me the vision of the throne," he said. "It was the first time I ever saw."

He left then, closing the door behind him. Full seconds passed before Tiallin heard him walk away. Tiallin did not move, just stood in the dark listening to the faint creaking sounds of the tree branches in a cold winter wind outside the thick walls then brought a shaking paw up to his face and slumped down, sliding to the floor. He suddenly wished more than anything that he could run freely along those branches once again, blissfully unaware and free, free from knowing anything more.

"Why…why me?" Tiallin whispered into the blackness.

"It's because you truly care."

The voice made him jump, and Tiallin shot to his feet, looking about. Lyrah, her body still half-hidden in shadow, gave him an apologetic smile. She was leaning out from an entrance that Tiallin hadn't known existed.

"You truly care about his plight in a way that others don't."

"You're—you were spying on us!" Tiallin shouted, not sure why he was so angry over it. Fury was rising within him all the same, and it seemed he could not hold back his next venomous words. "Do you have to stick your nose into everything?!"

Lyrah bit her lip and ducked her head momentarily. Tiallin did not quite have the grace to feel bad about it.

"I'm not, really," Lyrah fired up suddenly. "I just followed you here. And anyway, hark who's talking! It was *you* who told me to come with you and see if King Sirius was all right!"

"Yeah, well, why didn't you come on in then, instead of spying on me like that?"

"Oh, come now. You can't expect that I would have seen you two standing out here in an otherwise deserted corridor talking in hushed voices and thought it was okay just to intrude? Who could resist eavesdropping?"

Tiallin did not have an immediate response; he spluttered for a good minute before saying helplessly, "All this time? You heard everything?"

He got his answer from Lyrah's silence.

"And it's not because I *care*," he blurted. "Lots of people would've cared."

She only shook her head. "Not like you do, Tiallin. You have a habit of taking on other people's problems like they're yours. It must cause you a lot of stress."

"Well then, obviously you don't get it at all. We're all in trouble, not just the king. A couple of days ago, I had the life almost choked out of me by a huge gray who seemed to want to provoke me into lashing out with magic—who knows why—but I think I deserve to be a little stressed!"

Lyrah stared back at him, puzzled, and the sudden realization came to him that once again, he had neglected to tell Sirius of his encounter with the gray.

As he turned, indecisive, for the hidden door that would let him back into the king's chambers, he felt a paw on his wrist, and surprised, stared down at it. Lyrah looked up at him, her face open and honest.

"Please don't be angry," she said. "I really didn't mean it to be an insult, but you should know that you're not the only one carrying the burden of knowledge you're not sure what to do with. That door doesn't open from the outside," she added as she watched him grope around for a door knob.

Tiallin let his paw drop from the door and stared back at her, into those dark claret orbs and felt his mind go oddly blank.

"Uhm..."

Lyrah put a paw to her lips.

"I want to show you something," she whispered. "even though I'm not supposed to. That way we'll be even, all right?"

She tugged on his wrist and he fell into step behind her. Very soon it became apparent that they were headed for the door Lyrah seemed to have come from only moments before. It was nondescript, the last doorway in the hall, an excellent place to put something you didn't want anyone to find—but Tiallin could not begin to guess what sort of thing anyone would now have cause to hide in such a place. Or perhaps they were only going here for an even more secluded place to talk.

Lyrah led him over the threshold and he thought that this second guess must be correct—all that this room contained was an old loom and a mass quantity of yarn, lying tangled and disorderly on the ground. Someone had been working on whatever was on the loom, and though the poor quality of the light would not allow Tiallin to see what it was, it seemed as if they had been making good progress. He turned to Lyrah, but she was busy shaking the firefly lamps littered about the room into waking. As the little creatures within came to their senses, drowsy and irritated, a glow began to illuminate the room, growing stronger with each second until they were enveloped in warm yellow light. The light could not have been more welcome to Tiallin, who felt rather like he had been standing outside in the darkened corridor for a lifetime. He opened his mouth to ask Lyrah a question, but her tail brushed lightly over his cheek as she went to light the very last lamp and he was struck dumb. By the time he came around, she had turned back to him.

"I've been working on this for some time," she said, and Tiallin belatedly realized she must mean the tapestry, for he now saw that was what it was, the woven sheet draped over the loom, intricately woven and made with all the right colors, it seemed. But his eyes were riveted especially what was depicted on the tapestry. A white squirrel was suspended in a spattering of blues and blacks as if he or she were taking a leap from one branch to another. Indeed, to the lower right of the squirrel, Tiallin noticed the end of one lonely, flowering branch, but the eyes of the squirrel in the picture were not trained on this. Instead, they were fixed on some point above him. Tiallin looked for any distinguishing feature on the squirrel depicted, but it seemed as if it could have been anyone—his mother, his father, Zerrith, Sirius, even himself. Except that the squirrel could not possibly be any of them; the squirrel in the picture could not possibly exist. He, she...*it* possessed two long, graceful and feathery protuberances arching upward delicately from its snowy back, making it all of a sudden quite alien to Tiallin.

Lyrah must have noticed his long silence, for he felt her glance over at him worriedly.

"Tiallin? You don't think ill of it, do you?"

"Wings," he breathed.

Lyrah looked confused for an instant.

"Yes," she said after a time. "Wings. I gave him wings."

"Him?"

"The squirrel in the picture. I was commissioned to weave a tapestry for King Sirius. No one's supposed to know. You know he thinks he's finished with?"

"Yes," Tiallin said heavily. "I haven't missed that, funny enough."

"He must trust you a good deal then, if you find it so obvious. He tries to keep it on the low, normally. Anyhow, he wanted me to make a tapestry commemorating him in some way. No," She said, perhaps seeing his dumbstruck expression. "You misunderstand. It's tradition. All the kings of the past have had things made in their memory, a painting or a carving or a tapestry like this one. Such things are always made in advance, before their time has come, to prepare them and suit them to their liking. No one's supposed to see it before it is finished except for the king himself…it's considered bad luck."

Tiallin blinked. "Then why'd you show it to me?" He felt slightly uncomfortable with this new knowledge.

Lyrah looked to the side for a second, but in that one motion he saw a great anger revealed, some curling, bitter resentment under a surface that was tired of forcing restraint. He saw it in the way her jaw held and in the tone of her voice when she answered him.

"Because the king will never be able to see it, will he?"

Tiallin was surprised and confused.

"Well, that's not his fault really, is it?" he argued.

"No. I'm not blaming him for being blind. But he could be a lot more interested in the state of things! He doesn't show any interest in how his tapestry is coming along anymore. Earlier on, he was always asking for fruit to make the dyes, you remember...checking up on it. But now he's stopped completely. It's like he's forgotten this whole project exists."

"Maybe he's just got a lot on his mind," Tiallin suggested.

"You want to side with him so badly, don't you?" Lyrah snapped, and again he was taken aback. "I wanted to show you this because I thought you would understand. You're not the only one carrying secrets, even if you are the only one he seems to trust enough to carry them." The resentment was back in her voice, and she talked quickly now, as if she might lose her gall if she were to stop and consider her words. "You may be eager to take his side now, but there are things I know about Sirius that you don't. He...he tends to use people for his own purposes. Maybe I am wrong to be so bitter about it, but I have devoted a good portion of my life to this thing. It is easy now to think that he might not care about it at all, that in his sense of doom he has neglected tradition or that he only gave me this task to keep me busy. To find a use for me."

Lyrah paused and made a visible effort to calm her breathing.

"It's useless to talk about such things as if talking could change anything, isn't it? I spied on your conversation because I was interested. And *you* always seemed interested by what I was doing for the king. And now you know. It's nothing fancy, like your job...but it keeps me busy." She cast a glance over at the tapestry, hanging forlornly from its loom, its colors melding so effortlessly together.

"It's very lovely," Tiallin said. He said it to make her feel better, but he also meant it. Clearly it took someone highly skilled with trained paws and sharp eyes to put together such a piece of art—Tiallin was sure *he* could never have done such a thing in his wildest dreams. But something was nagging at him. The design of the tapestry, the choice Lyrah had made disturbed him for whatever reason.

"Why did you make him flying?" Tiallin asked, staring at the fabric as he spoke, embarrassed to meet her eyes. "Sirius doesn't approve of the old fables of salvation, does he?"

When he finally peeked at her from under his hooded eyes he was surprised to see that she was grinning now.

"He did not tell me what to depict, except that it must be representative of himself in some way. Sirius *used* to believe in the tales...you know that. He was Tamen Nunquil's greatest admirer once...but with Tamen's death and his subsequent condemnation, his belief went out like a slowly guttering candle. Besides, there are other reasons for the design...Tamen, for instance, hasn't got a tomb to his name."

As she explained, Lyrah crossed the room in a couple of steps and began to feel expertly along the back wall, as if she knew exactly what she was looking for. Tiallin watched, uncomprehending until Lyrah's paw stopped in its roving and closed over something that had been formerly invisible to his eyes. She pulled at the invisible grip and the whole wall shifted to the side with a loud grinding. Tiallin stumbled backwards in shock; when he looked back at the wall again, there was a chunk of darkness staring back at him and mischief twinkling in Lyrah's eyes.

"Come on," she said. Tiallin thought there were probably a million reasons that he should say no, but at the moment his mind could not summon a single one. He followed Lyrah mutely to the opening where they were met with a cold stone staircase.

Stone? In a tree? That is curious, Tiallin thought hazily. *I wonder who built...?*

But Lyrah's tail brushed his face—it *was* a fine tail, he thought once again, remembering his first glimpse of it in the king's chambers—and with it, his thoughts were also brushed aside.

The stairs wound down for a seemingly infinite length of time, until Tiallin became uneasy entertaining the suspicion that they might be underground now. Squirrels by tradition harbor an instinctual dislike for anything subterranean, and the thought of being under a mile of earth with squirming sinuous roots and the smell of dead leaves and whatever creatures might live down here was highly unpleasant. He attempted to block it out, to reassure himself—but surely the Great Tree could not have been this high? Perhaps he had just lost track of space and time; after all, Lyrah did not appear tense at all, and on what must have been the tenth spiral they had made, she stopped at last in front of yet another door. This one required no special trick to open, and after a brief moment of standing still as if to prepare herself, Lyrah did so, looking back to make sure Tiallin was still following. He straightened his back quickly, and made a stab at a fearless expression.

At first Tiallin did not understand what it was he was seeing in this next room. It was frightfully dark and all that met his eyes were what appeared to be rows upon rows of bleary, imprecise lumps of even deeper darkness. His eyes adjusted slowly, and when he understood at last, he felt he could have done without the knowledge.

"Is this a...crypt?" he asked, turning to Lyrah in disbelief, but she had bent beside the edge of the wall nearest them and was searching on the ground for something. She found it and straightened up, the lantern hanging from her left paw guttering into life. The dark shapes before them took on more definition now, and Tiallin saw that they were indeed tombs of heavy stone, set in four long rows the ends of which Tiallin could just make out, disappearing into the other end of the room still shrouded in dark. He looked back at Lyrah and her smile held an odd allure for him this time. The side of her face farthest from the glow of the lantern was cast in shadow.

"The resting place of all the kings of the past," Lyrah said, and a silence followed in which Tiallin looked away up the rows of unmoving stone filled with a dread sort of wonder. Why had Lyrah brought him here? Did she think he had doubted her when she had spoken of the traditions of kings?

Before he could ask her, Lyrah had set off again, this time down the row of tombs closest to where they stood. As she passed them she cast her light over them, so that Tiallin was able to make out the inscriptions upon each one as well as the personalized works of art that accompanied them. He became so absorbed in his analysis of each new stone face that he almost ran into Lyrah when she stopped suddenly.

"Except for one," Lyrah said, and Tiallin followed her gaze to the tomb directly in front of them. The flat, long rectangular surface was definitely blank all except for a lone engraving which read:

Tamen Nunquil, 43 s. (?)

Tiallin just stared at the stone for a long while before asking the new question that had come to his mind.

"Why doesn't he have a picture?"

Lyrah glanced at him then let her eyes fall to the tomb once more.

"That's what I wanted to show you. I wanted you to understand my choice completely in making the tapestry. Tamen believed in the story of our salvation, and he believed that we would achieve it. Unfortunately, because his body was never found, he was never confirmed dead, and tradition also holds that a king must be confirmed dead in order to have their tomb dressed. As you can gather from the inscription, Tamen was still rather young when he disappeared, in only about the middle of his reign. He had not had anything commissioned yet, so there were no works in progress left sitting about for the dressing of his tomb. I---well, I suppose you could say that I am making my tapestry partially in honor of Tamen as well, for unless tradition changes, it is clear that he will never get one all to himself." She dropped her head for a moment, and Tiallin, who had been attempting to look her in the face was at a loss for what she might be feeling until she said, "It's bad, isn't it? I'm sacrificing one king's honor, the king I should be serving faithfully, in honor of one who is long dead."

"No," Tiallin said abruptly, wondering at the same time whether he was being completely truthful. "I—I get it. Besides, like you said, Sirius did honor Tamen at one point. He's only bitter because Tamen's disappearance caused a lot of trouble for him. Granted, if he knew what you were making the design like…"

"No, it's worse than that," said Lyrah, and this time she looked angry with herself. Looking about for a moment, she propped the lantern she was holding on the surface of Tamen's tomb and sat down next to it heavily. "It's worse because I can't help thinking I'm also doing it for personal reasons too, reasons that aren't so honorable."

"Come on—

"No! Look, you don't know the half of it. I'm angry at him, Tiallin! I'm angry at Sirius, and I've been angry at him for a long time. He's rejected me and he doesn't even appreciate what I'm doing for him, this meaningless task he set me! You would think that with so many squirrels turned against him he would be a little more appreciative of everything—especially—

But she died into silence, giving the empty space to the left of Tiallin a hard stare.

"He uses people, Tiallin. You should know that. He used to be so obsessed with getting an heir that the first time he took a mate, he only wed her because she was magic. When their child was neither magic nor male, and the wife died, he grew even more desperate. Then he took a liking to a female under his rule, and under his age by a considerable amount of years. I don't know whether he really liked her or not, but he in any case, he requested to mate her instead of ordering it; she too showed faint signs of being magically gifted. She turned him down after a time, feeling that she too was being used. And those he chooses to serve him…well…I think Zerrith was smart to refuse."

Tiallin felt too numb to be offended. He had just worked something out in his mind as she spoke, and he stared at her unhappy face, lit up in the lantern glow, pretty as ever. Lyrah, seeming to know what she had given away, met his eyes boldly.

"You're the child, aren't you?" Tiallin said. "The one he had with the first wife."

She did not give him an actual answer, only leaned back slightly in her place on the tomb and continued to hold his gaze.

Tiallin had always wondered what Lyrah's place was in the Great Tree, where she had come from and why he had never met her parents. Now that he knew, he supposed it fit, though somehow he found it hard to imagine Sirius with any type of family. He could certainly understand Lyrah's bitterness better.

"Someday," she said, and her tone had switched to one of contemplation, her dark eyes softened with thought.

"The tapestry I made will be laid across a tomb next to this one…for all its color, it will live in darkness. Tiallin, it can't be soon."

She was looking at him intently, fiercely as though she had just seen him for the first time, and Tiallin felt a thrill of dread at what he knew she was referring to.

"Tiallin. I'm angry with him, it's true, but this creature, this Cumin is not someone I would wish on anyone. No matter what. We've got to do something!"

"Yes," Tiallin agreed, staring at the ground next to Tamen's tomb now. "But what can we do? Sirius only told me to keep the truth in mind, whatever that's supposed to mean. Well, you heard it all." He gave her a wry look. "He doesn't even know what Cumin is planning. It could be anything." Tiallin shrugged helplessly. "It doesn't leave us with a lot of options."

Lyrah would not be deterred.

"What about the squirrel? The gray squirrel you said attacked you, what was that about I wonder? Do you think it could be related to whatever ill plans Cumin has in store for Sirius?"

Tiallin opened his mouth to object, but closed it without speaking.

"His son was spying on me too, earlier," he said slowly, after a time. "At first I thought it was only because he was interested in me, the way a lot of the grays seem interested in us whites. I mean, they do it to Zerrith too, he says, when he's out on his walks wherever he goes. Maybe they know I'm close to the king."

He hoped this last statement had not rubbed against Lyrah the wrong way, but when he looked back at her she seemed to hardly have heard. She was staring off into space, biting her lip in an intent manner, her eyes slightly glazed over.

"Do you approve of what Zerrith is doing?" she asked finally, and Tiallin, not expecting this particular question, halted in the midst of his speculation about the grays.

"You mean the Byrd?" he asked after he had gathered himself again. "I—well...do you?"

He felt rather lame saying it, like he needed her opinion first to express his own.

Lyrah only seemed to consider a moment.

"No. I don't. I used to think it was all just an innocent pleasure of his he had taken up, but as its progressed he's been getting more and more...*obsessed*, Tiallin. It's almost like he's lost touch with all of squirrelkind."

"Yeah, well," Tiallin said. "Zerrith is like—"

"No, he's *not* like that," Lyrah said, and Tiallin thought he heard the threat of tears in her voice. She had been thinking about this for a long time, he knew. "He was always solitary and introspective and sort of...obnoxious that way, but not like this. Never like this. The way he looks at that *thing* he's created, you would think it's alive instead of made of some silly twigs and thatch and feathers. It's ridiculous. And today...he doesn't seem to care anymore, Tiallin, and however he might have seemed to you before, Zerrith always cared."

Tiallin turned away from the look on her face as she said it, but he could not pretend it did not exist, just as he could not pretend that the pang which he felt go to his own heart was nothing. But when he could bring himself back to think of the sense behind her words, he knew she was right. He remembered who Zerrith used to be, the games they had played in younger days; they had stopped playing those games long ago, but that was a result of growing up. It was only recently that Tiallin had begun to see what Lyrah may have been seeing for quite some time—for whatever reason, this one creation out of many was wreaking change upon his brother, and the change was not good. He recalled to mind Zerrith's face as he, Tiallin, had left his room to go to the aid of the king.

"I can do it myself", that's what he said. Like he didn't need us anymore. Like he didn't care for the king, or either of us. Well, if that's true, why did he invite us to help him in the first place?

"I've considered quitting helping him," Lyrah said suddenly. "I've thought about it a lot." Her eyes were bright as she looked at him straight on. "But I kept telling myself I was imagining it, because…I kept telling myself, anyway." Tiallin thought he saw her blush, but it was too dark to tell for certain. He felt a sort of warmness tingle in his own cheeks and hoped that her eyesight wasn't any better than his.

"If you see it too," Lyrah continued, giving no sign that she saw anything at all except perhaps Zerrith's face in her mind, "Then I believe I could bring myself to stop. I could tell myself that I am doing him a—a service by refusing to indulge this project any longer. If you saw it too…"

"I do," said Tiallin, perhaps too quickly. He was unsure of his motives and also prepared not to care if they were less than honorable for once. "He's been…different around me too. More distant."

He thought of the note Zerrith had left on his bed what seemed so long ago now, and the way he had felt deceived by this older tradition being brought back to life merely so Zerrith could apologize without apologizing. Because Zerrith could never say he was sorry, not out loud the way it counted. His insensitivity to what he meant to Tiallin made Tiallin feel cold.

Why did I keep your secrets? Why did I ever play your games?

"I do," Tiallin said again, firmly this time. He stared into Lyrah's face boldly. He had made *his* decision; let her make her own. "I do, and I am not going to help with it anymore. He said he could do it himself, so I'll just let him. I won't stop him, but I am through. You won't see me in that room tomorrow."

Lyrah looked back at him, and seemed to gain a sort of strength from whatever she saw there. Her eyes were quite dry.

"Don't worry about it," she said, "I won't be in that room tomorrow either."

"Don't do it for me," he said.

"I'm not."

And Tiallin was startled to find that he was leaning over, getting closer to her face, his paw connecting with the cool stone of the tomb below them, and in that moment he was glad that it was truly empty, that no one had found Tamen's body so that the honored king would not be below, witnessing...

Lyrah's breath smelled half of salt, half of strawberries. "I'm doing it for me," she whispered in his ear, and his paw reached out in the suddenly unstable darkness, touching on her fur. It was softer than he had imagined.

"Good," Tiallin said. "Good."

All around them in the stretching dark of the catacombs, the forever staring eyes of royalty past watched them with indifferent stares through an inch of unyielding stone.

In a place like this, every moment held forever.

CHAPTER XIX

It was near dark and beginning to snow when Edelle caught sight of the lights. There were only a couple of them, but they were as good as a city for she and Lute, who had been walking in endless winter with hardly a sign of habitation for days now. Despite what the gray had said about being not far from their destination, she had begun to feel that every day they traveled might only be getting them further away. Perhaps the white squirrels themselves knew they were coming and were forcing them away by way of some old magic. When they came upon the lights, she had to rub her eyes twice and look away and back a couple times as well before she could convince herself that they were real.

"Lute! Lute!" Edelle called, craning her neck around behind her: though Lute had made a fuss about her larger size causing them to go slower in the snow, it turned out that he was the one who had been holding them up the past few days. His coat was thinner and he did not seem to possess as much energy as she did for traversing long distances in these conditions; as a result, he had also become much grouchier, a change that she personally did not relish. Edelle supposed the clouting he had received from the snow in the act of saving the young squirrel earlier might finally be getting to him, but she wished he would go back to being the squirrel from before, minus the thieving of course. She had almost come to believe she could begin to like that squirrel.

"What's it now?" Lute shouted with unnecessary force, as if the snow were a barrier that required great strength of the lungs to communicate around.

Edelle turned around to face him.

"The lights! Lute, can you see the lights?"

She attempted to keep her impatience under control as Lute came puffing up to her. He squinted into the distance then nodded at long last.

"So?"

"So? We've got to be close to them, you numb wit!"

"Numb wit, that's a new one. And yer always telling me not to be crude...how do yew know it's them anyhow?"

"Hush. Don't you see what this means? Whether or not it's them, it means we're getting close to *someone*. According to that map of yours, we should be close to the land of the white squirrels, and if that's true, then someone who lives nearby is bound to be able to give us some direction."

"...If they're not enemy-types yew mean," Lute muttered, but he looked vaguely excited all the same and Edelle could tell that he had not thought of this. "Lead on, then."

Edelle knew it would be fair to give him a chance to rest, but the urge to find out what was plaguing those back home and to put it right was simply too strong to even stop momentarily now that they had gotten so far. Without another word, she turned and plowed her way through the snow, hopping in and out of drifts, closer and closer.

Lute, lagging behind, had to reflect on how annoyingly persistent Edelle had become. He hadn't rested much at all in the course of the last day or two, largely due to the fact that each time they took a break longer than an hour, she would become unbearable. He understood, now that he knew her story, and in a way he was just as eager to get to the whites...but it was a bit creepy trekking through what was not unlike a whole expanse of wasteland, and the subject of old Pember's death would drift in and out of his mind uneasily during long moments of silence.

The lights they had seen dimly up ahead might very well be their long-awaited destination, though he wouldn't wager too large a sum on it. Edelle certainly seemed to have high hopes for it; she kept turning around to see if he was following, which made Lute vaguely annoyed. He couldn't help thinking, though, that excitement was an expression that really suited her features.

When they got closer to the lights, Lute saw that there were only two of them. He got the feeling that whoever had them on was not meaning to attract any visitors and went to inform Edelle of this new thought process, but she was already racing full-tilt toward the first of the lights, emanating from a window shielded by bristling pine boughs.

"Hey! Hey!" Lute cried despairingly, then, "Cripes. She's never going to hear. And if she does, she won't listen, damn her." Honestly—who ran toward the houses of strangers with so little caution? On the chance that there were enemies in the place beyond, she would stand no chance if she approached things this way. Lute did the only thing left to him and ran, powering his aching legs onward with a sudden burst of energy he did not know he had in him. He managed to reach Edelle and to grab her by the tail just before she threw herself into view of the palely gleaming window, now clearly outlined only yards away. Feeling as if his legs would give out at any second, Lute gasped at her from behind. His lungs felt on fire from the cold.

"Are…yew…*insane?*"

Edelle, who had turned and was attempting to yank her tail out of his grasp, glared at him over her shoulder.

"What's your problem?"

"We can't just run up to them like that, I thought that was obvious."

"Maybe to a thief it is," she said rather haughtily. "I guess you've never been through a community on innocent premises, have you?"

"That's not—

Lute blinked, then squinted, thinking hard.

"Look, will yew just oblige me then and go about it in a slightly more…subtle fashion?"

Edelle looked at him a long time.

"Fine," she said at last, which had been the least thing he had expected, though Lute supposed this was rather foolish of him; he should never grow to expect anything from someone as unpredictable as Edelle. She was almost just as much a puzzle to him as Pember's death had been, or why some squirrels liked the taste of winterberries…but that was neither here nor there.

"So what do you say we do?" Edelle asked. It was so rare that she would ask him such a thing that he was not sure if she was mocking him.

"Erm…" he began, but the crunching of someone else's paws on snow and a far-off sighing sounded from close by and he froze.

"C'mon!" he hissed, taking Edelle's paw and pulling her toward the nearest cover, which happened to be a crumbling fragment of rock wall. Edelle, from her spot crouched beside him, looked confused only for an instant before her expression changed to one of understanding; she had heard it too. Whoever it was—for Lute didn't quite dare to look—sounded as if he or she were coming from the direction of the nearby trees, and the slow drag of their footsteps seemed to indicate that they did not have a fixed idea of where they were going. Lute held his breath and listened to the sound of the stranger's progress intently. Start, shuffle, shuffle, stop. Start, shuffle, stop. At this rate, it could take forever and a day for the unknown squirrel to pass them by. To give himself something to do, or because Edelle was beginning to do the same and he felt a ridiculous pressure not to look a coward, Lute craned his neck until he could just see over the very top of the wall. He didn't see anything.

Then Edelle whispered excitedly from beside him and he felt suddenly as though a large bucket of water had been dumped over his head, soaking him thoroughly in cold.

"Lute—it's one of them!"

Lute looked again, and he could see now what he had missed before. The figure making its leisurely way toward them from the trees was indeed a white squirrel. Lute stared.

From so far off, he could not make out too many details, but he could easily see why the appearance of this other had eluded him at first—the fur was so pale that it blended into the surrounding snow. Perhaps it was because he had heard tales of such grandeur pertaining to the white squirrels, but the one he saw before him looked rather smaller than he would have expected; his coat seemed fine and sleek even from this distance, his body impressively lithe, but in size Edelle certainly would have this squirrel beaten. Lute did not dwell on such things, however; his heart was beating rapidly and he could feel the same anticipatory stillness radiating off of Edelle without so much as looking in her direction. He wondered if she, too, felt the stirrings of fear in the pit of her stomach.

There could be no more doubt about it. They had reached the domain of the white squirrels.

CHAPTER XX

Tiallin kicked a chunk of ice off to the side and watched it skid across the surface of the snow, his thoughts scattering with it. He was not sure what to do and it was driving him mad. He had slept terribly late into the day and when he finally woke he had wished himself back asleep, for his waking hours were fretful and full of the odd sense that he had been trapped inside an hourglass somehow, one that had only now been set into motion. He could not rid himself of the feeling that something bad was about to happen, and he could only hope this sudden prescience were only an effect of the events of the day before and the things he now knew. The look in Lyrah's eyes when she had told him they needed to do something had awoken something in him that had previously been slumbering undiscovered. Tiallin could not shake the notion that something needed to be done perhaps faster than it *could* be done especially when he considered that they had as yet to form a cohesive idea of *what* to do in the first place. It was more than a bit infuriating, not to mention discouraging— and now there was the fear to contend with as well. He had meant to seek Lyrah out earlier to talk to her, but he had been afraid that she would notice his fear and think less of him for it.

They had both convened to discuss their options only the day before. Tiallin and Lyrah had sat together on a branch secluded by a cluster of pine needles weighted with snow on all sides and spoke in hushed tones as they discussed theories on what the perhaps not-so-distant threat of Cumin would try to do next to get at their colony.

"He's already had the fellow who carves the walls of his chambers killed," Tiallin reflected. "But Sirius thinks that was purely to frighten him, and that was some time ago." He shrugged helplessly, watching Lyrah's profile as she stared at the wall of balsam-smelling greenery in front of them. She looked thoughtful. "But we can't really infer anything from that."

Lyrah, her eyes still trained on the space directly in front of her, was silent for a beat of time. When she spoke, she spoke matter-of-factly.

"Unless we can assume that Cumin himself did not in fact kill this carver."

"But we *do* know—"

"Shh," she waved a paw at him, smiling somewhat mockingly. Tiallin suppressed a surge of annoyance, smothering it with his curiosity at what she had to say.

"It is a well-known fact that much of the time leaders, especially those who are filled with self-interest and care for their own preservation above anything else, will employ *others* to do their dirty work."

"Oh. You mean like servants. But what does that—?"

"Shush, Tiallin. Honestly. King Sirius seems to think, no doubt because Cumin is the one sending him the telepathic messages, that Cumin is coming for him himself, that the first sign of danger will be the arrival of this old squirrel. But what if Cumin is using others to do his bidding as well?"

Tiallin stared at her, a frightening thought looming at the corner of his mind. He did not know why he hadn't thought of it earlier; in light of Lyrah's words it seemed painfully obvious.

"The gray!"

"Hmm?"

This time she did turn to look at him, intrigue etched lightly on her features.

Tiallin plowed on, trying to keep his voice from trembling, though whether it was trembling with excitement or fear he could not tell.

"The gray who knocked me over and threatened me," he said, "he was very interested in what I did for the king. He must have seen me going to the Great Tree and waylaid me when I came back out—anyway, he asked about protections on the king's chambers…"

Lyrah's eyes were round. "He did?"

"Yes…" Tiallin tried hard to remember the exact words. "He asked if there were any…magical protections around the king's chambers, I think. He seemed to think *I* had magic, and he was interested. And of course I said—"

But Tiallin broke off. There was no room in his mouth for anything now but the terror crawling its ponderous way up his throat. He had said no. He had confided in the big brute of a squirrel that no, there were no such protections around the king. Tiallin let out an anguished groan, and the expression on Lyrah's face grew steadily more alarmed.

"What?" she said sharply. "Tiallin, *what's wrong?*"

"I don't—I didn't mean to—I was frightened for my life, and I wasn't thinking clearly! I told…" he stared down at his feet miserably, urging himself not to throw up. "I told the gray that there was no magic protecting the king! If he's working for Cumin, I just let slip that they don't have to worry about combating magic at all. He knows *I'm* not magic, he was trying to get it out of me by nearly killing me, in case I'd show my powers to save my life. So he knows that there are no protective barriers *and* that I'm no threat."

"Please, Tiallin," Lyrah sighed. "Anyone can make mistakes. It just turns out that yours could be severely detrimental."

Tiallin made a sound of despair.

"But you brought up a good point," she continued thoughtfully, "You and I are really the only white squirrels who attend to the king personally. The few others are grays, for the most part. Keeping in mind what Sirius said about how Cumin turned most of the grays against him when he became king and refused to share his rule, I think it might be possible that some of them are in league with the gray that jumped you, and therefore in league with Cumin as well."

Tiallin stiffened.

"You know—that would be really frightening if it were true, don't you think? But Sirius was telling me—" He paused, aware that he was once again betraying the confidence the king had put in him, "—how he was getting these feelings about some sort of threat to him close by, how people might be plotting against him from the inside. I guess it's what's made a lot of other white squirrels think he's not so sane anymore—they think he's paranoid. But if it is true… how would Cumin be keeping contact with his spies?"

Lyrah shrugged. "Maybe through squirrels from the outside, grays from the border like the one who attacked you. Maybe if the majority of them work for Cumin, they're the ones who report to him and carry orders to those inside. I've talked to some of the grays that work inside the Great Tree. One of them helps me with managing the supplies for my tapestry. I can't imagine he would be one of them, he's much too old to do any real harm, old Banker…" she trailed off. "But I guess we can't be too certain. And some of the others…"

"Some of the guards are definitely shifty," Tiallin said, nodding. "I think you have a point worthy of investigation. But what kind of orders would they be receiving? And why haven't they *done* anything yet, if some of them are already inside?"

Lyrah sat quite still, staring again into the branches before her.

"Maybe they're waiting for something."

Tiallin considered a moment, then shook his head in frustration.

"It just doesn't fit together. If the white squirrels around here aren't so wild about Sirius, why doesn't Cumin use *them* instead? I'm sure my dad would sign right up."

Lyrah gave him a sharp look at this last.

"Sorry. Nothing to joke about," he amended, even though he wasn't sure he'd been joking at all.

"No, it's not. But I think you just made a really good point, even if you didn't mean to, Tiallin. Why is Cumin not attempting to get the whites on his side? Is it simply because he himself is not a white squirrel and whatever he is doing is aimed not only against Sirius but against all white squirrels? Or…is it because he thinks Sirius has the white squirrels at his back and he has a lot more resistance to deal with than he actually does?"

Tiallin could not quite hide his amazement at how quickly and keenly Lyrah's mind seemed to work when she put it to figuring out such matters. He struggled with what she had said, feeling impossibly slow.

"Are you saying that Cumin might have missed the fact that not all of the white squirrels are behind Sirius?"

"Well, we've certainly drifted apart as a community over the years…the last time Cumin was here, things may have worked differently. The last time he was here in the flesh, he was thrown out effectively…maybe he thinks Sirius has a lot more going for him than he actually does. We need to change that."

"What? Change it? But how can we? You mean—"

Comprehension dawned on him, and he stared at Lyrah in unflattering wonder. "You mean you think we should *get* the other white squirrels to back Sirius?" Had she lost her acorns?

Lyrah smiled slyly at him in answer.

"But—but—what'll we tell them?"

"What we know."

At his incredulous look, she said "Well, with a little elaboration, perhaps."

Tiallin could not ignore his nervousness at the notion.

"But...where can we find the other white squirrels anyway? I've seen passing glimpses of them, but really Lyrah...it's always honestly seemed to me like we're the only ones. You and me and Zerrith and my parents. We can't lie to ourselves any longer," he said, and was astonished at how much anger he found in his tone. "We're not a community. We may once have been, but now there's nothing but the color of our fur that we hold in common. I don't think it's enough. How will we ever connect with them, let alone *find* them all?"

Lyrah was silent for a long time this time. When she finally spoke, her voice was soft, but she reached out and gave his paw a comforting squeeze.

"We found each other, didn't we?"

Now as Tiallin waded through the snow, he blushed to think of the feeling that had raced through him upon that contact. It was foolish, he knew...Lyrah loved Zerrith, and who would choose him over Zerrith? Creative, introspective Zerrith...Zerrith, who they weren't helping anymore.

That had been hard for Tiallin at first. Living in the same house as Zerrith, taking meals with him but no longer coming to his room afterward had to be one of the most awkward situations he had found himself in for some time—though Zerrith never did invite him after the incident with the king, and his manner on the few occasions that he and Tiallin did speak was cold. Tiallin was glad for it in a way; though he could never quite stop his brother's opinion from mattering to him, it was much easier not to regret his decision when Zerrith kept acting as if he were invisible.

Tiallin kicked at a more solid piece of ice and nearly tripped; it was immovable, wedged solid in the ground. Cursing silently, he snatched his hind foot up and began to massage it, falling over backwards in the process. Body aching and cheeks flushed in embarrassment, Tiallin clambered to his feet.

Then he saw it, out of the corner of his eye—a quick flash of movement, a darker hue over the blinding white of the snow. Tiallin stared at the spot where he had seen it, a dilapidated pile of stone that might have once served as a wall of some sort in seasons long past. His mind immediately went into defense mode—*spies*!

Feeling anger mount in him, Tiallin raced to the pile of stone, heedless of his own recklessness. Just let them try to jump him again, he would show them that he couldn't be made a fool of so easily!

"Spy on me, will you?" he shouted "Well, I know what you're up to and you won't get away with it! Tricked you into thinking I don't have powers, did I? Well, you just try to run away and see if I do!"

Coming around the other side of the stone wall, Tiallin froze, his bravado falling to pieces in the back of his mind. Not one, but two squirrels stood cowering between himself and the wall. One of them was even larger than him, russet in color.

A fox squirrel. Just like Cumin. Oh, what have you done Tiallin, you stupid, unthinking fool.

The smaller squirrel, a curious dark gray in color, looked scared quite speechless, but his fox squirrel companion swallowed once and began to speak.

"We—we come in peace," she said haltingly. "We don't mean to cause any harm. We would only like to see your leader."

The gray beside her jumped at her words as if he had not expected her to be giving that particular information away. Heart thudding madly, Tiallin smiled grimly at them.

"To my leader, eh? I don't think—"

"Tiallin! Tiallin, there you are!"

Tiallin turned, startled, to see Lyrah racing across the snow toward him.

"I went to your house, but you weren't there, then I went to the Great Tree—there's something I want to show—" Her voice cut off as she saw that Tiallin was not alone and she stared at the intruders. "...you," she finished weakly, and shot him a questioning glance. Tiallin turned his tight smile on her, and she looked directly at the strangers, addressing them with a cold formality that Tiallin had never heard from her before.

"This is not a very good time to be seen around here, you know," she told them. "There's two of us and there's two of you, but I would say we have the advantage, so you might just want to follow us quietly and don't try anything."

CHAPTER XXI

Felix marched down the never-ending road to his destiny, his mouth dry despite the abundance of snow around him. The others in his band would gather the snow to their mouths every so often, drinking it in to stay hydrated. He felt as if he did not need it himself. He could not explain it, but as steadily as the ground decreased between himself and his goal, Felix had just as surely begun to feel as though his earthly needs were few indeed. He supposed famine, as briefly as it had touched them so far, may have had a role in this toughened sensation, this not unpleasant feeling that he could simply go on forever, when all the others around him ceased. There was power in such a sensation, and he used the thrill to keep himself from the guilt he knew he felt at leaving his Father behind.

To be fair, there was no possible way the aged squirrel could have gone; he was weak and bound to his chair, a cripple. But the feeling of guilt had persisted, and so Felix clung to his illusions of invincibility out here in the snow—sometimes he even felt as if his father was there with him, with the rest of the colony marching for justice on the white squirrels. Impossible as such a thing was, the feeling he had always associated with his father being near was a hovering presence in the aura of impending victory draped like a cloak about them all.

Whether or not all of this was just some great delusion of grandeur brought on by the bitter cold and the position of leader he had somehow sidled into, Felix did not know. He did know that it hardly mattered. The only truth that did matter was evident in the horizon growing thicker with trees and in the purple, hostile tint of the darkening sky as well as the weary complaints rising up around him now. The truth was evident, yes, and the truth made him smile in grim satisfaction. They were getting close.

This is for you, Edelle, Felix promised her silent face in his mind. *For you, and a little bit for me.* But wasn't that how love was?

Closer, closer, ever closer.

It would only be a matter of days now.

When the white squirrel found them, Lute had been fairly certain that his life was over. And then Edelle had started talking and all his reservations disappeared; he was positive. How could she be so foolish, so full of nerve as to think that the white squirrel, young as he was, would listen to her? They had walked right into the arms of a potential enemy, and to make matters worse, yet another white squirrel had appeared and now they had no chance of outrunning their captors—none at all. He looked sideways at Edelle as they trailed the two white ones, but he could not tell what she was thinking. The female white squirrel kept looking back sharply at them to see if they were following.

Edelle was lost in a haze of wonderment and slow, deep-settling worry. These white squirrels did not seem too keen to help her. Perhaps she should have expected as much, but they seemed untowardly hostile and it made her nervous. She kept thinking of the way Cumin had come up here and never returned, of the old stories.

Should have known, should have known, Edelle's mind jabbered. Somehow she had fantasized the white squirrels to be kinder, that they might feel some guilt from days gone by and listen to her plea. *And maybe they will. Don't get ahead of yourself Edelle, they didn't even hear you out yet. And you* did *seem to be spying on them…*

Somewhat comforted by this thought, Edelle wondered if she should not speak; she had been told to be silent, so it was likely best to wait. The way Lute had looked at her, mouth agape, when she had simply asked to see their leader suggested that he thought her insane to have been so bold. Well, let him think what he wanted; this was no coward's mission after all. She might have expected a former thief not to understand such sentiment. Lute was used to running, and Edelle was used to not having to.

Edelle thought suddenly of the picture of Astrippa hanging on her wall at home and lifted her head a bit higher. Up ahead, neither of the white squirrels had spoken to each other, the uneasy silence spreading out to affect their wards as well. Were all white squirrels so strangely distant, even with their own kind?

When they had passed through a significant number of pine trees, they came out into a clearing in the center of which stood one large, overbearing tree, its needled branches drooping slightly to the ground from the weight of snow, making them look like long, outspread arms, sadly awaiting an embrace that was never to come. The male squirrel whom Edelle had heard called Tiallin, stopped and whispered something to his female companion. She seemed to think, then shook her head and whispered something back to him. He stared at her a moment before nodding, glancing behind him at Edelle and Lute. Lute flinched, but Tiallin only turned back around and shrugged. They began to walk again, heading to the lone tree, and then up its wide, scratchy trunk. Edelle gauged from their actions that a decision of some sort must have been made and followed with a mix of curiosity and foreboding. She sensed Lute trying to make eye contact with her and stubbornly looked anywhere but at his face, not even sure of why she was doing it. She was not even angry with him anymore, but there was too much to concern herself with at the present moment. Would the white squirrels give her a chance to speak? She certainly hoped so—if not, she would have to force herself on them, and she hated to think of the results of such a move.

Tiallin and the female squirrel lead them down a wide, gaping entrance hall, dark and drafty and unwelcoming, and then almost immediately into smaller and more labyrinthine passages, which twisted and turned so quickly that Edelle felt herself getting sickeningly dizzy trying to keep her eyes on each new door she passed. She soon became sure she was seeing things that weren't even there, and shivered despite herself.

Get a hold on yourself. There's enough real danger as it is.

The admonishment made too much sense to ignore, and Edelle sobered herself just as the two ghostly forms in front of them stopped at a small unobtrusive opening to their right. The female pushed the door open a crack and went inside. Edelle and Lute made to follow, but Tiallin thrust out a paw, barring their entrance. After a time that could not have been more than a couple of seconds, he let his paw fall again to his side and vanished into the doorway. This time Edelle did look at Lute, who shrugged. Though they still had not said a word, it looked as if the white squirrels meant for them to follow.

Edelle stepped inside the room, not sure what to expect, but all she found was a few firefly lanterns set on tables and an old loom. The female white squirrel was running her paw along the wall at the back of the room distractedly, glancing back at them only now and again. Finally, she seemed to grasp at something invisible, and the wall moved aside. Lute jumped back, nearly knocking over a rickety table behind them. Tiallin had come around behind them and was now standing with his back to the door.

Blocking our exit.

Edelle stared at the opening in the wall, but all she could see was blackness. The female white squirrel simply stared at them from her spot by the opening. Edelle shook her head.

"No." Her throat was dry, rendering her voice a tiny croak. The female narrowed her eyes, and Edelle heard the male, Tiallin, close in on them from behind. They were trapped. Gulping down the musty air, she closed her eyes and felt her heart hammer in her ears. Lute was already starting down the stairs beyond the opening. Edelle followed.

No sooner had they gotten on the other side of the door then it was closed, with a grating of stone, and she turned in a rush of panic to find only more blackness meeting her eyes. The white squirrels had gone, and all that was left for the two of them was the descent.

It was then that Edelle gave in. She had felt it coming on for a while now, but she had controlled it up until now, like every other time in her life since she had been five seasons and her father had left, left her alone with an infant brother and the uncertain promise of something beyond the life she inhabited and the mysterious smiling face of Astrippa upon her wall. But now at last it had won her over, the demon that she had created a tough exterior to avoid, pressing itself into her mouth like warm, lifeless cotton and choking her, clouding her mind until it was either go insane or let it out. The space where Astrippa had hovered so strongly in a field of certainty and promises taken for granted had blurred, the flame of unwavering belief and her scorn for others who did not possess it went out, and suddenly she understood those others all too well...

Edelle's next breath came out long and labored, choppy and retching. She held her sides, staring down at the place below her, where there might have been stone or there might have just been black, black like the pits of hell, down forever.

"No," she moaned in that breath, or she thought she was saying something like it. "No."

Yes, the tilting black seemed to smile up at her. *You knew it all along.*

Lute broke out of his own fearful reverie at the sound of a sob, so pitiful and full of a terror he hoped he would never encounter that it made his veins freeze in his extremities. He did not know where to turn at first until he saw, or rather felt Edelle waver on the step next to him, and reached out just in time to keep her from toppling down into the unknown.

"Hey," he whispered, husky and soft, astounded at how much his heart suddenly ached. "Hey." He wasn't sure she could even hear him--was the stiffening in her body because she resented his touch or because of something that was beyond her to control?

After a long moment, Edelle's body relaxed, but the relaxing was somehow more terrifying than the stiffness, for it felt like the victory of doubt, of the ultimate plight of one who has lost all pawholds. After several moments of this, standing in the dark holding her limp form close to his (how was it that she felt so light now?), Lute wondered if she had fainted. Then he felt her shudder again and realized she was crying.

"It's...useless..." Edelle whispered. "It's...just as I feared. I'm so...so scared. I k-knew it all along. No one's there."

"Someone will come. It's all right, hey, someone will come. This is just for now. Someone will come."

And though he had never felt the stronger of the two, Lute held her to him, letting the salty wetness of her tears seep into his fur, and waited out the darkness for them both.

CHAPTER XXII

"Where are we going?" Tiallin gasped, struggling to keep up with the no-nonsense pace Lyrah was cutting through the woods. They seemed to be headed to a part of the forest Tiallin had never explored before; he supposed Lyrah knew her way around like the back of her paw, what with all those times out with Zerrith in younger years. The thought of his brother at the present moment was unwanted, and he pushed it aside, fishing for something else to focus on. And there was plenty else: the prisoners they had taken, for one. Tiallin did feel bad leaving them down in the catacombs, but Lyrah had seemed so certain of it that he hadn't wanted to argue. They *had* been spying after all—he would have bet a great deal that they were somehow connected with Cumin and was not disposed to risk that point of view by letting them roam free. One of them had even asked to see Sirius.

Lyrah had wanted to show him something, and he supposed that was what she was about to do now, though he did wish she would speak. She'd been oddly silent the whole time—at first, Tiallin had simply put the blame on their hostages, for the finding of whom he had begun to feel rather proud. But now the hostages were safely behind stone walls and still Lyrah kept her peace. Yet, he had been sure she was about to tell him earlier... Hopping over a fallen tree branch, Tiallin tried again to get something out of her.

"Lyrah, if you don't mind—"

Lyrah whipped around rather violently and put a paw up to her mouth urgently. She stood there frozen for a second or two, listening, then dropped to all fours and positioned herself so that she could speak into his ear;

Tiallin immediately became overly conscious of how close they were.

"While you were sleeping this morning, I remembered a place I'd been before, about two minutes' walk from your place. Last time I was there, we saw some others. I saw one again this morning, so I'm guessing some of them live around here."

Tiallin did not need to ask what she meant by 'others.'

"We?" Does that mean you were with—

"Yes, I was with Zerrith. He talked to some of them, then. Like he'd done it before, only in passing, and they seemed friendly enough, if distant, maybe a bit snobbish. There was a certain squirrel among them, though…oh, I doubt he'd be here now. The others didn't take to him too well."

"If they're friendly, why're we being so quiet?" Tiallin asked, perplexed.

Lyrah looked at the ground as though it had suddenly become very interesting.

"Well, they were friendly enough to Zerrith. Like I said, it seemed like he'd come across these particular few squirrels before in his meandering. But they kept looking all suspicious at me, and I got to feeling uncomfortable. Zerrith took a while to notice, but once he did, he brought me back." She smiled wistfully at the memory, and Tiallin felt an inappropriate need to push in with something irrelevant, but his tongue grappled uselessly on the roof of his mouth before falling dormant again behind his teeth.

Instead, Tiallin stared around at the trees to either side of them.

"Lyrah?" he asked. "Do you have any idea how we are going to get them to listen to us?"

Lyrah smiled. "No. Not much at all. But I've got an inkling of something that'll just have to do."

Tiallin could not make himself feel as reassured as she seemed to be by this small comfort, and when they had gone a bit farther and caught their first glimpse of another body in the woods beyond, he found that his paws were shaking. Lyrah noticed too, and gave him a look which said very clearly to hide them. Tiallin complied, grasping both wrists in opposite paws behind his back until he had regained control of himself. For a moment it seemed as if whomever they had seen had gone away, until a branch creaked close by, bent under the weight of another.

Without a word, Lyrah scampered nimbly to the end of the branch on which they had been standing. He heard her make a surprised little sound, and she turned back to him, motioning impatiently now with a free paw.

Tiallin came and joined her in looking. At first he saw nothing, and wondered if she was having him on. Then he saw that her eyes were not focused on the ground at all, but on a low branch of a stout pine not three yards from where they sat craning their necks. On the branch were seated four ghostly white figures, huddled in a semi-circle. The way their heads nodded up and down every now and then indicated that they must be conversing with one another. Tiallin felt faintly foolish for staring so long at them, but he was so accustomed to only the few other white squirrels he knew that to see others, and so close by all along...it was amazing! He cast a subtle glance over at Lyrah, and was gratified to see that he was not alone; she too was gazing raptly at the group slightly below them. After a moment longer, she turned her head away and addressed Tiallin again.

"I'm going to go talk to them."

"Don't you think we ought to...?"

But Lyrah had already started over, climbing down the trunk of the tree rather than leaping in order not to startle the strangers into hostility. They appeared to notice her approach once she reached the base, stepping bravely over a twisted root poking out of the ground and stopping to meet their hard scrutiny. Tiallin's heart was pounding for her, and ignoring the pulling in his stomach, he followed the path she had taken and stood slightly behind her, refusing to look away as the gleaming sets of pink eyes took him in as well. There was simple surprise on some faces, suspicion on others, and on the face of one particularly elderly looking squirrel there was even something like anger. It was this squirrel who broke the silence that had fallen among them.

"Well now, what are you two young things looking at? It's rude to stare, don't you know."

The squirrel next to him, heavyset but possessed of kind features, placed a paw lightly on the old one's shoulder.

"Easy there, Katrank," he said firmly, speaking as one would to a favorite grandfather, a touch of playfulness about his mouth. "They are not doing us any harm. Hi!" he directed this last to Tiallin and Lyrah, and strode forward, keeping his air of friendliness but also positioning himself so that his bulk blocked out Katrank and the two others, nondescript, tall squirrels who could have been twins.

Lyrah stepped forward to meet him.

"Hello," she said. "I am Lyrah, and this is Tiallin Stormskiln. We don't live too far from here."

"Stormskiln, eh?" The paunchy squirrel looked Tiallin up and down. "You do look a good deal like your father. I know him a bit, by and by."

Tiallin didn't know what to say to this. He and his father had never been on the best of terms, and ever since he had begun to work for Sirius, they had grown even further apart.

"Er," Tiallin cast about for something to say to this. "It's nice to meet you, um…?"

"Dielnan." The large squirrel burst out with a hearty chuckle. "You're definitely your mother with the manners though, aren't you? A lot slower to speak, too."

Tiallin grinned. His nerves were quickly beginning to ease around this squirrel. Dielnan flapped a paw over his back at the three figures standing motionless and rather cold behind him.

"This is Loren and Hael," he said, indicating the tall look-alikes. They continued to stare impassively at Tiallin and Lyrah, which made Tiallin wish Dielnan would stand in front of them again. "You've already meet Katrank."

"Are you all family?" Lyrah asked.

"Family? No, no. Katrank and I do live next door to each other. Loren and Hael…well, we've only just met them. Recently, Loren was injured by a—"

"Yes," Loren said, his voice smooth and clipped, and Dielnan trailed off awkwardly. He looked at Tiallin and Lyrah, and, perhaps to cover up for this faltering moment, spread his paws wide.

"So what is it that we can help you with? Since you've told us you live close by, it can't be that you're lost."

"It could be that they were sneaking," Katrank said, still sounding testy at being disturbed.

"We weren't sneaking," Lyrah said quickly. "We just want a word with you."

"About?" Even Dielnan looked reluctant now.

But Tiallin turned to Katrank. "Katrank, you could probably be of the most help to me here. Were you around in the rule of Tamen?"

Katrank blinked, then snorted with apparent indignation. "Of course I was around. Seven seasons I was, when I was inducted into his service. It was a great honor."

"And, er, did you…like him?"

"*Like* him, boy, where are your brains at? I loved him." His expression went grave as he added, "Tamen Nunquil was the best ruler we have ever seen. Sirius was a big follower of Tamen's principles, at least at first. He…had a different way of dealing with things, though. Just a while back, he locked up a squirrel, name of Zirreo, because he was spreading around that white squirrels were no different than any other kind. Granted, that's blasphemous in ways I suppose—I certainly wouldn't entertain the notion—but Sirius locked the guy up in one of the back rooms in the Great Tree, and well…they say he's still got him imprisoned there, if he's alive. It's that kind of stuff that gives squirrels mixed feelings on Sirius, they tend to go thinking he's unstable, that he no longer stands for anything his predecessor believed. Reasonably speaking though, it may not be all Sirius's fault that the end of Tamen seems to have marked the end of our community…like I said, it isn't like he didn't fight for it. Tamen's a hard act to follow, even if he was wrong..."

"Who's to say he was wrong?" Tiallin butted in. Lyrah turned to him, surprised, and from behind Dielnan and Katrank he could see Loren or Hael raise an eyebrow slightly. Ignoring this, he pushed on, giving himself no time to think on what he was saying; he was not even sure what had made him speak out in such a way, and to pause to ponder would be to lose his nerve.

"Tamen preached the idea of a special type of salvation for us white squirrels, a way that we could be brought back to the position of Astrippa's messengers and to be released from this earth."

"We know, boy. Go on," Katrank waved a paw impatiently.

"Well, that means of salvation was becoming united with other types, other races of squirrels. That's what Tamen believed, and he followed this well. Well, what if we've got to be united among ourselves as well? We were on the way to this during Tamen's reign." Tiallin half expected someone to call him out on this, to remind him that he had not been born until after the reign of Tamen, but no one said a thing. All eyes were trained on him.

"Things broke apart with Tamen's disappearance. I understand that none of us were there personally for the end of it all, with the exception of Katrank. What we know, we know from our parents, or from what history would tell us. Most accounts say that Tamen was mistaken because we were not given wings and ushered back to some other world we can barely remember. But we were scattered after the reign of Tamen, mistrusting not only all the squirrels of color who had begun to live harmoniously with us, but ourselves and one another as well, and most of all Sirius himself." A couple of the listening squirrels averted their eyes at this.

"But here is what I think," Tiallin said, his voice rising with his growing conviction. "Maybe the conditions for salvation were never quite fulfilled. For even back then, as hard as Tamen worked to build a perfect community, there was poison amongst us. Someone who was not desiring of peace, or respectful of tradition. Someone who wanted power above all else. Someone who would have done anything to achieve that power...even kill a well-loved king." He looked at Katrank again. "Do you recall the name Cumin?"

A sharp intake of breath and a nod later, the old squirrel had dropped his crusty exterior. "Yes, I do remember him as a matter of fact. Not a very nice type towards me, acting as though the few seasons he had on me set him apart by a hundred leagues. But a lot of others liked him. I don't understand, though…" he gave Tiallin a quizzical look. "He was only an orphan."

"I have something to tell you," Tiallin said. "And it is imperative that you believe me."

Dielnan's mouth was working nervously and Loren and Hael even had the decency to look faintly interested when Tiallin finished relating Sirius's story to them and the danger he believed they now faced from an unvanquished and dangerous enemy.

"So… what can we…I mean…" Dielnan looked awkward for a second before saying, "Well, oughtn't we leave, then? I mean, it's all very well and good and I'm deeply sorry that Sirius is in danger, but it doesn't concern us."

"You're wrong there," Tiallin said sharply. Catching himself, he closed his eyes and willed his blood to cool, to quit its sudden mad race to his face. "Can't you see, it's you who have really killed Tamen! You and me, and all of us! Sirius believed in him too, our king was never the enemy! If we get more white squirrels and band together, we can meet whatever is coming and defend Sirius and avenge Tamen's death by defeating his murderer. Then perhaps we will prove ourselves redeemed, worthy of Astrippa's fabled gift. But yeah, I guess it's up to you." He shrugged jerkily. "Either grab your last chance to be selfless, to get something grander than you could ever imagine, or live to be old and remember running away and letting Tamen's ideas die with the last king."

Lyrah moved ever so slightly next to Tiallin, and he felt her discomfort. For once, he did not feel the same; he was not the insecure one. He had broken all his promises, spilt all his secrets; he had stood here and spoke harshly to those who could kill him, outnumber him if they chose. But he had kept the most important promise: he was serving his king. Let them do what they would.

Old Katrank was the first to move. He looked up from the spot he had been staring fixedly at on the snow beneath him and brought his eyes to meet Tiallin's challenging stare. His voice shook as he spoke.

"I will defend against this danger with you, Tiallin Stormskiln. These days, any day might be my last day. I would like to spend it doing something I will be proud of. That Tamen would be proud of. I'm sorry to have misjudged you."

Tiallin expected someone to step up and challenge him, but Dielnan was nodding his head slowly, resolutely, and Hael suddenly spoke, her voice surprisingly soft.

"We will do this, too."

It was more than Tiallin could have hoped for. He opened his mouth to thank them all, but Loren cut across, still cool and reflectively distant.

"We know where a lot of the others live now. Come with us, and you can tell to them what you told to us."

Tiallin obeyed, but as they turned to follow the lithe form of Loren, he could not keep from looking at Lyrah any longer. He was concerned that she might be angry with him for taking over from her, that he might have ruined her plans. But when did look, she was looking back at him; her expression was nothing he had expected, and judging from the way she quickly looked away again, he knew he wasn't supposed to have seen. Of one thing he was certain: there had been nothing disparaging in that glance.

When Tiallin walked back to his house that evening, he felt like a different squirrel. Together he and Lyrah and the others had convinced a large number of white squirrels—nearing thirty all told—to fight alongside them should danger come. And though he had spoken of this danger as a possibility, he knew it to be a certainty. The feeling was still there, the almost instinctive crush of dark coiling around his thoughts, ever present, so close. He did not know whether the feeling came from the inexplicable bond Sirius had placed him under; it didn't really matter anyway. It no longer frightened him. He supposed that might be the difference in how he felt now: he was no longer frightened. But it was more than that too—it was as if a heaviness, a great part of him had winked off into some other dimension, leaving him clear-headed and decisive. There was nothing left to hold him down.

Coming around to the pine he called home from a different angle than that to which he was accustomed, Tiallin's gaze fell on a familiar upper branch, now visible from this fresh perspective. Where the branch came to meet the trunk was hidden from view, making it appear as though it were reaching out into the sky, slowly pulling away from the pine's possession on it, shaggy limbs dipping down amid the pink and orange hued sky to touch the setting sun. Atop the branch, a figure he knew too well sat very still, faced away from him, tail relaxed out behind him, resting level with the wood. It was then that Tiallin felt a very small pang in his chest, a feeling that was like hunger and yet not at all. Shaking it off, he continued inside, resolving to tell his family what he had told the others the very next day for he was exhausted beyond belief.

CHAPTER XXIII

Edelle shivered. In the darkness directly below her she could see the stairs, but only a grand total of two before they disappeared into the black. Her eyes had to work even to see these, for the shimmer of light that dispelled itself from an uneven chink in the rough stone edges of the door was weak and inconsistent.

But there was a light. It had been a day, or two, or possibly three—it felt impossibly long—since they had had contact with anyone else. The outside world felt so distant now that she was almost indifferent to the thought of it. Her only aspiration for some time now had been to get the white squirrels to take mercy on her colony. Now they had locked her up and very likely left her to starve without waiting for an explanation of her presence; to believe such creatures capable of mercy was naïve to an extreme.

So, her mission ended in failure, her anger and fear having succumbed to the uncaring company of the stone around her, she waited. Lute was waiting too, but she did not think he was as calm as she was now—she knew it, she could feel his nerves burning away in silence next to her. For Lute, it would be a waste to die. Death would only be saving Edelle from having to witness the death of so many more...

They took their meals on the step between them. During one such time, Lute had suggested they go farther down, explore to see whether there wasn't some hidden way out of their enigmatic cell, but Edelle had stomped on the idea immediately. One of them could too easily fall and never find their way back up again—and who knew what was awaiting them down that flight of stairs? For she was sure in a prison of this design, the idea was to eventually get the prisoners to stray downward and be lost forever amid whatever gruesome torture implements existed below.

And so they had stayed in the very same spot for days, quietly wondering how long they could also stay sane and knowing that if they moved too far from the door they would be lost forever. There was no light, no one inhabiting the room beyond, no beacon, however small, to guide their trembling paws back.

Until now.

"Do yew see that?" Lute whispered cautiously, voice a bit rusty from keeping silent for so long. The small light caught his profile and she squinted at it.

"I do."

A noise issued, soft and clunking, from the other side of the stone. It was barely audible but it made both squirrels stiffen.

"Get to the side," Lute hissed, and before she could even manage to feel resentful of his instruction, he pulled on her arm sharply. She moved over.

"Someone's coming in."

Lute and Edelle stood on the uppermost step, just out of range enough so if the door were to slide open they would remain in shadow. Lute was right. Edelle was stunned—was someone coming to get them at last? A short series of muffled bumps and then a moment of silence passed before the grating of stone upon stone sounded, slow, deathly slow, as if whoever was on the other side were trying to keep quiet. The yellow orb of a firefly lantern poked through the opening, the paw holding it barely visible to them from their hiding spot. Despite her earlier thoughts of doom and gloom, Edelle's heart sped up.

The squirrel in the doorway moved inward at last, down one step, then two. The light from the upheld lamp cast its glow over the newcomer's face, and Edelle experienced a brief moment of confusion.

The old gray squirrel bobbed his head from side to side and shook his lantern to encourage the captive creatures within, then began to move ponderously down another couple of steps. In his paws there was a length of string which he continually fondled, muttering under his breath. His words were either too low to hear or not words at all. Lute and Edelle turned to one another simultaneously. It was frightening, the chances of being caught were ninety to one, but if they did not act now, they would be trapped here forever. With renewed inspiration, Edelle eyed the square of openness illuminated by the lantern light which was slowly receding and grasped Lute's paw. On this signal, both squirrels darted out from their shadowy cove and through the opening into the next room in which Edelle could just barely make out the shape of the loom and the tables they had passed on their way in. She paused only for a second to give thanks to Astrippa that the gray hadn't turned and seen them before running in tip-pawed trepidation to the door of this room, also left agape, and through into the hallway beyond.

Which way, which way did we come in? She wracked her brain for the answer but it did not come. Lute appeared at her side, breathing quick and exhilarated.

"C'mon," he said, and made the choice effortlessly for her, taking a left, his near-black, thin body melting into the dark. Edelle followed without question or argument, every ounce of her being focused on getting out of this place.

She hadn't gone a yard further, however, when she ran into Lute again.

"Why did you stop?"

"Edelle—there's a door here! It's small, but it's open a bit and I can see through and cripes, it looks incredible! The walls…"

Her incredulous look was lost on him in the dark.

"Lute, we need to get out of here! At any second, someone could—

Lute's mouth tugged upwards in a roguish grin.

"What else could happen to us? I'm just going to check it out real quick-like."

She opened her mouth to cut him off with some derisive remark, but she stopped herself. Cumin hadn't run away all those years back, why should she? If they were caught she would simply make sure she got a chance to be heard out before she was dumped once again in their prison…then, maybe then, she would try the stairs. The old gray squirrel seemed to know where he was going, so perhaps it was not torture that had awaited them after all. The gray's appearance confused her, though—she hadn't thought white squirrels would associate with grays…

"I don't think there's anyone in there…" Lute said, in reference to the door in front of them. A scratching, as of someone walking on wood, sounded off down the hallway, and made them both jump. Lute pushed open the door a moment after and boldly stepped through. Edelle stood behind him on the other side, half expecting a shout or a loud noise of some kind, but when all was silent it became clear that Lute must have been right.

"Move over," she hissed at Lute's back, for he was standing immobilized in the way of her passage.

"Oh…sorry. Edelle…look at…just look at these walls."

The *walls?*

And then Edelle was inside, closing the small door behind her for good measure, and she saw what he meant. *The walls*, indeed.

Whoever had carved all of the intricate depictions and scenes she saw before her must have had a skill far greater than most, to say nothing of a patience beyond comprehension. Small pricks of wintry sunlight had filtered through the cracks in the lofty makeshift ceiling, alighting by chance on one or another of the carvings and drawing her attention to them; she would stare at one fixedly before moving to another. Here, squirrels were pushing a boat down to a raging swell of river, or sea…here, a giant fly-dragon was being slain by a crowned elder…it seemed to her that the walls were talking in muted excitement, each panel with its own story to tell, and if she only knew how to listen she would find the stories just as real as anything else.

Lute seemed even more engaged than she. She would not have expected a thief to care for such things, but he stepped closer until he was standing right in front of the wall, lost in a sort of trance. Edelle tore her gaze away and walked around the perimeter of the grand room. What kind of place was this? The air spoke of not years but centuries, and the very atmosphere was filled with a calm anticipation, the hundred blank raised wooden eyes at its perimeter all silently confirming her thought. Here was a platform, a slightly raised portion of the floor on which a table rested, a simple thing in the vast openness. Her eye caught on a covered object, a bulk lying beyond the platform and Edelle moved to it as if pulled by some gravitational force, unthinking. Placing a paw on the top of the canvas, she seemed to think for a moment before pulling it off and letting it fall to the floor…

In front of her now stood a throne, carved in a very similar manner to the walls around them. Edelle could not spend forever looking at this however, for her mouth had gone dry and her tongue felt stuck to the roof of her mouth. On her first attempt to speak, she failed and had to start over. Lute heard the funny sound erupt from her throat and turned, an odd mist clearing from his eyes as he noticed the mingled awe and horror in her expression.

"Lute, I think we're in the king's chamber."

CHAPTER XXIV

Tiallin woke to an unpleasant impact in his side and a burning sense of urgency, the latter of which sent him tumbling out of bed in a mess of twigs and wool blankets. Lyrah's face swam before his bleary eyes and it took him a moment to recognize the image as something familiar. The open fear in her eyes coerced him out of his disorientation much quicker than her hitting him had.

"What, what?" He found that between the words it was hard to draw breath, and now he could feel the faint tugging, the tingling that signaled his bond with King Sirius...

"Someone's coming, Tiallin. I saw them! They're marching toward the Great Tree, there's a lot of them, I couldn't waste time, I've already told everyone to get bows from the armory. Tiallin they look big!"

"Big?"

Tiallin was up and running for the door. Lyrah followed.

"They were right there, just over the horizon. We knew they'd come of course, but not now, we're not ready...oh, Tiallin, it's too soon. It's just too soon."

Tiallin stopped his mad dash down the stairs and turned to face her, taking her paws in a fluid, sure motion that shocked some inner part of him. Mastering his voice, he said, "No. It's not. We'll be ready."

He stared hard into the deep velvet red of her eyes, daring her to believe. A flush crept over her features and, at a sound from downstairs he whipped around and began to rush forward once again. Tiallin had almost reached the door when a blur of fur shot across his vision and he found himself facing Iskla. His mother was terribly pale; she did not look herself.

"Tiallin, I need to talk to you."

"Mother, I can't do it now," he said, trying to slide past her. Lyrah looked strained and apprehensive, but Iskla did not seem to register anyone else in the room but the two of them, mother and son, even as another motion from beside the kitchen table told him of his father's presence as he joined them, tense and brooding.

"Where's Zerrith, Tiallin? Where is he?"

Tiallin blinked. "Zerrith? I thought-- But Lyrah was shaking her head.

"No, he is gone, Tiallin. I checked, briefly, before I went to get you because..."

Tiallin turned from her and she had the sense not to continue.

"He's gone, Tiallin, and so is that thing of his he was working on!"

Tiallin stopped fighting for the door for a moment, trying to register the oddness of the statement. Even now, Zerrith was off in his own little world...for the first time, he felt a burst of something like real hatred for his brother.

Iskla was looking back and forth between he and Lyrah now, her eyes desperate.

"What thing? What is he working on? You need to tell me what's going on, Tiallin. I *know* something's not right, don't try to tell me it's not—"

"Mother, I can't explain now, I've got to go! We'll all be in trouble if I don't, I promise I'll come back and—"

"You're not going anywhere."

The unexpectedness of the deep voice took Tiallin by surprise. His father had crossed the room to stand in front of him in a few strides.

"It's for him, isn't it? Whatever you're doing? You've been his squirrel ever since you started working for him. Or perhaps I should say, *under* him. He's been making you do things all along, hasn't he? You're not loyal to anyone but him anymore, and I know it. He's poisoned our family, he's poisoned this colony—

"*Datin*," Iskla warned, but Tiallin's father merely jerked his head in her direction to silence her.

"He wants everything. Damn it, Iskla, you should know. First it was you, he wanted you for your *gifts*, he thought you had something. When he couldn't get you, he went for Zerrith, he thought Zerrith might have *had* something too...don't tell me you don't remember! A *spark*, he called it, said he *sensed* it, thought Zerrith might even be his *heir*! And now, now he's gone for Tiallin."

Face twisted in anger, Datin grabbed at Tiallin's arm, hard, and held him there just feet from the door and freedom. "Well, Tiallin's *my* son too, and he *hasn't* got it, that I'm sure of."

"You're raving." Iskla's voice was cold.

Ignoring this, Datin turned his full attention to Tiallin, shaking him by the arm. "What does he want you for?"

"Let go of him, Datin."

"He wanted you, Iskla, he would have taken you from me—

"I would not go." Iskla's voice was like ice. "You're assuming I would have gone."

And then something happened that Tiallin did not understand: suddenly Datin gasped and stumbled back, though nothing visible had repelled him. His grip slipped from Tiallin's arm; Tiallin knew he should run, but he could not will his feet to move somehow. Instead he continued to stare at the scene in front of him, at the two squirrels he had once kidded himself into believing he knew. Iskla's eyes were gleaming with anger and then she was gone, out the door. Lyrah, Tiallin suddenly saw, was also gone; she must have left, snuck out some upstairs window. He thanked Astrippa for that, hoped that she had been able to get their brigade ready in time for whatever was on its way. It was only when Datin rose unsteadily to his feet in a way that suggested he had had too many Dew Frosts earlier and stumbled toward Tiallin, eyes glinting madly, that the latter was able to unglue his feet from the floor and run for it.

As he dashed away across the frozen ground, Tiallin only glanced back once to see his father standing at the door, backlit by the light from inside, leaning out as if he were too tired to go any farther and bellowing at the top of his lungs.

"Iskla! Come back! ISKLA!"

Tiallin went faster.

When he reached the Great Tree, he saw them there: all of those who would be fighting for the colony of the whites. For a while, as Tiallin panted up to them and fell in alongside Lyrah at the head of the crowd, it seemed as though they had a chance, and a queer sensation of being far away, as though he suddenly knew with certainty that he would look back on this day someday in the future as just another thing survived. He was a bit surprised but gratified to see old Katrank up front in the ranks, clutching a sharp wood spear tight, his lips set in a grim line as he eyed the horizon. Hael, Loren and a few dozen others spanned out directly behind him. They had come against the rationality of their solitude, they had come for one common purpose. A pride in his own kind awoke in Tiallin, and he thought of what Katrank had said about the one squirrel who had said the whites were no different. It seemed degrading and low in that moment, that they should be no better than their spiteful attackers that he knew he could never make himself accept it. And then Lyrah nudged him in the side, whiskers aquiver, and he followed old Katrank's gaze out over the horizon. At last he saw them, and a great fear blossomed in the region of his stomach, eclipsing any of his former excitement.

The enemy was not only big, but there were a lot of them, and they were coming on fast. He was handed a white hewn bow from somewhere beside him, which he accepted, never taking his eyes off of the group approaching him. They were fox squirrels, he saw that now. Large, well-muscled and coming relentlessly near, now he fancied he could see the glint of hunger in their eyes. Was it history repeating itself exactly as Sirius had said? The thought of the King flashed across his mind in a jagged spark of worry. Where was Sirius? Tiallin hoped he would not come out—did he know what was being brought to his doorstep? He thought of asking Lyrah but knew it was too late. A voice from the sea of invaders carried to him across the still, cold expanse of sky.

"Beware, white ones! We are coming to end your lives!"

They were crazed, and as they got within sufficient range, Tiallin could see they had been suffering. He wondered at how they had had the strength to come this long way across Firwood, wondered even as anger was mounting inside him at this shapeless rabble, this hate-fueled mob.

"Curse you!" Tiallin shouted, raising his voice above their noise. "We have not done a thing against you. This is your last chance to turn and go home."

Another of the fox squirrels yelled out boldly, derisively. "Your magic doesn't scare us!"

A pike, long and deadly, came tearing through their midst without warning. A noise from behind Tiallin caused him to turn; Hael was standing, her weapon by her side forgotten in her shock, one paw clutching her shoulder in an attempt to staunch the flow of blood now trickling out from beneath her paw. Loren, in his place beside her, had eyes hard as stone. Picking up the pike, he snapped it wholly in two and flung the halves at the opposing side one after the other with astonishing force. One of the fox squirrels dropped and did not get up again.

Now they were within a couple of yards, and Lyrah lowered her voice to whisper in Tiallin's ear.

"We've got to lead them up into the trees. We're hopelessly outnumbered, it's the only way."

Tiallin nodded dumbly. Turning around, he called to the others to follow, trusting the ones nearest him to pass his message on. Then he paved his way through a compliant mesh of bodies and leapt a considerable distance up the trunk of a sturdy pine. He was halfway up when everyone began to get the idea and others started to do the same. Most among them had bows as their weapon of choice, and this way at least they could stave the fox squirrel colony off for a little while, perhaps deplete some of their number while they were still on the ground.

Situated high up in his perch, Tiallin shot down at the sea of squirrels he knew neither by name or face, trying not to linger on the brutality of what had become necessity. The cloud of squirrels swelled out into the forest, shouting angrily and began to throw javelins and spears up at them, some already leaping onto the trees and taking their chances at being struck down.

They all hate us, Tiallin thought. *They all hate us because they think we're starving them.*

Tiallin nocked another arrow onto his bow, sighted and let loose. He hit his mark. A fierce young fox squirrel not five feet from his branch fell thrashing to the ground where all further movement was thankfully stilled. He knew they had to do it, knew it was needed. But a tiny part of Tiallin still nagged him, quivering in the corner of his mind like a scolded child.

Would Tamen have wanted this? Truly?

But maybe there were things even Tamen could not have foreseen. After all, that was a long, long time ago.

CHAPTER XXV

Lute walked up and down the length of the walls in the great throne room, unable to halt his examination of each and every panel—what did all the images mean?

When the enormity of Edelle's declaration of their whereabouts had settled over him, any lingering doubt was swept from his mind on their origin.

"Edelle," he said, not knowing why she should care but needing to tell someone all the same. "This is what Pember did for the white squirrels. These are his carvings. Cripes…" he stared, transfixed.

Edelle came to stand beside him.

"This was all done by your...teacher?"

"Yeah. I'd recognize his paw anywhere." As he said this, Lute reached out one of his own paws and placed it lightly on the swelling of a carved boat in the panel in front of him. "S'mazing."

Edelle nodded, reverently leaving the beauty of the carvings to silence. From far off, she thought she heard the faint sounds of something happening beyond the walls of the tree. Lute, still staring straight ahead, did not seem to be hearing.

"He had something, he did. Pember had a…he had a gift."

This time the sounds of turmoil from outside rose in pitch, and Edelle knew there was no chance she was imagining them.

"Lute," she said sharply, "Lute. I need to get out of here. I think there's something going on outside. The king's not here, and I need to find him. I'm not going to hide anymore. The action is outside, and that's likely where I'll find the king."

Lute, whose sight up until now had been continually locked on the carvings, turned to her finally.

"What d'yew mean?"

Instantly, she tried to quell his unease.

"Don't worry. I won't ask *you* to do anything. You're more than welcome to stay here, but I've had this weight in my chest ever since I left home. I want it relieved. I want it relieved now. If the king isn't going to find me, I'm going to find the king."

Lute was fully attentive to her now. His mouth felt strangely dry, and he had to wet his lips twice before speaking.

"Yer not leaving me here. Wait--! Don't go, this is stupid, you're not going to—"

But he knew it was no use. She had already turned her back and was heading for a large set of double doors, more obvious than the one they had come in through.

Following her to them and then through, he found they were standing in some sort of entrance hall, and the chill nip of the air here could only mean they were close to being out at last.

...Right out the front door and into the arms of the enemy. He felt as though he would throw up in his mouth, that if Edelle could only read his thoughts she would turn around immediately at the fear he felt. *More for her than me*, he realized, and was this what it was to be brave? To not fear for oneself, but fear double for the ones you loved?

Love?

Good one, Lute boy.

The opening to the outdoors came up before them, small and surprisingly unimposing. Edelle stuck her head out but did not go any farther. Hoping against hope she had changed her mind, Lute knew as well that this was an impossibility with Edelle and that her hesitation probably meant there was something worse outside than that which they'd left inside.

Worse. How could anything be worse?

He got his answer not a second after, when he peered out himself. A sea of white squirrels lined the branches outside, the nearest ones only a yard or so from them so that Lute was at once afraid of being spotted and fired upon. Indeed, they were all armed with fearsome weapons, ivory bows and arrows. Sitting as they were on the frozen snowy branches, the only thing not cloaked in white seemed to be their eyes, glinting red as poison berries.

But Edelle was looking down, and when Lute followed her gaze he saw that the white squirrels were not the only ones up in arms. A whole parade of fox squirrels, squirrels just as large and burnt red in color as Edelle, were circling the trees in which the white squirrels perched, some beginning to climb rage emanating from each movement of their powerful limbs. Then Edelle spoke, her voice filled with wonder.

"They're at war."

Lute didn't know what it was that made him want to laugh at the most improperly horrible of times (*It's 'cause yer a loon, Lute boy,* Saecka's voice echoed at him from his mind), but laugh he did.

Luckily Edelle did not seem to hear him, and when she spoke again he fully understood her awe.

"That's my colony."

But even these wide-eyed revelations were not enough to prepare them for what they would witness next.

Tiallin paced the branch on which he stood, throwing a desperate glance over to Lyrah, who was busy defending the tree next to him. He knew they should start moving to one side, to attempt to lead the fox squirrel clan away from the Great Tree, but they were quickly becoming surrounded, and there was hardly enough space between them and the enemy to abandon their weapons long enough to execute such a move. The fox squirrels were climbing the trees to all sides of them, and spread out as the others were, Tiallin got the sense that the whites had fallen into a trap, that they were being surrounded. He watched a few of the fox squirrels scale a clump of close-growing pines in an attempt to get level with him, and as he waited for the squirrels in question to reappear closer to him, sighting his bow as he did so, something entirely unexpected greeted his ears from the very spot he was focused on. It was a voice, a voice he knew very well, speaking in an indignant tone of oblivion.

"Watch it, you're going to scare her! She's my creation."

Out of the corner of his eye, Tiallin saw Lyrah turn in the middle of grappling with a foe, her eyebrows raised in incredulity. She had heard it too.

Only a moment later, Zerrith stepped out onto a long branch under the naked, cold sun, and he must have realized at last what it was he had walked into, for he looked around, first at Tiallin, then Lyrah, then the numerous others, all of whom had paused to stare back up at him.

But they were not staring at Zerrith alone. As Tiallin's older brother took a few more steps out into the open, so did the thing behind him.

The Byrd was gigantic. It walked with an odd hop-skipping motion, its legs appearing scaled and grotesque in the unflattering waning of the winter daylight. The sun slid behind a cloud and the Byrd, feathered and massive, sharp-beaked and clawed, surveyed them all, its orb-like eyes flat and wary. Without warning, the creature let out an unholy sound, a shriek which caused several squirrels to drop their weapons and huddle in terror. The Byrd cocked its head, turning toward the movement and clicking its beak. Its multicolored plumage puffed up menacingly, as if to mirror its creator's indignation.

It's real, it's real, oh Astrippa, it's alive.

Tiallin wondered faintly through the screaming in his mind at this immense power that had been kept a secret for far too long. Sirius had suspected it…he had wanted a magical heir…

And then someone, Tiallin could not see who, let a spear fly at the thing. As big a target as the creature presented, the thrower was clearly frightened out of his mind and his unsteady paw failed him; the spear went whistling past the Byrd's rounded head, harmlessly clattering off of a tree behind where it stood. Tiallin could have sworn in that instant he saw panic in the creature's eyes, a familiar emotion in the demeanor of this thing that should not even exist. Zerrith drew himself up beside the Byrd, anger flashing into life in his eyes.

"Don't you dare—you have no right to—

Then a lot of things happened all at once. Someone, a fox squirrel, lurched forward suddenly with the intent to attack. The Byrd shifted, growing ever uneasy and Zerrith stepped in front of it, bringing a paw up to its neck in a protective gesture. But the Byrd had had enough. In that second, it turned in a mad flash of feathers and color, deadly sharp beak slashing downward in one single savage stroke. Tiallin watched as his brother, gored on the spot, gushing blood, stumbled backward, just keeping balance on the branch. Zerrith teetered only a moment, just long enough to bring his paws up to the gaping wound in his chest, his expression one of puzzlement, before he toppled over, losing footing on the slickness of his own spilled blood to fall downward. He died before he hit the ground, breaking his body on a protruding branch some feet below. Tiallin heard the crack only faintly in the pounding madness of his head.

Some of the squirrels craned their necks in the silence that followed to see below them, but the snow appeared to blur everything and the ground was so littered with debris that their efforts proved fruitless.

The Byrd was in a full-out panic now, hopping from side to side in a strange, savage dance, shrieking at the top of its voice, mournful and depraved. Tiallin, bow forgotten, stared into its flashing eyes and felt ill. But the nightmare was fated to end as quickly as it had begun. Someone from the perimeter of the battle scene, someone with a solid, unshaking paw had shot an arrow. Hardly any of the onlookers, frozen in fear as they were, saw it until it had completed its purpose. The arrow buried itself clean through the Byrd's neck at an upward angle, piercing the place where its brain would have been. Caught in the middle of another shrieking wail, the beast floundered for a second before its beady eyes clouded over in death. Slowly the claws eased their grip on the branch below, and it fell backwards, appearing oddly light and somehow fragile now with no carriage of life to weigh it down. The Byrd fell slow but deliberate, straight through the foliage below to join its maker.

Tiallin and Lyrah, frozen in place only feet apart, stood dumbly as the fighting slowly crept back into action around them. If it were not for the sheen of dark red covering the foot of branch nearby, they might have come to believe in a matter of seconds that the last two minutes had never happened at all.

From their place in the entrance of the great tree, Edelle began to back away slowly, trembling all over. She could not understand what she had just seen—what sort of creatures did the white squirrels have under their control, what strange and unwieldy powers? She could feel Lute watching her, frightened.

"Lute," she finally said. "I don't know whether I can go out there anymore. Something's changed, as ridiculous as that may sound. Things…don't feel right."

A bit of an understatement. She felt as though she were going to faint. The mysterious, god-like white squirrels were waging a battle with her own colony, but she did not feel as reassured by the presence of her fellows as she might once have been. Instead she felt small and scared and as if she were just now realizing she were part of something much bigger than herself and her own issues. Something it would be wiser to walk away from than to meddle in. But how could she, when she had come all this way?

Lute, sensing her total bewilderment, took charge.

"Look, er, why don't we just go back inside? It's just about deserted in there and now I guess we know why. Maybe we can think better away from all…all that," he finished lamely.

He was surprised and a bit dismayed when she didn't even begin to argue. The two of them turned and began to go back the way they had come.

Tiallin saw them leave from his vantage point up above, one gray—or black,

he couldn't tell from the distance—and one fox squirrel, and felt his blood, already gone cold, freeze in his veins like so much ice. He did not see how he had not thought of it before. They were in great danger.

"Lyrah!" he shouted. "Lyrah!"

Something in his tone must have conveyed just a bit of the urgency he was feeling, for Lyrah gave a mighty heave to the fox squirrel she was fighting, pushing her off the branch with what seemed extraordinary strength, or just the result of confused emotion. She was over beside Tiallin in a second.

"What is it, Tiallin? You look as though you're going to faint dead away."

Tiallin tightened his lips grimly. "I just might. I need to go, right now. You must stay here and hold everyone together. I think I've just figured out the rest of Cumin's plans. Oh, I've been so dumb."

He started out across the branch. Lyrah stood where he had been, confused, wanting to follow but perhaps granting him his way in light of what had just happened. He was thankful for it; he would need absolutely no delay if he were to get there on time. The gray squirrel who had attacked him days ago had asked about wards for a reason. All of this show was only a decoy, a distraction to keep them all busy while Cumin could get at the king. What a fool he was, fighting around out here with Cumin's manipulated lambs like it did any good when the real enemy might be—and likely had been for some time now—inside the Great Tree itself.

He just hoped he was not too late.

CHAPTER XXVI

Edelle dimly wondered where it was she was going as she retraced her steps, following Lute back through the chill, barren, entrance hall. Oh, they were going back to the throne room—she knew this, but beyond that there was nothing to aspire to, and life was a puzzling blank. She had come to save her family and her colony, but now her colony was here, in this very place, seemingly come to save itself. She hadn't wanted that. How could they hope to hold off the white squirrels? Numbers were nothing against the brutality of magic, and the stuff was tangible on the air here. She wondered if her grandparents were out there, and little Bench too, but the thought was nothing less than horrible and she closed her mind against it.

Edelle followed Lute through the large double doors without another thought—they would wait here. Wait here until it was all over-- and in her present state of exhaustion it took her a full two minutes to realize that they were no longer alone.

The figure across the room from them was standing very still, staring around as though lost. It took her even longer, and getting a bit closer to realize that she recognized his form, the curve of his cheek, the fine, tawny fur. How many times, after all, had she watched from somewhere hidden up above as he crawled over the branches of trees across the clearing back home? But now she remembered her last encounter with him, and on the verge of crying out bit her tongue. He had no reason to take kindly to her.

He had no reason to be in here either, she could not help thinking, when the rest of the colony was outside fighting—had he known she was here? She merely watched him for a while, moving neither forward nor back. She watched him stand by the small hidden door in the back wall and turn his head this way and that, and then finally, inevitably, he saw her.

He looked almost confused at first until she said his name. "Felix?" Breathless and soft, a question in itself.

His eyes grew wide and he took a step toward them.

"Felix? Who's Felix?" Lute spoke awkwardly loud, a sour note in his voice. But Edelle ignored him, suddenly bounding to close the space between she and the other young fox squirrel.

"Felix, what are you doing here?"

"Edelle, it *is* you. It's...you?" He still looked inexplicably disoriented, but now fear was evident in his tone, and he seemed to glance down, face slowly going white as his paws clenched at his sides.

"Of course it's me. But what's wrong? You look as though you've seen a ghost."

Felix half-shrugged and then stared back into her face pleadingly.

"I don't know, I think I might have. You—you're supposed to be—dead." His head shot up and he seemed to see Lute for the first time. "Him! He was the one! He—was supposed to have killed you! I thought—

"Sorry to disappoint you and all," Lute sneered. He had recognized the young squirrel at last; the memory inspired no fond thoughts.

"Edelle," Felix gasped, turning back to her. "Edelle, you need to go. Quickly. Oh, Edelle, I'm so sorry. So, so sorry.

Edelle only stared at him. "Felix?" She moved to put a paw on his shoulder and he jerked away violently.

"Go away, Edelle, you need to go. There's...there's been a mistake. I...I'm scared, Edelle. You need to go. Something terrible is going to happen."

Edelle snorted. "And it isn't already? I'm not going anywhere. Just last time we met you were begging me to stay." He flushed and she went on, louder. "You told them, didn't you? You told the colony where I was going after I told you not to! And after I told you—"

"No, Edelle." Felix was looking about wildly now, and she wondered whether his mind might be deteriorating. He was sweating and his fur was standing up at the nape of his neck. "No, Edelle, I thought you were dead, gone from me forever—"

"From you? I don't even know you!" Edelle screeched hysterically, aware that she was getting worked up for no reason. She grabbed Felix by the shoulders and when he tried to pull away, something flashed in his paw as it unclenched to keep his balance. Lute shot in front of her, bowling Felix to the side with the sheer force of surprise and taking the knife from him, holding it up to the light.

"I can't believe it," he croaked. "It was *you*. *You* killed Pember, didn't you, you filthy yellow creep!"

He dove at Felix, knife held in front of him, just as the big double doors creaked open behind them and Edelle turned, helpless to stop what was happening before her, to see their new guest enter the chamber purposefully and close the doors behind him once more.

The king of the white squirrels wore no crown upon his head to identify him as such, but Edelle knew at once that this was who he was; his tall, calm majesty was not at all belied by his slightly stooping form or the misty pink eyes that stared above them all at the wall beyond. From the scramble of movement at her feet, Lute let out a startled cry and pulled free of Felix, whom he had had pinned to the ground a second before. Edelle was so preoccupied with the king's presence at the door that at first she could not see what had caused him such alarm, but when she looked again at Felix, she saw.

Felix was changing. The flesh around his face began to pulse as though his very skin were alive and breathing, then to squirm, and finally, in a characteristic so nightmarish that Edelle could only stare in numb horror, too shocked even to scream or to throw up, it began to *tear*. Then Felix began to scream, and the sound filled the whole chamber, all-consuming, trapped, terrified. There was a sound of tendons snapping and flesh ripping, and the screams, the screams permeated everything, and when Edelle finally tore her gaze away her eyes went to the king once more. He was standing in the exact same place as before, head cocked as though he needed to concentrate to hear the sounds of Felix's anguish. She thought he looked faintly disgusted. Did he know what was happening right in front of him?

Then a worse thought came to her—was *he* doing it? Was it the king who was tearing Felix apart by magic for entering his chambers?

But then Lute said her name, and his voice was so unusual and small that she looked back again against her will.

The squirrel who was straightening up before her was no one that she had ever seen before, and nothing made sense until she saw the mess he was standing in—the mess of what had been Felix. This new squirrel was old and bent like the king, and one of his legs was twisted so that she could not see how he could be standing unless it was by magic of some kind. The sight of this new fox squirrel made her feel a deep, innate fear in the pit of her stomach like she had seen blackness itself inverted and found inside something more permanent and much less desirable.

Then the king moved from his position by the doors at last, just a step before he stopped again. A smile that held no trace of pleasure whatsoever twitched into being on the side of his face.

"I see you have made good your promise, Cumin. You have come at last."

Tiallin raced through the crowd of clattering, fighting squirrels, once or twice having to stop in order to throw someone off of him and take the defensive. He went through the mass of bodies like they were simply impediments put in his path to spite him, long blades of tough grass in a wild field, grass that could cut, could make him bleed—if he did not cut them down first.

And then he was up the Great Tree, up and through the entrance hole and still running. He knew the path by heart, and sure enough, here were the doors, solid pine looming up in front of him. He reached out for them before he got there, bringing his paw to rest on the grainy surface, almost halting for one final second before he pushed them inward and greeted the scene before him.

Edelle stood, looking between the white king and the other squirrel, the old one who stank of foul things and rot.

Cumin.

The name resounded within her; she knew that name, knew it well. It did not make sense to her—this could not be the same Cumin who was praised as the savior of her fox squirrel clan. That Cumin was long gone, dead…

"Sirius," Cumin said, and his grin was ghastly. "It has been so long. But we've done all our catching up, haven't we?"

Sirius's mouth did not move from the straight line he had set it in.

"Yes, it has been a while."

"Oh, Sirius, so few words," Cumin sighed. "Don't be so pretentious, you never were like that. Would you prefer it if we skipped straight to your demise?"

"You will not have this colony, Cumin."

"Oh, I don't want this colony, not anymore." Cumin's face twisted into an ugly sneer. "No, you see, you're not so impressive anymore. Ever since Tamen *left*—

But Cumin suddenly broke off, letting out a noise of surprise. He stumbled backwards several paces, head hitting the wall hard, and fell to the floor once more. Sirius spoke again, betraying no hint of the exertion this move had cost him. His words were cold and stiff.

"Do not speak of Tamen."

Cumin got up from the floor surprisingly quick, leering, and then closed his eyes, exerting his mind. Sirius was slammed backwards this time, with a force so great that Edelle was sure he must have been knocked unconscious. But a minute passed, and Sirius was back up again, visibly shaken and gripping the wall behind him for support. Cumin moved in on him, and as he did so the king of the whites slid along the wall away from the sound of his footsteps.

"Is that all you have for me, Cumin, after all this time?" Sirius mocked, even as he scooted one step away for every step his opponent took. But Edelle could see that the white king was winded; it was not a fair match—though they were both older than she could guess at, Cumin seemed to possess more energy, more power somehow within his withered frame, not to mention the simple advantage of the gift of sight.

"It's not all I have at all," Cumin chuckled darkly. "But I didn't know you wanted to see—aha—metaphorically speaking, of course—my best. I doubt you will really appreciate it, Sirius, but perhaps I ought to do it, just so there are no—He shot a look at Edelle and Lute, "interferences."

Cumin then did something so fantastical that Edelle thought she must be imagining things at first. He brought a paw up to his mouth and breathed upon it. When he slowly unfolded it, inside was a small, flickering flame. Cumin let the fingers of his other paw play over the dancing fire with no visible pain, then put his mouth to it once again and blew it to the ground. The result was tremendous. Roaring, deep orange burst up from the ground. Edelle jumped back, but the flames pursued an easy circle around the spot where Sirius and Cumin stood, closing she and Lute off. Sirius, feeling the heat a bit belatedly, was forced to come forward from the wall fast. Cumin continued to talk as though nothing had happened, as though the flames were not inching closer, growing higher every second. Edelle wondered whether Sirius could feel that he was being ensnared. With every step he took, the fire seemed to follow him, enwrapping him mercilessly in its licking maw.

"Learned some new tricks, Cumin?" Sirius said. "Magic is not something to be played around with so lightly. It was this that you could never understand, this that would have made you an ill-fit king."

"You have a throne I see, Sirius," Cumin said. Sirius's words seemed to have angered him but he was evidently trying not to show it. "That must be a new adjustment, eh? Last I knew you, you were still in that phase where you believed the throne actually *detracted* from the king. Not that it won you the popularity, the *love* you so desperately sought. Oh, but wait...that looks like Tamen's old throne. You *didn't*, did you? Getting materialistic in your old age?"

Sirius's brow raised.

"I have no idea what you are talking about," he said, and Edelle saw that it was the truth—perhaps Sirius believed the throne still covered, or perhaps he was truly unaware of its presence in the room.

"Salvation, Sirius," Cumin said. "It's what you preach, it's what Tamen preached. You white squirrels, messengers of Astrippa. Just waiting to get your wings and go elsewhere. Away from all that, away from us. The mission of the white squirrels. Oh, you and your white squirrels, how you have irked me. But as long as just one of you is alive, you see, you will keep trying to fulfill that damned fable like it's some prophecy; as long as you cling to this pathetic Pinewoods colony, your mission can continue, you can try all you like to live as Tamen said and get your reward."

"What do you want, Cumin? If you don't want the colony, tell me that." There was more than a trace of weariness in Sirius's voice.

"What do I want?" Cumin asked. "What do I want? Shall I show you?"

He closed his eyes as if to concentrate again, but this time no invisible shove came to push Sirius. Instead, the king's face went blank, his mouth drawn in a slight frown. He remained frozen and time seemed to halt for a time as his breathing grew shallow. Then, without warning he flinched backward. Sirius's paws went up in front of his face and he waved them around frantically in a pitiful motion of distress. Then he screamed, and Edelle knew she had never felt more for anyone than she did for the king in that moment.

"No!" Sirius screamed. "No! No! No!"

The flames around him were licking up the ground in front of him, and the heat pushed Sirius backwards, right into the throne of Tamen Nunquil. Straightening up, he gripped the arms of the great chair hard and tipped his head back, knocking it against the wooden throne hard, as though trying to rid himself of whatever nightmare vision Cumin had planted in his mind. Edelle watched helpless, all but forgotten in the corner of the great room, caught in the crumbling of a great era that had never been hers to know. She was vaguely aware of Lute sitting somewhere off to her right, staring blankly down at the knife glimmering on the floor feet from them. His eyes were distant, as though he did not truly see the scene being played out across the room from them.

The knife. They had forgotten that.

A desperate impulse flashed through Edelle's mind and she got up from where she was seated and went for the blade, praying she wouldn't be seen.

Tiallin thought at first that the flames were an illusion; they were everywhere at once, and there were squirrels he didn't know—wait, those were the two captives he had taken the day before, and how had they escaped? It didn't matter. Fire with no evident origin was surrounding a carved wooden throne, its majesty breathtaking and fierce, enveloped as it was in the destroying red glow. And upon the chair sat King Sirius, his image wavering in the heat like a vision. But Tiallin knew that this was no mere vision. This was real. As though he needed further proof of its reality, he heard a sound beside him, a muffled little cry, and saw his mother from the corner of his eye. His mother, Iskla, of all the squirrels to appear, of all to have followed him. He did not know how long she had been standing there, even though he himself had just arrived. Time made no sense here, in this chamber where the walls were devoted to history; time bent with the heat strokes made visible by the fire and made Tiallin feel like he might be sick.

"Surrender, Sirius," a chill voice spoke from next to the blaze. An old fox squirrel stood, twitching his tail lazily from side to side and smiling in an amused fashion that was at total odds with his voice.

"No!" Sirius screamed. "No! I will not!"

Cumin (for Tiallin knew it was he) seemed to grow bored, and clicked his fingers. The fire licked greedily up the throne and enveloped it at once, along with its occupant. From inside the blazing inferno, Sirius shouted one last time before the sounds he made were thankfully drowned by the cracking of the enchanted flames.

"I will not! I will not see!"

Iskla put her paws up to her mouth and held them there. For a while, her body swayed forward as though she would rush headlong into the fire, then she turned and put a paw on Tiallin's arm.

"Come with me, Tiallin...we need to leave this place."

But he was shaking his head.

"No, mother. I'm staying here. I'm staying because I'm going to kill *him*."

Iskla stared at him for a long moment, and tears gathered in her eyes. She nodded, turned and ran. He never saw her again.

Tiallin turned back around just in time to see Cumin heading for the back passageway.

No...you will not escape...!

With no plans in his mind on what he would do, with nothing to fill his head but mind-numbing shock and hate and a sense of loss so profound that he felt its pressure in his throat like bile, Tiallin gave chase. There was no way

Cumin could live to see another sunset, not after what he had done. A world which allowed that would be one not worth living in as far as he was concerned, so Tiallin threw himself rashly at the old squirrel while his back was turned in retreat, wrapping an arm about his neck and hanging on, pulling him downward...

Cumin let out a hiss of annoyance, and slashed out at him with a free paw. The supposedly crippled old squirrel possessed an inordinate amount of strength. He hit Tiallin across the cheek, and Tiallin dazedly felt the warmth of his own blood trail down his face. The fox squirrel took Tiallin by the arm and pulled him close. His breath smelled of rot and old things and burned just as the room around them burned, threatening to overtake them all....

And then Tiallin felt a burning within himself as well, sharp and excruciating. He cried out, and to his bemusement, Cumin staggered backward a step, staring at him a moment in confusion, and something that might have been fear. It was this expression that would remain fixed in his eyes for all eternity, for a line of red appeared suddenly at Cumin's throat and he fell as though pulled slowly through the air by the sheer force of gravity to land at the ground, at Tiallin's feet, bleeding freely.

Edelle brought the knife in her shaking paw down and let it drop to the floor. She stared at Cumin's body as though it were a puzzle she could not quite understand.

"I'm sorry," she said to Tiallin, but he thought he must have misheard her, for surely there was nothing to be sorry for...but then, before he could say anything back, the burning within him started up again so fierce that he squeezed his eyes shut against the pain and the red and the heat, hoping that the sound he was hearing all about him was his own screaming. When he dared to open them, when it seemed to have subsided again, the fox squirrel female was gone… the carved knife, lying slicked with blood, the light of the fire dancing hypnotically along its blade, remained as the only evidence of her presence. Then the pain took him again, and it was worse than ever before. He was going to burn inside before the burning without would ever reach him. Tiallin's mind began to fuzz over and his vision to blur, and it was only when he noticed he was seeing Cumin's body at a horizontal angle that he realized he must be on the ground. Tiallin raised his head but the burning persisted, growing ever more intense, in powerful agreement with the burning world around him, and then his head fell to the floor once more and he lost consciousness altogether.

"Tiallin! Tiallin, please wake! Oh, Tiallin…"

It seemed to Tiallin only seconds later that he opened his eyes to the absence of pain and the presence of Lyrah's face just above his own, tight with worry. The hall around them was still burning, the fire impossibly tall now, blocking out any hope of passage back through the entrance hall. How had she gotten here? Hadn't he told her to stay back?

"Tiallin…?" There were tears on Lyrah's face.

"He's…" Tiallin spoke, his voice a thin rasp. "…gone. He's…gone."

"I know," said Lyrah softly, looking down at the body of Cumin, dangerously close to being devoured by the flames.

Tiallin shook his head; she did not understand. He tried to speak through the heat, but it seemed to suffocate him, trivialize his every attempt to communicate to her what he meant, the new emptiness in his chest, his previously burning nerves now numb, the evidence of a connection broken, lost, never to return.

Sirius had let go.

"Tiallin, please don't be angry. I had to come back for you," Lyrah said, her voice breaking.

"The...battle?"

"As good as lost." She turned away a moment. "We tried. But we've come off worse, Tiallin. There were very few surviving when I left. I had to go back, though."

"I know," he cut across her gently, slowly picking himself up from the floor and moving up against the wall and away from the fire. "So where do we go from here, Lyrah?"

Lyrah turned from the wall, staring at the fire surrounding them on all sides, pressing in and scorching their fur. If they stayed a minute longer, they would start to burn from the heat of the air alone. She pointed at something behind Tiallin, and he turned, remembering the door as he did so. A surge of something like hope went through him, and he pulled it open, feeling the wood scorch his paw as he did so. He reached for Lyrah's paw and they went through together; not long after, the fire crept up to the threshold, the sounds of wood crackling and popping loud in their ears. In the covered passageway, they found an impediment they hadn't counted on—the thick gray smoke flowing into the hallway had no immediate means of filtering out of the tree. It was fast building up around them, stifling their attempts at breathing, so that talking became too much to risk. Tiallin tried hard to remember which way he had gone that day so long ago when he had been listening outside this very door, the day Sirius had brought him to service ...But there was not time enough to think, and Tiallin felt the smoke creeping treacherously between the cogs of his mind, slowing it. Offering a prayer to the ever-silent Astrippa, he at last chose the right, moving through the thickening air,

Lyrah behind him, silent and trusting. A loud snapping caused him to look back once; dimly through the smoke, he saw that the fire had spilled out into the corridor behind them, cementing their choice. Not saying a thing, but clutching one another's paws a bit more tightly, they kept going.

CHAPTER XXVII

When Edelle broke out into the noise and confusion that was the outside world, Lute close behind her, she felt a numb relief so welcome it almost brought her to tears. The chill air was no longer drear but a thing in itself symbolic of life, so when she looked about her and remembered, saw all the bodies strewn out on the ground below, she was merely confused.

Squirrels were leaping to and fro, spiraling up trees and leaping among them, the fire of a battle being brought to a close still high among them. But some were turning now to look toward the Great Tree with a question in their eyes. Edelle, who had not put enough distance between herself and the Tree yet, did not see what it was they were seeing. Recognizing the face of one of the squirrels who had turned, she called out to him.

"Jonip!"

His head whipped around and he did a double take. A friend of her grandfather's, Jonip had held Edelle on his knee during the long slow summers of days past. Now he looked simply weary, clutching his bow to his side loosely.

"Edelle Craswotch?" Jonip said uneasily. "Is that you? Is that really you?"

"Yes, it's me—But she broke off in alarm. "Watch out!"

The lithe body of a white squirrel had materialized from the foliage behind them, holding a spear aloft.

Jonip turned to face his attacker, and Edelle, acting on an impulse, shot between them. The white squirrel was so startled at this type of interference that he merely blinked at her for a moment. She took that moment to speak.

"Everyone needs to stop killing each other. There's been a terrible mistake, Jonip."

"What do you mean?" Jonip's eyes were narrowed; a born warrior, he was not taking them off the white squirrel for one instant.

"I mean that you were lead into this under false conditions. I'm not sure what's going on, but I know the white squirrels didn't intend us any harm, I *know* it, Jonip. You must believe me."

"They said that," Jonip replied evenly, his tone suggesting that he did not entirely believe it was true. "Before we attacked. But—

"It's true," the white squirrel who had risen to attack him said, and Jonip's eyes flew back to him immediately, glaring. "You've got that one thing right, at least."

"Now you listen to me, I've got you at the point of my—

"You've been deceived," the white squirrel cut across him heedlessly. "But then, perhaps so have we..." He stared out at the bodies of his fellows around them with a sadness and an anger so intense that Edelle backed up a step into Lute, who moved away mechanically, still lost in some reverie of his own. He was acting odd, she thought, but then Jonip spoke, before she could wonder more at Lute's odd behavior.

"Would you mind telling me then, *how* we are mistaken?" he asked the white squirrel challengingly.

The white squirrel looked away from the bodies on the ground and shrugged sinuously. "We were not the root of your troubles. The root of your troubles was among you and led you into war against us to achieve his own means."

Cumin, Edelle thought, and in the jumble of confusion in her mind, something began to clink into place.

But Jonip was looking to her now, suspicion high in his voice.

"Is this true, Edelle? How could anyone but a white squirrel," he laced the last two words with contempt, "possess magic so dark as to poison every bit of food in our colony's possession?"

Edelle could only shrug helplessly. "I don't know." But in her mind she had gone back to the king's chamber, seen the fire flow from Cumin's paw and encircle the king, heard him scream until the pain became too much for noise. "I don't know, but I do know that he did. I saw it. I saw everything. It was one of our own, Jonip."

Perhaps her face had betrayed some sense of her thoughts, for Jonip was looking at her carefully. "Edelle," he said. "What happened back there, in the Tree? Were you imprisoned?"

Edelle shook her head, not in denial so much as impatience. "I can't talk about that now, don't ask me to talk about it. Just round up those of our colony left alive and get them to stop, get this whole thing brought to a halt before we're all killed. Please."

Jonip looked like he might say something, then he only nodded once, and turned to leave. It appeared that most of the battle had spread out away from the Great Tree, for it was in this direction that he ran. The white squirrel sighed, and dropped his spear to the ground. Then he said, "If you wish, I could explain. If you want to hear. But I heard it from Tiallin first, so I may not have everything straight." He stopped, and looked around, beyond she and Lute. "Where is Tiallin? Was he in the tree with you? Is the king safe?"

Edelle felt a heavy weight settle over her suddenly, and she finally turned to look back. The Great Tree was smoking, heavy clouds of gray issuing from its openings, knotholes and doorways. The sinking feeling increased, for Edelle knew that if anyone at all was still inside, they were likely already dead.

CHAPTER XXVIII

Tiallin and Lyrah stumbled down the passages of the Great Tree, struggling at the same time to breath. The smoke had become almost so thick that they could not see one another clearly, though they were feet apart, and the unvoiced thought in both of their heads was becoming more and more persistent. *Wrong way.*

They had to find a way out. If they did not find a way out soon, they would perish, suffocate to death on the smoke and have their bodies be burnt away by the ravaging fire once it caught up to them. The fire was taking the Great Tree from the inside out, and they needed to beat it. But every door they came to was barred, locked tight, and unobtrusive. Surely not ways out…and several times the passage would split, and they would be forced to decide on the second, to take one turn or another, until Tiallin was sure they were lost beyond hope. But they stumbled on; when he stopped, Lyrah started, pulling him on, and they worked off of each other like this. He was disoriented, becoming dizzy with the fumes, by turns forgetting where he was and imagining that he knew where he was going and taking a sudden change in direction.

Lyrah knocked into him by accident and muttered an apology.

"Tiallin…we should rest."

There was nothing he wanted more than to say yes, to take her to him and rest forever.

"We're almost there, Lyrah," he reassured her, voice sounding cloudy and muffled to his own traitorous ears. Then he ran into another door; it was not locked, simply barred with a heavy piece of wood. His heart quickened. There was nothing for it. They had at last reached a dead end.

Tiallin began to grope, to pull at the piece of wood, cursing the ineffectiveness of his weakened paws and arms. Lyrah joined in and together they strained at the obstruction, conscious all the time of the heat growing at their backs. Sooner than they expected, the bar gave way, splintering as it fell to the floor, and the door swung inwards, dispelling them in an untidy pile in its opening.

The room they found themselves in was small and empty of any material comforts, giving it the likeness of a cell. Through the smoke that was already flowing heavily through, Tiallin made out the form of another squirrel across the room from them. He was young, and wearing an expression of ludicrous calm as he surveyed the new occupants of his space. The walls of the room held no escape, no way to the outside world.

"Please," Tiallin gasped, but the smoke and his tiring resistance to the heat would not allow him to form another word.

The young squirrel surveyed them a moment longer, then got up and seemed to walk away from them.

"No!" cried Tiallin, his vision dimming even as he reached out a paw, imploring. Lyrah shuddered by his side, face turned into his fur.

But the young squirrel did not leave. Instead, he knelt by the wall opposite them and whispered something that sounded faintly like a song Tiallin had heard somewhere, long before...it calmed him, and the corners of his mouth nearly curved up. Smiling, now? How could he be smiling now?

But something was happening to the wall; it seemed to shimmer for a moment before Tiallin's eyes; the young squirrel raised his paws and put them next to one another on the wall deliberately, then began to stretch them apart. A hole began to widen between his paws, a hole that looked out on sky and Tiallin thought he could feel the faint nip of the cool winter air on his skin. Lyrah made a small sound of contentment against his chest.

The strange young squirrel looked at them then. His eyes were intense but friendly.

"Come," he said. Then, "Hurry. I cannot hold it long."

Tiallin did not think he could rise at first, but he managed somehow, bringing Lyrah to a kneeling position beside him. They began to crawl together, each pausing to help the other up when they began to fall. The squirrel waited patiently for them by the hole he had made with his paws, which were still resting on either side of it like a frame. He must have felt the heat growing more intense, and Tiallin knew somehow that the fire was on the verge of entering this very room now, but the squirrel kept his silence and did not tell them to hurry again. When at last they reached the edge of the opening and felt the breeze ruffle over their fur, Tiallin drew on a new supply of strength and stood, taking Lyrah's paw in his and feeling her responding squeeze. Even as he felt a new energy flow through him, he turned back.

"Aren't you coming with us?"

The young squirrel only smiled, his face sad in a way that seemed beautiful beyond comprehension.

"I can only hold it open for you now. I cannot hold it open for myself," he said simply.

Tiallin knew that he should protest, but already Lyrah's feet were traveling through the hole and he was coming after, and then they were there at last.

"I told you we'd make it," Tiallin said, enjoying the feel of the soft breeze over his face, and Lyrah nodded against him.

"It *was* true," she said, after some time. They just stood there as though to ponder these words, letting the breeze play lightly with their fur.

They had forever, after all.

CHAPTER XXIX

For the third consecutive day in a row, Edelle did not remember where she was upon waking. Then everything fell into place, and she was overcome by joy and relief in equal measure all over again. If she never broke this new cycle of greeting the day, she would be happy with that. The past weeks had been such an ordeal, they had seemed like months really. She could hardly believe that she was on her way back home to Bench and her grandparents at last. Still, she could not help but dwell a bit upon the fact that their number had decreased considerably—the whole colony had come up to Pinewood, and only a sad score and a half straggled back. Over the days, she had forced herself to become acquainted with the losses, to devote time to remembering each one of them in a different shade of fondness.

Still, she supposed, the white squirrels seemed to suffer more still. Only a handful of them had survived the battle, and there was a certain sad guilt in knowing that they were truly gone, perhaps forever, their great tree burned to a hollow black shell, spectral and eerie in its clearing in the woods. That clearing had been a blessing, she reflected, or else the fire would have been allowed free reign over the forest.

The memory of such distant, mystic creatures as the white squirrels stayed imprinted in her memory, even as she went about her ritual of waking up, the mundane chores of washing her face in the stream they were camping by and breaking her fast on the food —the wonderful, delicious, mouth-watering food—taken from the homes of some of the more accommodating whites. They had insisted that they did not need it, had seemed anxious to be out of the area for good; most of them had even left before Edelle's colony had. There was a desperate sadness in their solidarity, something they shared but at the same time were kept from sharing between them. They had all left, and they had gone separate ways. The companionship they may have shared dissolved so easily, or perhaps their shame or their sorrow had torn them asunder, scattering them on the wind to an even more ethereal existence, fading to nothing over the years as slowly they would be forgotten in the minds of all the colonies of normal squirrels. Until their very existence itself might seem a question, or more a fable. Edelle pondered these things in broad daylight, her feet dipped in the stream.

She thought of King Sirius, someone she had never understood. Now she wished she had had the chance to know the mysterious king.

She thought of Felix, blinded in his love for her, and controlled by a power far beyond his comprehension, used as a vessel for evil. She wondered what he would have been like, what the real Felix was like, the one unpossessed by Cumin. In some other life, some other story, would she have fallen for him?

She marveled at the narrowness of her views, of how she had in her foolish piety, condemned again and again. She had continually thought the worst of each new face she encountered, never thinking twice about her flash judgments. She would change it. Or perhaps she had already changed. She would go home and appear the same to her grandparents and to Bench, who would squeal with joy when she picked him up and spun him around and went off to tell him a story with a plate of fresh berries by their side, evidence of a curse broken. But she would have changed, and her morals would be wiser, her tongue gentler, her spirit at peace. Since she had left the dark stairs on which she had been imprisoned with Lute, she had felt increasingly sure that the panic attack she had experienced then might finally be her last.

Lute. That was another thing.

The fact of the matter was, Lute had been curiously withdrawn ever since they had stumbled into the king's chamber and he had gazed upon the wall carvings therein. She had tried to talk to him, feeling guilty for her negligence during the battle; he had been a better friend to her than she deserved. But he would only answer in short sentences, as though he weren't interested in talking at all, and his eyes were almost always somewhere else, as though it pained him to look at her. After a while, this had annoyed her so much that she had ceased trying to draw him out, and had left him to whatever it was that preoccupied him so.

Still, she would have liked to say goodbye to him. When her colony had been ready to move on, they had waited for her as she searched everywhere, including the tree Lute had adopted as his place to sleep in the days after the battle. But he had not been anywhere she looked, and finally it had been time to go; she hadn't wanted to hold anyone up.

"Edelle, you ready to go?" The voice of Jonip brought her back to the present day.

"Yes," she said, feeling the tingling of longing intertwined with anticipation moving through her all over again.

Jonip smiled. "Good. It looks like if the weather continues to behave, we may get there late afternoon. Won't that be nice?"

Edelle grinned broadly. It certainly would. Of all the things to feel, she thought as she followed him to go rouse the others from their respite by the stream, there was nothing near as perfect as the feeling of coming home.

Far away, doubling back over the land to Pinewood, the Great Tree of the white squirrels stood like a spectral guardian over the rest of the surrounding forest. The Tree was completely black, hollowed and burnt, one whole half of it cracked away and dissolved to ashes, the passageways inside it destroyed, rendering the passages below ground inaccessible. The uppermost room, the former chamber of the King, stood empty, cupping the warm blast of sunlight that streamed downward on this most unnatural of winter days. Or almost empty, for there was a single occupant in the room, standing by the one remaining wall of blackened carvings, the series of which ended on a curiously blank spot, a square just big enough for one more.

Lute had noticed the space that day he had been here with Edelle. He had wanted to point it out, but there had been too much else to do, and anyway he doubted she would have cared. She had gone; he had realized this a couple of days ago when he came down at last from working. He would have liked to have seen her off, he supposed, but lately it had been hard to be around her at all. Her spirits had improved, and that was good, but he would never know what to say to her again now that they were not in desperate danger. Now that she had no need of him, he could not pretend that she felt anything toward him like what he had begun to feel towards her. So perhaps it was better this way.

Lute straightened up and backed away from his work, squinting against the bright glare overhead.

Blasted sun, he thought, disgruntled. *It decides to show itself just as there's something needs doing all precise-like.*

But gazing at his work, he had to admit that he had done himself proud. And the sun had its uses. Days ago, it had enabled him to find the knife, and that had been a stroke of luck. Granted, it had taken some risky searching about in the ruins of the other half of the room, and the handle of the knife, with its depiction of the bees and flowers that had taken him so long had completely burnt away, leaving him with nothing but the blade to work with, which had been tricky in itself. But given all that, he had managed, through careful toiling, dedication and much sweat, to wrest something from the wood that was turning out to rival all of its blackened neighbors in their timeless glory.

"How's that for grand, Pember?" Lute whispered, leaning back on his heels in satisfaction. He paused for a moment, considering carving his name somewhere, but instead settled for sticking the blade in the right hand bottom corner of the picture, like a period.

The last square depicted a large, winged animal with a fierce beak and scaled feet and claws. Its wings were spread, its round eyes strangely alive—he had smeared some ash there, two black dots of it, for an extra touch. The thing was flying up over a forest and a field, dizzyingly minute miles below. These things had taken all of the last two days on his part, with little eating or sleeping to punctuate the process, but today his paw had a different concentration, one he had saved for last.

The rider on the back of the Byrd was a white squirrel, young, with a small, thoughtful mouth and intense eyes. This squirrel was not holding onto the animal as it pursued its upward course, but his arms were spread ever so slightly instead, as though he too was preparing to fly.

The eyes, Lute knew, were the most important, so he had saved them for last. He remembered them from that day, from the bloody, striking scene on the branch he had just happened to witness, and had spent an hour on them alone in order to depict them true.

The eyes—they communicated to him now in the unbroken silence of the finished wall, the last word breathed in an era, but more. They were hard to depict, precisely, and impossible to forget.

They were the future.